Koesler tried to stall for a bit more time. The person seemed to be making a move to leave. "But you see, if you don't confess any sin and express your sorrow for it, I can't absolve you."

The laugh was loud and utterly mirthless. "The fool," the person shouted. "thinks he can . . . absolve the devil!"

With that, the person was gone.

Koesler heard the church door close. He did not frighten easily . . . but he was genuinely frightened.

===

KILL AND TELL

A FATHER KOESLER MYSTERY

WILLIAM X. KIENZLE

BALLANTINE BOOKS • NEW YORK

Library of Congress Catalog Card Number: 83-25791

ISBN 0-345-31856-0

This edition published by arrangement with Andrews and McMeel, Inc.

This is a work of fiction and, as such, events described herein are creations of the author's imagination. Any relation to real people, living or dead, is purely coincidental and accidental.

Manufactured in the United States of America

First Ballantine Books Edition: March 1985

Gratitude for technical advice to:

Sgt. Roy Awe, Homicide, Detroit Police Department
Rudolph Bachman, Ph.D., Clinical Psychologist
Ramon Betanzos, Professor of Humanities, Wayne State University
Jim Grace, Detective, Kalamazoo Police Department
Donald Grimes, Director of Pharmacy, Deaconess Hospital
Sister Bernadelle Grimm, R.S.M., Pastoral Care Department, Samaritan Health Center
Dr. Richard Hoffmann, Director of Pharmacy, St. Joseph Mercy Hospital, Pontiac
Nancy E. Kelley, Management Consultant, Motion Picture and Advertising, ASIST Corporation
Timothy Kenny, Principal Trial Attorney, Wayne County Prosecuting Attorney's Office
Marj Jackson Levin, Staff Writer, *Detroit Free Press*
George Lubienski, Attorney, Probate Specialist
John Malone, M.D., Mt. Carmel Mercy Hospital
Werner Spitz, U.M.D., Wayne County Medical Examiner
Donald Worrell, Assistant Director, Mt. Clemens Public Library

Gratitude to those priests of the Archdiocese of Detroit who have helped in the research of all my books thus far. For the sake of their ecclesial careers and by mutual agreement I shall not mention them by name.

Any technical error is the author's.

With special thanks to my editor at Andrews and McMeel, Inc., Donna Martin, who has—figuratively—lived with Father Koesler through six volumes of murder and mayhem, and who deserves a Nobel Peace Prize for diplomacy, tact, and patience—and most of all, for caring.

FOR JAVAN

KILL
AND
TELL

1.

THE FIRES OF HELL.

Why did he invariably think of hell whenever he encountered fire? It didn't matter whether it was a house afire, a fire under a pan on the stove, or a campfire. Always hell. It must be all those years in parochial schools and the good old Baltimore Catechism, he concluded.

"Why," the Catechism would ask, "did God make you?"

"In order," the Catechism would respond, "to know Him, to love Him, and to serve Him in this world and to be happy with Him forever in the next." And little Frankie Hoffman and all the other little Catholic kids would memorize not only the Catechism's answers, but its questions also. It was only many years later, when Mr. Francis Hoffman became a junior executive in a major automotive company in Detroit, that he reidentified his personal goal in life: to become chairman of the board of his company—of The Company. And to do whatever might be necessary to get there.

"We call this our 'batch,' Mr. Hoffman," explained Amos Culpepper, the black manager of the glass plant. "It's got all the ingredients used in making glass, plus a goodly amount of cullet—glass that's discarded along the way in the process.''

Hoffman stared at the grayish powder being almost imperceptibly pushed into a fiery furnace that was radiating enormous heat. ''How hot is it in there?''

''Oh,'' Culpepper answered, ''anywhere from 2,450 to 2,800 degrees.''

Hoffman gave a low whistle. Once, he had forced himself, because he thought he had needed the discipline, to view a cremation. Till now, he had never experienced a similarly intense heat. If one approached the furnace too closely, the waves of heat were enough to literally take one's breath away. ''What would happen if you put a man's body in there?''

Culpepper chuckled. ''Someday soon somebody would be looking out of a car through him.''

Hoffman experienced a shudder. He had begun this day with an ominous feeling that had intensified as the day wore on. Breakfast had culminated in an argument with Emma, his wife. And it had not helped that for days he had been dreading this assignment given him by Charlie Chase, his immediate superior. He had complained to just about anyone who would listen about having to review the operation of The Company's glass plant. He would get Chase for this. Oh, yes, he would.

In the meantime, and for some inexplicable reason, the blast furnace was making Hoffman extremely nervous. He moved away from the batch and around to the side of the furnace where the heat was only slightly less intense. The considerable entourage that accompanied this VIP moved with him.

''This is your first visit here, isn't it?'' Culpepper said.

Hoffman nodded.

''That's why I'm taking you through our process step by step, right from the beginning.

''Now, this area here is what we call the tin bath. The

mixture is liquid now, and in this phase, it conforms to the perfectly smooth surface of the tin."

The heat, though less than that at the open furnace, was rapidly becoming unbearable. Hoffman led his entourage farther into the plant. "God, this is hot! When do you shut it down?"

Culpepper shook his head. "Never."

"Never!"

"Shut it down and the walls'd break up. Runs twenty-four hours a day, seven days a week. Furnace lasts six, seven years; then we rebuild it."

It was Hoffman's turn to shake his head. He was beginning to understand why the plant's annual budget was in excess of $35 million.

"Now," said Culpepper, "this is where the glass is stretched and sized."

"What are those things? They look like anti-aircraft guns."

"They're tweels. They're the robots that stretch and size the glass. A good bit of our operation is automated. More every year. Imagine by the time I retire most everything'll be done by robots."

In spite of himself, Hoffman was growing interested. Like many men, he easily became fascinated with machines that carried out automated functions. He could easily stand and watch by the hour as a machine carried out human, sometimes superhuman, tasks.

He became aware of a marked drop in temperature.

"Not as hot, is it?" Culpepper sensed his relief. "This is the annealing process. We relieve the stress on the glass by lowering the temperature gradually. The glass is cooling. But," he added quickly, as he saw Hoffman approach the emerging thin, smooth glass, "you wouldn't want to touch it yet. Still quite warm."

Hoffman, hands now inserted in trousers pockets to avoid further temptation, stepped away from the glass.

A series of revolving cylinders conveyed the glass rapidly forward to a point where it was cut for the first time. The process was, again, automated. Two cutters, acting in tandem, were propelled alternately across the breadth of the glass. "Primary cutters," said Culpepper. "Looks real simple, but actually they're a little monument to engineering. Looks like they're cutting on a bias. But what they're actually doing is compensating for the movement of the glass through here."

Hoffman initially found the cutting process engaging. Once again, he was drawn by the automation. Now, informed of this special technological achievement, he became engrossed in the operation. Gradually, he became aware he was standing directly in the path of one of the cutters. As the razor-edged blade raced repeatedly across the glass's surface, each time it stopped abruptly and automatically, only inches from his navel. He looked at Culpepper with a challenging grin.

The manager correctly interpreted Hoffman's smile. "Never fails. The blade'll always stop at that precise point. Every bit of automated equipment we've got in the plant is monitored by fail-safe devices." His smile exuded confidence.

Maybe, thought Hoffman. But he wasn't convinced. As fascinating as he invariably found automation, he also firmly believed nothing was fail-safe. As long as humans were involved, and the thing was made up of parts, and Murphy's Law remained ubiquitous, machinery would find ways to fail.

Hoffman could not identify what was making him edgy, but he could not deny the feeling. The incredible heat of the blast furnace; this automated cutter, which, were it to break loose from its arm, undoubtedly would kill him—everything seemed to contribute to his sense of nervous foreboding.

The group moved along the production line.

"These are the cord wood cutters," Culpepper pointed. "Now the glass's in rectangular shape. It'll be cut one more time into the desired windshield size further on down the line. See? Some of the glass has already been broken or damaged. Well, these guys," he indicated workers wearing heavy gloves and positioned on either side of the conveyor, "pull off all the spoiled glass and just let it drop down there, where another conveyor going in the opposite direction takes the glass back to the beginning where the cullet becomes part of the batch all over again."

The glass that survived all this cutting and jostling was carefully removed from the conveyor system by workmen, again heavily gloved, who stacked the glass in wooden brackets. The brackets were then manually loaded on dollies and transported to the next stage of the operation.

"And here," continued Culpepper, as the group reached a rather congested area, "is where the glass is shaped into the windshield." Sensing Hoffman's interest, Culpepper let the machines do the talking for a few minutes.

Ingenious, thought Hoffman. Untouched by human hand. A robot with four arms extending from its control box, the arms bent downward where suction cups replaced hands . . . hands that picked up the bracket glass, a single pane at a time, then swung it to another machine. The robot then positioned the glass carefully and precisely on the table of another robot. The well-oiled "finger" of the second robot, armed with a glass cutter, traced the shape of a windshield on the glass. The outside rim fell off, and a perfect windshield would be delivered to the next worker in the chain.

Yes, Hoffman had to agree, in time this entire operation might well be totally automated.

"Like a mother picking up a baby," commented Culpepper, having allowed time for Hoffman to become mesmerized by the robots. "Its sensors establish the limits of how far it moves the glass, and then it counts the pulses before laying the sucker down right on the exact spot. Amazing, ain't it?"

The two men were by no means alone in the fascination with the robots. The eyes of the entire entourage were riveted to the process.

Something was wrong. Culpepper sensed it rather than reasoned it. His right arm shot out, catching Hoffman on the shoulder, knocking him to the floor.

Instead of delivering the glass in its usual herky-jerky fashion, the robot's arms swung in a smooth, forceful, fast arc, passing through the space just vacated by Hoffman, and stopping only when it smashed into a nearby pillar.

Culpepper bent to the visibly shaken Hoffman and helped him to his feet.

The robots ground to a halt. Someone had cut the power. But Culpepper seemed the only one interested in Frank Hoffman. The technicians and engineers were absorbed in their machine, trying to figure out what had caused a fail-safe device to fail . . . and only incidentally, come within a hair's-breadth of killing a man.

"What we've got is a bad case of axis runaway," stated a tall, laconic Bill Kelly, the glass plant's chief engineer.

"Could you explain that a little more fully?" asked one of the two black Detroit police officers who had responded to the call.

The officers, Kelly, Culpepper, and Hoffman stood near a worktable in the plant manager's office.

Kelly nodded. "The robot is programmed to make suction contact with the glass, raise it from the bracket, and move it to the cutting machine, counting the pulses on the way. At the exact count of the exact number of pulses, it lowers the glass to the cutter. Instead of moving on its axis to the count of pulses, it lost its programming entirely.

"In layman's language, all hell broke loose."

The officer suppressed a smile. "And can you tell us how this could happen?"

Kelly nodded again. "Y'see, the type of material used for this silicone chip is a metal oxide semiconductor. We know it as just MOS. And, y'see, if an external, static-type current is applied over the MOS, it'll fail—in a completely unpredictable way." He looked from one officer to the other to make certain each understood.

"So," the officer said, as he finished writing on his notepad, "this 'external, static-type current' could come about accidentally? Or would someone have to bring it about intentionally?"

"No; it could happen accidentally."

"Could you think of any way in which this 'axis runaway' might be deliberately caused?"

Again Kelly nodded. "Sure. Somebody could enter a sequence in the computer programming the robot's probe—or arm—to run away and break its sequence."

"I see. But if someone were to enter such a sequence in the computer, an expert like yourself would be able to find it?"

"No," Kelly scratched his chin, ". . . not necessarily. Anybody who could program a switched sequence like that could also program the computer to erase the sequence from its memory."

"Just like that?"

"Just like that. A couple of numbers would do it."

"I'll have to bow to your expertise," said the officer, "and admit that it's possible for someone to program this robot runaway and also to erase the memory of this programming from the computer. But if Mr. Hoffman were the targeted victim, how would the programmer know the precise moment when Mr. Hoffman would be standing in the exact spot where he could be hit?''

"Now," Kelly replied, "I'd have to guess. But my guess would be that if someone—someone clever enough to reprogram a computer—were out to kill Mr. Hoffman, it could have been done anywhere along the line. A little shove into the furnace. A failure of the glass cutter. Any number of 'accidents.' With Mr. Hoffman standing in the path of the loading robot, with everyone's eyes on the robot's procedure, anyone easily could have slipped over to the computer controls and quickly reprogrammed it. It would require only a few seconds. Oh, yes; it could be done easily.''

The officer, seemingly satisfied, nodded. But he would later question the men who had been working in the area to see if any of them had noticed anything or anyone unusual in the vicinity of the control box.

For now, he turned to the plant manager. "Mr. Culpepper, what kind of security do you have in this plant?''

Culpepper looked embarrassed. "Well, none, really. There are no uniformed guards—or plainclothes guards, for that matter. We try to keep our eyes open, but it's almost impossible. The other day, I saw somebody wandering through, taking pictures, so I challenged him. Turned out he was on assignment by The Company and nobody had notified us. But, just about anybody can come through here, especially if he or she is wearing work clothes. Nobody wears identification tags. And the place is so big nobody knows everybody else.''

"So, if this thing had been caused by someone who reprogrammed the computer, that person might or might not be working here?''

"Right. Or, for that matter, if somebody did

reprogram the computer, he or she could have been hired by someone not at all associated with The Company.''

Kelly leaned forward. ''One thing puzzles me, Amos: How in hell did you ever guess that the probe was out of control? I mean, a split second later and we would have had a major league tragedy.''

''I'm not sure even now.'' Culpepper, still shaken by the incident, shook his head. ''The arms came up just a fraction too fast. And, when the probe missed its first pulse count . . . I . . . I just reacted.''

''A lucky reaction as far as Mr. Hoffman is concerned.'' He turned to an obviously angry Hoffman. ''Mr. Hoffman, who knew you were going to make this—uh—operating review today?''

''Just about everyone. It was common knowledge around my office.'' Hoffman paused. ''And I guess I complained about it enough so that most of my friends and co-workers knew about it. Why?''

''Because we can't be sure yet what we've got here. It's either a very dangerous industrial accident, or attempted murder.''

''Murder!'' Hoffman reacted as if he'd never before heard the word.

''It's a possibility, especially since we know that this—uh—axis runaway could have been programmed.''

''Murder!'' He shook his head. ''That's impossible.''

''Not impossible, Mr. Hoffman. If Mr. Culpepper had not reacted as quickly as he did, that machine either would have sliced you in half or battered you into that pillar. Either way, you would have been dead. And if someone actually programmed the robot to act as it did, then that's attempted murder.''

''My God!'' Concern began to replace anger.

Both officers sat down across the conference table from Hoffman. ''I think it would be to your advantage,'' said one officer, ''to take a little time and try to come up with a list of people who might want to do you harm. If it was an attempt at murder, there's a big problem.''

''What?''

''If it was merely an accident, it's The Company's problem. If it was attempted murder, you and we have a bigger problem.''

''Yes?''

''Whoever did it may try again.''

⚙

In a brief time, Frank Hoffman would repress this incident from his consciousness.

But there would come a time when he, and others around him, would be forced to recall it vividly.

2.

"Later this afternoon, I think I shall attempt suicide."

Louise Chase sipped her coffee. Early morning coffee was important, nay essential, even on a day that might include suicide.

"Not the irrevocable sort, mind you, like jumping off the Renaissance Center or dousing myself with some flammable substance and setting myself afire." She shuddered. "No; something more subtle. Like a slight but decisive overdose of sleeping pills followed by a desperate phone call to one of my friends."

Louise looked across the breakfast table at the *Wall Street Journal* that separated her from her husband. "What would you say to that, dear?"

"What? Oh . . . sounds good to me, dear." Through long practice, Charles Chase was programmed to respond without being sidetracked from his reading.

Today's *Journal* seemed to contain nothing but bad news. Even what usually passed for the light item that regularly appeared in one of the center columns of the front page was grim. Some New York clinicians had concluded that the rays given off by word processors, including the ones used in newspaper offices, were carcinogenic. It was getting to the point where living could be harmful to life.

Charles could well remember when word processors came into vogue in the seventies. They had seemed such useful mechanical toys. Who would have thought then that they might prove to be one more nail in the casket of Western civilization?

Well, for the moment, it was no more than an allegation that remained to be proved. And, he knew, the industry would fight the investigation every step of the way.

The rest of the *Journal*'s news went downhill from there.

And not the least of the bad news concerned the automotive industry. Sales were down for everyone, even The Company. Nor was the foreign market, once The Company's strong point, holding its own.

Often, lately, he found himself second-guessing his move into The Company.

A graduate of Cass Tech and Lawrence Institute of Technology, Charlie Chase was a local boy who had become the epitome of the self-made man. For a relatively brief period, he had worked in design for the Ford Motor Company. Then he had struck out on his own, forming a privately owned automotive plant, then nurturing it into the major supply source for most of the domestic industry.

Then, nearing sixty, he had been lured into The Company as general manager with the implicit guarantee that if all went as anticipated, the presidency would be his.

But all had not gone as expected. Charlie could not put his finger on it, but it was more than the poor state of the economy. He had just not been able to get control of the reins. The reason remained a puzzle to him. It was as if there were some shadowy force that foiled him at every important juncture.

There was no doubting it, this was a serious threat to the financial future of the Chases. At least on the level to which they had become accustomed. He had risked everything on the leap from his own business to his new uncertain future in The Company. Now, he was able to think of little else.

"If whoever I call doesn't respond in time," Louise continued as she buttered her toast, "I shall, of course, be dead. But that should be no barrier to a Christian burial. I understand the Church now considers suicides to be at least temporarily unbalanced and will therefore grant Christian burial. And of course I shall leave no suicide note that would compromise the situation."

This was the first time Louise had tested her theory that her husband seldom paid attention to what she was saying. Right now, Charles was, depending on one's view, either passing or failing the test with flying colors.

"When one considers burial," Louise continued, "as of course one must, I should prefer being cremated. That also, I understand, is permitted by the Church now.

"Then, what to do with the ashes? Perhaps you could sprinkle them here and there throughout Mira Linder's Spa. Goodness knows, I've been under so many mud packs at Mira's, it seems only fitting that I should become part of the mud." Louise shivered slightly. "Oh, how ghastly, even for make-believe . . . strike that last sentence." Then, raising her voice a decible, "How do those plans strike you, dear?"

"What? Oh, first-rate, dear."

The test had gone on long enough. Too long. She smiled sardonically and tried to remember when genuine communication had last passed between them. It had been, she was forced to admit, a long time ago.

But then, things had been difficult from the very beginning. They had married—despite solid opposition from both sets of parents—when Charles was in his early twenties, Louise in her late teens. She had done secretarial work, using her salary to support them and putting him through L.I.T.

Shortly thereafter, he had become successful—very successful. At several points during their marriage they could have stopped to smell the flowers. At no time did they. For Charles, there had always been an established set of priorities: his work, his family, his Catholic faith. Even though their two children were now grown and moved away, the priorities remained fixed.

Now, Charles was worried. He had been worried since shortly after joining The Company. Louise could not understand the reason for his worry. Nor had she been able to relieve his anxiety.

There was, as far as she could see, no reason for his fears.

Now at the nineteenth pay grade, he made in excess of $300,000. He would receive at least half that much each year in retirement, along with an annual new car and special health care insurance. Their future was secure. If only he would learn to relax.

But he could not. And she knew it even as she knew she could not do anything about it. Something was wrong, something he had not been able to resolve at work. And work remained the first of his priorities.

"Do we have anything on for this weekend?" He folded the *Journal* and drained his now nearly cold cup of coffee.

"Saturday night."

"What?"

"A dinner party."

"Where?"

"The Mercurys'."

"Oh, no; not again!"

"Sorry. But Em wants us to come. And since Frank is your right-hand man, I thought . . ."

"Must be something haywire in Frank's family. Imagine: his sister marrying an actor. And an Italian to boot!"

"Now, now; don't get upset. Em promised that Angie wouldn't invite any of his show business friends. There'll be just a few people, most of whom you get along with very well."

"Oh, all right . . . but just the same, we ought to be more in control of our own time. Weekends especially." His normally dour expression appeared drawn. He ran the fingers of one hand along a temple, slightly disturbing the trim but abundant straight white hair.

"It won't be so bad; you'll see," she said, encouragingly.

She followed him as he went to the hall closet, put on his topcoat and hat, scooped up his briefcase, and headed for the garage. At the breezeway, he paused and turned to her, with a suddenly concerned look. "What was it you said you had planned for this afternoon?"

She smiled. "It's my volunteer day at Veterans' Memorial Hospital."

"Oh . . . oh, yes. Well, do be careful."

3.

THE BALL WOULD HAVE TO PLAYED OFF THE back wall.

Angie Mercury raced to the rear of the court. But he badly misjudged the ricochet. Instead of a lively rebound, the ball all but dropped limply off the wall. Fooled by the feeble bounce, Mercury stumbled, falling heavily against the wall.

"Careful," Frank Hoffman cautioned, "mustn't damage the merchandise. In your case, that's all you've got."

Mercury kneaded his right shoulder. "Never mind. Just serve."

Hoffman retrieved the small black hard rubber ball and took his place at the line. "Twenty serving fifteen." He raised his racket.

The ball caromed off three walls before Mercury played it.

From then on, the two men positioned themselves in the rear of the court, content to return each other's volleys, each awaiting an advantage.

Finally, Mercury played a shot off the back wall that carried high against the front wall. The ball should have rebounded high off the floor. But the bounce was surpris-

16

ingly low. As if anticipating this phenomenon, Hoffman charged, easing the ball against the front wall, where it hit low and dribbled weakly along the floor.

"Game!" Hoffman announced unnecessarily, triumph unmistakable in his voice. "Want to go another one?"

"OK: one more."

"I'll just get a drink of water," Hoffman said, as he headed off the court. "Want some?"

"No, thanks. I'll pass. It's too late for water and too early for a martini."

Alone in the court, Mercury focused on the ball, now lying dormant. Something was wrong—but what?

He picked up the ball and squeezed it. It seemed firm enough. He bounced it a few times, paying careful attention to the height of the rebound. Aha! He held the ball up even with the top of his head, which was about five feet ten inches from the floor, then dropped it. It bounced little higher than his waist.

He'd never before come across a racquetball so lifeless. Yet it wasn't an old ball. Indeed, from its surface condition, he judged it to be new.

Frank must have fixed it, or had it fixed . . .

But why? Why would anyone tinker with a racquetball?

It took only a few more seconds to arrive at a tenable conclusion. Hoffman was spotting him seven, almost eight years. And while his brother-in-law took great pains to stay in good shape, when it came to that many years' difference between the late forties and the mid-fifties, the gap was considerable.

Hoffman had closed that gap to some extent with a deadened ball. One that would not rebound in a lively fashion. One that would not have to be chased all over the court. And—added advantage—Hoffman would be the only one who knew about the altered condition of the ball.

Hoffman had to win. He could not abide losing.

Mercury smiled scornfully.

Hoffman needn't have gone to such an extreme. Mercury had had no intention of winning, even if he could have. There was no advantage in embarrassing one's meal ticket.

All things being equal, Mercury and Hoffman would have been fairly evenly matched at racquetball. And Mercury intended no more than that: to keep the game close.

In a few moments, Hoffman would re-enter the field of combat, announcing the amount Mercury now owed him in betting debts, including the just-concluded match.

Whatever the sum, it was academic. He didn't have it, and the way his career was running, he would not have it in the near future . . . if ever.

However, next month, as was his monthly habit, Frank Hoffman would slip a substantial check to his sister Cindy, who happened to be Mercury's wife. And the Mercurys would once again be solvent.

Mercury felt like something between a kept woman and a subsidized medieval artist. The situation was so distasteful that he tried not to think about it. But it was impossible to avoid this predicament when confronted by Frank Hoffman with the bill owed Frank Hoffman. And, thought Mercury, here it comes.

"That brings it to $175." Hoffman briskly re-entered the court, slipping his hand through the leather strap of his racquet. "Want to go double or nothing?"

Mercury shook his head. "No. No; the regular wager will be fine." He'd have to absorb the coming game loss, but he didn't have to be a masochist.

"Suit yourself."

The game moved along predictably, with Hoffman pulling out to an early lead and Mercury not far behind. What made this distinct from the previous game was that

Mercury now knew the secret of the dead ball and was thus able to play it more knowledgeably. Thus providing him with enough secret laughs to equal a moral victory. Moral, of course, would be his only victory.

"Twenty serving nineteen," Hoffman announced, breathing more heavily than usual.

Hoffman served. With absolutely nothing to lose, Mercury aimed his return at the small of Hoffman's back. The ball caught him squarely on the right buttock.

"Hinder," Mercury called.

"OK." Hoffman glanced at Mercury, whose aim ordinarily was so accurate that Hoffman strongly doubted that he had been hit accidentally.

Hoffman served again. The volley continued for almost thirty seconds. Then Mercury tried for a kill shot that fell short and skipped against the wall.

"That's two hundred bucks even, Angie." The superiority in his tone was almost palpable.

"You want it in cash, or will a check do?"

"You'd better wait till next month." Hoffman dribbled the ball several times. "I get as much bounce out of this ball as I would from one of your checks."

"But barely."

"How's that?"

"Never mind."

The locker room of the Collegiate Club, one of many private clubs to which Frank Hoffman belonged, supplied virtually everything: soap, shampoo, towels, shaving equipment, and attendants who could fetch, among other things, drinks. Hoffman and Mercury each ordered a Bloody Mary.

Sitting before their adjacent lockers—Hoffman's permanently assigned, Mercury's rented for the morning— the two stripped off their sweat-saturated clothing.

"So, Angie, are you gainfully occupied currently, or are you—uh—'between shows'?"

"I'm doing *Two for the Seesaw* at the Book Cadillac."

"That old cripple still around? I must have seen it ten, fifteen years ago."

"More like twenty if you caught it early. Bill Gibson wrote it in '59. But with a cast of two, it works well in a dinner theater."

The Bloody Marys were served. Hoffman signed for them.

"That's it?"

"What?"

"That's it? No ads? No commercials? No films?"

Mercury wondered where this line of questioning was leading. "They're supposed to start shooting *The Rosary Murders* soon. The whole thing's being filmed locally. My agent says I'm a cinch for the lead."

"Angie, Angie . . ." Hoffman smiled and shook his head. "Your career in the entertainment industry—to overstate the importance of that field—is what we in the automotive world would describe as low pot."

"Low pot?"

"Low potential. You're always on the verge of something without ever getting there. All those years of—for want of a better word—vaudeville. And dragging my poor sister into your act. Then a Grade B movie career, a few TV shots, a couple of national ads. And now, local dinner theater—with nothing on the side. I don't have to tell you you're not making it. Ever think of getting a job? I mean one with a paycheck fifty-two weeks every year? We in Detroit make cars, you know. You could join the crowd."

"Tell you a story, Frank." Mercury drained his glass, realizing too late it should have been water. He was too thirsty to properly nurse alcohol now.

"There's a big circular table at the Press Club," Mercury proceeded. "It's never reserved; anybody can sit at it. Well, this one day, all the seats are occupied. This one guy smells a terrible odor. It turns out to be the guy next to him. 'Is that you that smells so bad, buddy?' The other guy acknowledges that he is the source of the odor.

" 'Don't you ever bathe?'

" 'Sure.'

" 'Then how come you smell so bad?'

" 'Well, I work in the circus . . . washin' elephants. Every once in a while, when I'm behind the elephant, washin' away, an accident happens—and that's where this smell comes from.'

" 'That's terrible! Why don't you quit?'

" 'What! And leave show business?' ''

Both chuckled.

Each clad only in a towel, Angie's around his waist, Hoffman's around his neck, they made their way to the showers.

As they showered, Mercury studied Hoffman, who lathered like a model in a TV commercial, vigorously and without benefit of washcloth. Hoffman was probably the only person—at least the only one Mercury knew—who lived in about the same style as TV models, with a measure of soap opera thrown in.

Although Hoffman unarguably took excellent care of himself, there were a few extra ounces of flesh here and there around the waist and in the buttocks. And his pectoral muscles were starting to sag. Perhaps his six-foot-three frame was beginning to settle.

But he was handsome. The white at his temples set off a full head of otherwise jet-black hair. He reminded Mercury of a middle-aged Stewart Granger. But then, Mercury had a habit of comparing everyone he knew to show business personalities.

For instance, Mercury knew that he himself resembled Dane Clark—with perhaps a bit more of a receding hairline.

"What's on your agenda for today?" Hoffman asked as they dressed.

"I've got an interview with Dave Newman on WXYZ radio at eleven this morning."

"Sorry I won't be able to catch it."

"Then my agent has set up a few interviews with some ad agencies and a reading with Jimmy Launce. He's gonna open a new show at Botsford Inn."

"Another dinner theater!" Hoffman finished buttoning his vest.

Mercury shrugged. "Any port in a storm."

They exited into the parking lot. The Collegiate Club squatted between East Jefferson and Woodbridge in the distant shadow of the Renaissance Center. Both Hoffman and Mercury would take the Lodge Freeway out of downtown Detroit while the heavy traffic was stop-and-going its way into town.

"Well, Angie," Hoffman called out as he eased himself into his car, "win a few today!"

Mercury smiled. Yeah, he thought, I might just win a few today—and if I do, it won't be with a ball that's been fixed.

4.

Ratigan steered his car into the parking lot of Bennett's Courtyard Restaurant adjacent to Mount Clemens' McKinley Airport. "How about it, gentlemen—hungry?" He switched off the ignition.

"Famished," Conroy replied. Koesler's hearty nod seconded the motion.

The three clergymen, in mufti, waited in the foyer for the hostess to direct them to their table.

Bishop Michael Ratigan, in his late fifties, was a relatively lean six-footer, with ample straight salt-and-pepper hair, a florid complexion, and a rather aggressive bulldog expression.

Father Robert Koesler, five years younger, was some three inches taller; at 220, he was perhaps ten pounds over his desired weight. He wore bifocals and his once-blond hair was now gray.

Father Charles Conroy, three years younger than Koesler, had long ago surrendered to good food. Pear-shaped and slightly uncoordinated, at five-six, his weight was more befitting a six-footer. A fringe of gray ringed his balding pate.

An educated guess from any onlooker would be first that the three men had played golf—the tip of Conroy's

golf glove stuck out of his rear pocket—and second that if
they could get away for golf on a Wednesday, they had to
be either clergymen or physicians.

In due time they were seated. Koesler ordered Chablis;
Conroy, scotch neat, and Ratigan the first of many martinis, all of which he would hold well.

They had, indeed, been golfing, at a small, nine-hole
course some three miles north of Port Sanilac, at about
the thumb's knuckle joint, Father Koesler had explained
countless times. (Michiganians, whose state resembled
the outline of a hand, invariably pinpointed their various
locales through the use of the hand's anatomy.)

The choice of the course had not been Ratigan's. He
would have preferred—and could easily have arranged
for—something more gracious. Both both Koesler and
Conroy had insisted for the sake of nostalgia: As semi-
narians, they had spent many summers as counselors at
Ozanam, a nearby Catholic boys' camp, and had, thus,
played the course many times.

Ratigan had reluctantly gone along with the choice. A
rarity for the bishop; concessions were not his way of
life.

"Well," he said, as the waitress departed with their
drink orders, "was it worth playing that cow pasture just
for old times' sake?"

"God, the memories!" Koesler shook his head.

Conroy sighed. "Yes, it's hard to forget."

"What is?" asked Ratigan.

"The summers we put in as counselors," Conroy replied.

"That's right," said Ratigan. "I keep forgetting you
two were 'campers.' "

"Four years for me," said Conroy. "But I couldn't
hold a candle to you, Bob. How many years was it?"

"Nine summers."

"Nine summers!" Ratigan repeated. "My God! I

didn't know you made a career of it. Here I was spending
my seminary summers earning big bucks landscaping
rich people's property. And there you guys were, getting
pennies for babysitting a bunch of snotty-nosed poor
kids.''

"We may not have had children of our own, but we
certainly paid our dues," said Conroy.

"It didn't begin all that altruistically—for me, anyway,'' said Koesler. "I and some of my classmates
planned on being lifeguards for the summer. We were—
God!—seminary sophomores when we took the Red
Cross course. Then we had to submit our proposed summer jobs for the approval of the rector . . . remember
those days—when the seminary controlled even summer
vacations?''

"Yeah," said Conroy. "That was a different era.
Nowadays, the seminary faculty spends the summer on
their knees just praying the students will come back for
another year.''

"Well,'' Koesler continued, "the upshot was that the
rector vetoed our requests to apply for jobs as
lifeguards—at least at a public beach. He did, however,
tell us we could apply for jobs as lifeguards and counselors at one of the Catholic boys' camps.''

Koesler paused to allow the implications to sink in.

A low chuckle began deep in Ratigan's throat. "Ah,
yes. What is it you may find on a public beach that you
will never find on the beach of a boys' camp?''

"Exactly!" Koesler affirmed. "The lesson was that
while it was all right to save girls' souls, it was not all
right to save girls' bodies!''

All three laughed.

"From a nice warm pool in Detroit to the frigid waters
of Lake Huron,'' said Ratigan, "even for high school
sophomores that was a pretty stupid decision.''

"What choice did we have?" said Conroy. "It was

Ozanam—or Camp Sancta Maria way up in Northern Michigan.''

"Well," said Ratigan, "I hope you guys enjoyed life in your camp subculture. It's odd, now that I come to think of it: You wanted to be a lifeguard at a beach where you could flex your muscles and impress the girls," he glanced across at Koesler, "and you ended up at a place where girls were barred."

"What's so odd about that?" retorted Koesler. "That's the way things were in the seminary. At least back when we were students."

"Right," Conroy agreed. "Remember Father Sklarski giving us our pre-vacation spiritual pep talk? One year he told us the prescribed clerical distance from anything feminine was a foot. Another year, the distance had shrunk to six inches. Eventually, he got down to 'Look, but don't touch.' "

Koesler chuckled. "But it never got more intimate than that."

"What's odd," said Ratigan, "is that you asked for permission to take a job that would put you in 'proximate danger' of being in the presence of girls—'the enemy' as the seminary would have it. Save the mark, if one of them got in trouble—or pretended to—in the water, you'd have had to actually touch a girl. And there would go your priestly vocation down the drain—and all because of a cross-chest carry." Ratigan was smiling.

"In Red Cross training," Koesler smiled too, "they told us it was better to hair-carry girls."

"I know your type. Anyway, your request for such a 'dangerous' job was turned down. While I asked for—and got—permission to spend the summer with Mother Nature. Watering and mowing lawns, trimming shrubs, pruning trees, and the like. And, as a completely unhoped-for, unlooked-for bonus, I got the girls."

Conroy's mouth dropped open. "You *did*?"

"Who do you think gets someone in to landscape their property—Mrs. Murphy on Twelfth and McGraw? Not hardly. It's Mrs. Grosse Pointe. And who stays home all summer while the landscaping is being done—Mr. Grosse Pointe? Not hardly. He's off earning enough to keep the family in Grosse Pointe and in gardeners.

"So, it's Mrs. Grosse Pointe and her nubile daughters and their swimming pool . . . and their gardener!''

"You mean you—"

Conroy wasn't given the opportunity of finishing his question. "Just as you two and all of us," said Ratigan, "I did not promise chastity until a year before we were ordained priests."

"But—"

"As to the rest, gentlemen, I believe I will plead the Fifth Amendment."

"You should have written down your experience as a guide for us who followed you through the seminary," said Koesler.

"What! And ruin all those lovely summers you were able to spend with the kiddies at camp?"

"And all the while, you were the lifeguard at the pool!" Koesler shook his head.

The waitress returned with their drinks. She did not bring menus. This threesome seemed to be good for one or more additional rounds.

"So, how do you like it at St. Anselm's?" Conroy sipped and shuddered as the scotch's warmth suffused his small round body.

"Just fine," Ratigan, who had been in residence at the Dearborn Heights parish during the past three months, replied. "It was kind of Bob here," he nodded, "to invite me."

Koesler smiled and shrugged. "It's like, Where does a 600-pound gorilla sleep? Where does a bishop live? Anywhere he wants."

"Not true." Ratigan chuckled. "At least not true to-day. And especially not true of a mere auxiliary bishop. After all, I'm not Cardinal Mark Boyle, Ordinary of the Archdiocese of Detroit. I'm merely a helpin' bishop."

"Waiting impatiently for his own diocese," Conroy interjected.

"Not at all." Ratigan sipped the martini. "Being an auxiliary is one very good way to learn the virtue of patience. I may very well spend the rest of my days in Detroit offering the sacrament of confirmation to kids. Unless," he nodded at each of his two companions, "outside of emergencies they start letting priests do that too. In the meantime, it was good of St. Anselm's beloved pastor," again he nodded toward Koesler, "to allow me residence in his parish and his rectory."

"It really was nothing, Mike. You know how difficult it is to find a warm clerical body these days. It's good to have the company. And, as I've said before, as far as I'm concerned, you can stay as long as you like."

"Thanks, Bob." Ratigan raised his glass in salute. "Not only is it good to be with you, but the parish is central to the section of the archdiocese for which I'm somewhat responsible. So it's very convenient. Far more convenient than the downtown chancery office, which used to be central before they split the archdiocese into regions."

The waitress returned. In response to her question, each of them would have another drink. And, yes, they would like to look at the menu . . . which would refer to her as a waitperson.

"By happy coincidence," Koesler drained his wineglass, "St. Anselm's is also convenient to a couple of your closer companions."

"The Hoffmans! Yes, indeed, that was a coincidence. That they're parishioners does make it convenient."

"The Hoffmans?" Conroy looked surprised. "Not Frank Hoffman! The auto executive?"

"Yup. Frank and Emma Hoffman of automotive fame," said Koesler. "And their friends and fellow parishioners, Charles and Louise Chase."

Conroy's mouth hung open. "The Chases! I've read about Charlie Chase so often I didn't think he was real. But he doesn't live in Dearborn. The Chases are in . . . where—Bloomfield Hills, aren't they?"

"Oh, come on, Charlie," Koesler chided, "don't pretend you've never heard of parish shopping! It must go on even at Patronage. You've got to have some of those old parishioners—Poles and Italians—coming back to the old neighborhood on Sundays."

"Well, yes, of course. I just never thought of somebody like Charlie Chase as a parish shopper."

"What did you think, then: that if the Chases didn't like their territorial parish, they'd go buy one they could live with?"

"Funny thing," mused Ratigan, "there was an article on that just the other day in the *Journal.*"

Ratigan, thought Koesler, might not have been the only clergyman who was a regular reader of the *Wall Street Jorunal,* but he was the only one Koesler knew. The *Journal* had definitely added a touch of class to St. Anselm's mail delivery since Ratigan had moved in.

"Actually," Ratigan continued, "I'd forgotten till I read the article that the tradition of belonging to the parish within whose territorial boundaries one lives goes all the way back to the fifth century."

"You may have forgotten it," Conroy remarked, "but I don't think I ever knew it. I thought it began in the early part of this century with the establishment of the Code of Canon Law."

"Nope. More like fifteen centuries. The article said

the practice of parish shopping was almost unheard-of until five or ten years ago.''

Koesler guffawed. "I don't think the writer of that article ever heard of Father John Roth, of happy memory.''

"Roth?" Ratigan tried to place him. "Wasn't he the pastor of some parish in Garden City?''

"Exactly. St. Raphael's. If parish shopping did not predate Roth, then he certainly launched it. He used to perpetuate pleasant practices like forbidding couples with small children from occupying newer sections of the church—so the little darlings wouldn't ruin the new pews.

"And when parishioners parked their cars across the yellow lines marking parking places, Roth had his ushers go out and slash the offenders' tires. And that must have been . . . oh, some thirty years ago when I was an assistant at St. Norbert's, the neighboring parish. We had our hands full trying to stem the tide of parishioners trying to escape the wrath of Roth—families who were very definitely parish shoppers.''

The waitperson returned for their order. After quickly consulting the menu, Ratigan ordered the filet and another martini. Koesler ordered chopped sirloin and Conroy the prime rib; each declined another drink.

"And that was back in the days when you needed a letter from the pastor of your proper territorial parish granting permission for the switch,'' said Conroy, picking up the conversational thread.

"The article in the *Journal*,'' said Ratigan, "noted that only about half of those who describe themselves as Catholics regularly attend Mass now. And in the midsixties, that figure was more than 70 percent. The article also said—and I imagine it's true—that most pastors welcome anyone who comes.''

"It is true," said Koesler. "We're a mobile society now. Nearly everybody who comes to Mass on Sundays, at least in the suburbs, drives. It is not that difficult to drive a few extra blocks, or even miles, to get to the parish of your choice rather than your territory. I know we have people who live in St. Anselm's parish attending Mass elsewhere. As well as people coming from outside the parish. Instead of Norbert or Anselm or Raphael, they just ought to name parishes St. Conservative or St. Liberal."

Conroy chuckled. "Which would Anselm be?"

"I'll answer that," said Ratigan. "St. Right-Down-the-Middle—with a bit of a hook to the left. Very representative but ordinary liturgies with good, solid homilies."

"Gee," said Koesler, elbow on table, chin propped in hand, "you read that just about the way I wrote it."

Ratigan grinned, then began eating his tossed salad. "Of course, I don't approve of parish shopping. I don't suppose any of us really does. The philosophy behind the territorial parish is as sound now as it was in the beginning. Parishes, at least the nonethnic ones, are set up to serve a given territory. What happens when a Roth comes along? People go shopping—burdening other parishes that weren't set up or prepared to care for the swelling number of parishioners. Meanwhile, for lack of contributors, Roth's parish sickens, maybe dies. As, eventually, Roth must do. Then we have neither a Roth nor a St. Raphael's. But then," Ratigan made a helpless gesture, "when you have a couple of the caliber of Charles and Louise Chase . . . well, then, we're back to where does a 600-pound gorilla sleep."

"But are people like the Chases and the Hoffmans all that active in the parish?" Conroy was first to finish his salad, as he would be first to finish each of the courses.

"As active as they can be, I guess," Koesler responded. "Actually, the Chases have been parishioners much longer than the Hoffmans. Unless I'm mistaken, the Chases were charter members of St. Anselm's. Lived in the parish when it was founded, long before I was assigned there. Used to be quite active until they moved out to Bloomfield Hills.

"The Hoffmans aren't that active. But they are, I guess, busy with lots of other demands. Actually, I don't know why they haven't moved out of the parish. They certainly can afford to."

"They're making a statement, Bob." Ratigan knew the Hoffmans much better than even their pastor did. "On the one hand, they live in an adequate house. On the other, Frank has a master plan for his life and a timetable for accomplishing that plan. He intends to climb to the highest rung of The Company. And as he climbs, he will move to the appropriate neighborhood, join the appropriate club, and so forth. For the moment, Dearborn suits him nicely."

"That's very interesting." Koesler felt a twinge of embarrassment at not having been let in on that little secret. But then, he reflected, a pastor is not necessarily a friend to be invited in to share secrets. Bishop Ratigan was that friend. "For a long while, I simply assumed that the Hoffmans would move, if only to put more space between them and Angie Mercury. There seems to be no love lost between those two."

"Indeed there is not," Ratigan affirmed. "If it were not for the strong bond between Frank and his sister Cindy Mercury, the relationship between Frank and Angie would never have existed." He speared a piece of filet. "In any event, we may just get to see this entire cast of characters interacting at the dinner at the Mercurys this Saturday. You're coming, aren't you, Bob?"

"Indeed I am. I intend to go and see who eats what."

5.

LOCKED INTO A SPACE CAPSULE-LIKE STEAMBOX, a towel wrapped around her graying red hair, she faced a sign that ran the length of the rectangular room. The sign read: TIRANA'S APHRODITE CLINIQUE DE BEAUTÉ. And beneath that: Tirana shares her Albanian beauty secrets with you.

There was little to do but read the sign—over and over—while hoping that the attendant who had fastened her into this cabinet would remember to return and unfasten it while she was still medium rare.

"Wasn't it Saint Lawrence," Louise Chase commented, "who, facing martyrdom by being roasted on a gridiron, said to his tormentors, 'You can turn me over now; I'm done on this side'?"

"Feel that bad, do you? Just hang on," Emma Hoffman reasured her, "it can't be but a few minutes more."

"It's not possible they could have forgotten us . . . ?"

Em shook her head and allowed a tight little smile to escape briefly. "Not likely. They haven't lost a customer yet. Can you imagine the fat headlines if Madame Tirana ever lost one of her VIP patrons?"

"Never mention that word in here," said someone in another steam cabinet.

"What word?" Em couldn't turn to see who had spoken.

" 'Fat.' "

"Oh."

The roasting ladies in the various steam boxes drifted in silence into their solitary thoughts. Only the soft sound of pressurized steam was heard.

This was Louise's first adventure into Tirana's famed clinique in the swank North Plaza of the Orchard Lake Mall. She was there at the invitation of Emma Hoffman, a Tirana regular.

The relationship—Louise and Emma's—was an odd one on more than one level.

As longtime parishioners of St. Anselm's, they had, of course, known one another for many years, though not well. Their husbands' backgrounds were in the auto industry. Each man was a self-made success: Chase as a supplier, building up his own company until it was the largest of its kind in southeastern Michigan; Hoffman as a mechanical engineer, graduating from the University of Michigan and later earning an MBA from that same institution. He had joined The Company immediately after graduation and worked his way up in the Plastics, Paint, and Vinyl Division to his present position as general manufacturing manager.

In the automotive pecking order, through all those years, Hoffman's had been the higher position because he was an executive with The Company, while Chase, no matter what his personal wealth, had been merely a supplier. Then, suddenly, the pecking positions were reversed when Chase was absorbed into The Company. Though the two were in comparable management brackets, Chase was now a level above Hoffman. And that

spelled a significant difference, not only in salary but—
which most galled Emma Hoffman—in perk levels.

Chase could and did belong to the prestigious
Bloomfield Hills Country Club. Although Hoffman
could have afforded a like membership, particularly
since his wife had an inherited fortune of her own, he
would not have been welcomed by the members of the
BHCC, by whose standards his position in The Company
simply was not high enough to warrant such membership.

Hoffman was a member of the equally exclusive but
somewhat less prestigious Orchard Lake Country Club.

So there they were, Louise Chase thought as she sim-
mered, crisscrossing each other at so many points in their
lives.

All things considered, she concluded, it was a miracle
that the two men got on as well as they did. Everything
indicated there should be so much friction between Chase
and Hoffman that their relationship would ignite and ex-
plode. But Charles had assured her that, contrary to his
expectations, Frank had been a continuing source of help
in the nitty-gritty workings of The Company—even to
making available his own most trusted advisers.

For all of this Louise was grateful.

"Come now, ladies; eet ees time." The attendant
opened the boxes containing Louise and Em's stewed
bodies. "All tze pores are now made open."

Louise considered the attendant's accent to be an ersatz combination of Italian, French, and gypsy.

The attendant ushered the two women into a smaller
room containing several massage tables. The decor was
all in blues and pinks. The carpet was plush. And there
was something about the walls. . . .

Now that Louise thought about it, there was something
about all the walls in Madame Tirana's Clinique. She had
been aware of something odd from the moment she'd en-

tered the place. Suddenly, she put her finger on it: There were no corners. Only curves. How appropriate—and evocative—in an establishment dedicated to the restoration of feminine shapeliness.

Emma, in a practiced maneuver, hoisted herself atop one of the tables and lay face down awaiting the ministrations of her masseuse. Louise, shorter by several inches than Emma and awkwardly trying to hold the large towel about her, required and received assistance in mounting the table. No sooner were the women situated on their respective tables than they lost their towels.

This shocked Louise. She was a regular patron of Mira Linder's skin care salon, where some sort of covering, no matter how minuscule, was used whenever possible. Whereas Tirana's philosophy admitted a good measure of nudity. All of which was not perhaps as compromising for someone like Emma, who, by constant vigilance, had preserved a body any fifty-year-old woman would be proud of.

Louise, nearly ten years older than Emma, and not nearly as diligent, suffered sags, rolls, and other ravages of slight indulgences as well as of gravity. Pound for pound, hers was not a body that justified feelings of outright shame. On the other hand, she did not fancy parading around in the nude to the degree common at Madame Tirana's.

"Vee vill dig out tza vorries and tza tensions," said Louise's masseuse in an accent she took to be a combination of German and East European.

Moans of relaxation escaped both Emma and Louise as their masseuses kneaded, rubbed, and pounded.

"Unt now, you vill please to turn ofer," Louise's masseuse suggested after nearly half an hour.

Somehow, Louise thought, when Germanic people make suggestions, they come out sounding like commands.

Louise, now on her back, experienced a cool substance oozing over the entire front of her body from neck to toes. There seemed to be more than one attendant applying the ooze. But in the face of a light directly above, she could determine neither the number nor identity of the slatherers. Nor, for that matter, the nature of the substance.

"I beg your pardon," said Louise," but what is it that you're rubbing on me?"

"Eet ees Madame Tirana's spezial, oonique masque. Eet ees tze spezial breast facial."

Louise decided to let that mixed metaphor pass. In good time, she was certain she would be given a face facial. "But what is it made of?" she persisted.

"Oh, eet ees blend of—how you say—potato peels, carrot greens, and crushed peach pits." This in a triumphant tone.

Louise thought about that for a moment. "But . . . but . . . that's garbage!"

"Don't ask. You shouldn't have asked," Emma murmured from under her coating of Madame Tirana's masque. "Just let them put it on. It's good for you."

Louise asked no more. She remained silent during the rest of the breast facial, the face facial, and the hosing off that followed.

Then she and Emma, still nude, were led to a whirlpool bath. Many nude women were already in the large, circular bath, most of them propped against the edge of the tub, most of them appraising each newcomer. Rarely had Louise felt more embarrassed. She quickly submerged next to Emma, grateful for the cover of the bubbling water. "How did you ever find this place?"

"Impulse. I was driving by and I noticed the sign. It looked interesting, so I came in. I tried it, I liked it, I joined it. Just impulse. Like I do almost everything."

Impulse, thought Louise, How typical of one born to

wealth. Probably never had an unfulfilled wish in her entire life. If you feel like it, do it; if you want it, get it.
Even if she hadn't married an auto executive, Em's
inheritance would have enabled her to live in wealth. The
type who could afford the luxury of doing whatever she
wanted on impulse.

Louise could remember the lean years. Growing up on
Detroit's near east side, the daughter of a Packard die
cutter. Not in abject poverty, but certainly not in wealth.
Lots of stew, leftovers, hand-me-downs. Marriage to an
auto worker like her father. The formidable drop in income when Charlie started his own business. More years
of financially straitened living. Finally, success. Now,
and for many recent years, virtually no money worries.
But the early days had left their mark. Almost everything
she did was carefully planned. Almost nothing was done
on impulse.

Her reverie was disturbed by a voice above and behind
her. "So, it is a new chickie, yes?" Louise was at a loss
to place the accent.

"Madame Tirana!" said Emma. "What a surprise!
Yes, this is a new one: Mrs. Louise Chase."

"Not the life's companion of Charles Chase, the auto
executive who is forever in the papers!"

"The very one," Emma affirmed.

"Someone should have told me! Such things can be
important!"

By squinting, Louise could just see the newcomer
through the water vapors. She looked like an older—but
well-preserved—sister to Marlene Dietrich.

"How has it gone for you this day, Chickie?"

"Oh, fine." Louise—certain she would never return—
tried to be as noncommittal as possible.

"Oh, good! Well, you just rest in the Albanian waters
. . . did anybody tell you, Chickie, that the waters you
rest in are imported from my homeland?" Madame Tirana

did not pause for a response. "The Albanian waters will
take out of you all the badness and all the bugs. You will
feel better than well. I will be by and see you when you are
in makeup. Just rest, Chickie!" And Madame departed,
leaving Louise to wonder how Madame Tirana could possibly import anything from a country that had no diplomatic relations with the U.S. However, she contented
herself with, "Manic, isn't she?"

"But good at what she does," said Emma.

There is no disputing tastes, thought Louise. "Speaking of getting bugs out," she laughed, "I wish I could get
the little beasts out of our greenhouse."

"Black Leaf 40," said Emma.

"What?"

"Black Leaf 40. Spray it on at night and by the next
day . . ." Emma raised her arms out of the Albanian
waters and spread them. ". . . all gone. Cindy Mercury
told me about it."

"Cindy? I didn't think you and she were . . ." Louise
hesitated, ". . . friends."

"Oh, I have no problem with Cindy." Emma submerged again neck-deep in the bubbling water. "After
all, she *is* Frank's sister. It's that actor," she verbally
italicized the word, making an epithet of it. "If only he'd
get a decent job . . . or at least live within his means. As
it is, he's nothing but a parasite. And Frank is the host."

"Isn't there anything you can do?"

Emma shrugged. "I've tried. God, how I've tried. But
every time, Frank puts on his best bullheaded German attitude. He says he does it for his sister. And there undoubtedly is some truth to that. But I suspect he also gets
a kick out of keeping Angie on a string. It's like feeding
gin to an alcoholic. Money goes through Angie like a lax-
ative through a chicken. With Angie, and most of his fellow thespians who are 'between shows' more often than
in them, it's all a matter of image. Whether they've got

money or not, they've got to live in the big house, drive the big car, and always pick up the tab. I've seen Angie pick up a check when I knew he had barely enough to bail his car out of the parking lot." She paused. "It's not that we don't have the money . . . though even Frank, with his money alone, would have a difficult time supporting both our families in the style to which we all, particularly Angie, have become accustomed. But one day I'll have my way in this. And I think Frank knows it."

She lapsed into silence. All was still but for the sound of Albanian waters.

Louise had decided to follow Madame Tirana's advice, Chickie, and just rest. But her attention was taken by a new entrant to the whirlpool. Till now, she had been oblivious to the other occupants. But this newcomer was so outrageously gorgeous, Louise could not help but notice her. "Would you look at that one?" she said as the newcomer began descending the steps into the water.

"Who?" Emma opened her eyes and tried to focus through the mist.

"The blonde just getting into the water."

Emma appraised her quickly and grudgingly but objectively. "The thing that young woman has got to remember," she said as she again closed her eyes, "is that as we are now, she one day will be."

Louise watched as the blonde took a place directly across from them, settled into the water, and steadfastly studied Emma.

For the remainder of the time they were at the spa, including their session in makeup, the blonde was never far away. And the whole time she rarely took her eyes off Emma.

Louise wondered about that.

6.

"THANKS FOR TAKING THE EIGHT O'CLOCK MASS for me." Father Koesler snapped on the roman collar and fastened the clerical vest at his waist.

"Not at all," replied Bishop Ratigan, as he watered his plants. "My schedule is rather fluid today." He snorted. "No pun intended. But I have to see old Bud Davis later this morning. Talk about a fluid schedule: I've got to talk old Bud into going out to Guest House."

"Bud having trouble with the bottle again?"

"Yeah. Bad show this time. He was scheduled to take a funeral day before yesterday. But he had the granddaddy of all hangovers. And his assistant finally just refused to cover for him again."

"Don't tell me Bud took the funeral!"

Ratigan nodded sadly. "Made a mess of it. The bereaved were furious. Went to the parishioners. Special meeting of the parish council. Council president phoned me.

"Finally got hold of Bud yesterday. Had to threaten him with everything from hellfire to suspension . . . but he finally agreed to see me today."

"A pity. He's a very talented guy."

"May be a blessing in disguise."

"How's that?" Koesler slipped into his suit coat.

"Finally get him out to Guest House. Place does a great job of rehabilitating alcoholic priests. Percentage of success stays phenomenally high, year in and year out."

"That's true . . . but have you given any thought to how you're going to get him out there? All he's agreed to so far is come down and see you."

Ratigan smiled. "Bud's not the only one going to be at the meeting: Ted Neighbors will be there too."

"Bud's best friend!"

"Yup. Ted's going to take him out to Guest House after our meeting."

"I see. He will be hung immediately after a fair trial."

"Only way to get it done."

Koesler slipped his topcoat on and nodded toward the greenery over which Ratigan was hovering. "How's it doing?"

"As they say at the hospital, 'as well as can be expected.' By the way—and again—it was very nice of you to provide this greenhouse. Very generous."

"Don't thank me. The parish council approved the expenditure. Besides, this wing of the rectory was empty. It makes more sense to convert it to a greenhouse so things can live in it rather than just let it rust out."

"Nonetheless, it was you who introduced the matter before the council and you who strongly supported it."

"Not really." Koesler sipped the last of his coffee. "Sometimes I think that my introducing a resolution is the kiss of death."

They laughed.

"Actually, I think they're so proud of having a real

live bishop living in St. Anselm's rectory that they'd give you just about anything you wanted. Catering to your green thumb is just not that burdensome.

"But, I suppose, once a landscaper, always a landscaper."

"Aren't you grateful that doesn't apply equally to camp counselors?"

"Absolutely. I paid my dues taking care of kids."

"Say," Ratigan began as Koesler turned to leave, "what are you doing up so early, anyway? I thought when you asked me to take morning Mass, you'd be sleeping in."

"Hardly. I want to be at the auto repair shop when it opens at 7:30."

"You taking your car in *again*? You might as well leave that Cheetah at the shop and rent one of theirs!"

"The warranty is about to run out. And the weather stripping has pulled loose from the door again. I want it fixed while it's still under warranty—and before winter sets in."

"Well, good luck. But I'll bet this won't be the last time they have to tuck that insulation in . . . just the last time under warranty."

"I'm not going to cover that bet."

"Besides," Ratigan called out as Koesler exited, "with parishioners like Charlie Chase and Frank Hoffman, why do you have to keep dragging that car down to the repair shop? They build the damn Cheetah!"

Koesler drove down Outer Drive to Ford Road to Telegraph. The latter was one of Detroit's responses to the Indy 500. Drivers on Telegraph gave consistent added proof—if any were needed—that it was a dog-eat-dog world.

As Koesler found the middle lane, following his phi-

losophy—in all things moderation—he reflected on Ratigan's parting shot.

Now that I think of it, I'll bet Charlie and Frank don't
have to go through this.

7.

FRANK HOFFMAN WAS IN A DECIDEDLY FOUL mood. And his mood was exacerbated by the fact that the weather stripping had pulled loose from the door of his car and a late October chill was making him decidedly uncomfortable.

The day had begun badly. Em had picked this morning to complain about the amount of time he spent away from home. She had demanded to talk about it "right now!" Which had led to another argument as well as a maldigested breakfast.

If that weren't bad enough, he had just lost two out of three racquetball games to a young subordinate. Even the ploy of the deadened ball hadn't worked. There was definitely something to be said for young legs. But there was also something to be said for the power of superior position—as this young man would soon learn when he was passed over for promotion and did not receive the merit increase he was anticipating. If the young man were as bright as The Company's hierarchy had been led to believe—he had received a high pot rating from the recruiters—he would quickly learn when and to whom he should lose gracefully.

He had been so angry at losing at racquetball that he

had not dried himself carefully after showering. And now, this chill wind blowing through the door was completing the job of drying his hair—he never wore a hat—and threatening incipient pneumonia.

Jefferson Avenue dipped beneath Cobo Hall and became the John Lodge Freeway.

Hoffman's anger at the early events of this young day had led to a general impatient frame of mind. So, as he drove out of the chute onto the freeway, he accelerated much more than necessary and well above the speed limit. His right front and rear tires plunged sequentially into a yawning pothole. Even in this well-suspended vehicle, the impact rattled his teeth.

Damned potholes! And it's not even winter yet. The constant fluctuation of temperature in the typical Detroit winter would soon create new and incredibly large potholes in the city's streets and freeways. Sometimes it seemed futile to even try to build decent cars when the roadways on which they had to travel would rip them apart.

He barely had time to reflect on the monster pits that threatened to swallow his products when he swung up and off the freeway onto West Grand Boulevard. Only several blocks east was the Fisher Building with its famed golden tower that was attractively illuminated at night. Employees of The Company worldwide invariably referred to the Fisher as The Building.

Hoffman tapped the horn. A huge door opened upward.

"Harry," Hoffman said to the attendant who hurried toward him, "the goddamn weather stripping is loose."

"Yessir, Mr. Hoffman. We'll get right on it."

He left his car in Harry's care. Before Hoffman would see it again, it would be cleaned outside and in, gassed and serviced—and the weather stripping would be tucked securely into its mount.

Hoffman strode quickly through the huge long vaulted main floor of The Building. But instead of turning toward the elevator that would have taken him to the thirteenth— the executive—floor, he continued out of The Building and across Grand Boulevard, past Topinka's to a nondescript little eatery whose exterior was painted a cheery yellow. Inside, he easily spotted the man with whom he had the appointment for which he was right on time.

"How goes it, Al?" Hoffman slid into the booth.

"Just fine, Mr. Hoffman. How about yourself?"

"Don't ask. This day had better improve quickly or I'm going to cancel it."

Uncertain how much humor was intended, Al considered a chuckle, but settled on a concerned frown.

The waitress appeared with menus, which Hoffman waved aside. "Just two coffees."

Al had assumed they would breakfast. He definitely desired more than coffee. But he said nothing. He would try to get something to eat later. If not, it didn't matter. What mattered at the moment was to follow his superior's lead.

"Nice day for late in October," Hoffman commented.

"First-rate, sir."

"Who do the Lions play this Sunday?"

"The Vikes, sir. The Minnesota Vikings."

"Hmmm. Did I ever tell you what happened the day the Vikes were late for the game here? Not many know about it. I got it from one of our guys in St. Paul."

Al shook his head and grinned in anticipation of this—or any—anecdote that Hoffman would deign to tell him.

"You remember the day, don't you—when the Vikings showed up half an hour late for the game?"

Al nodded eagerly. "Who could forget it? National TV, and all the viewers got to see for the first half hour was the Vikings warming up. They got fined for that, didn't they, sir?''

"Sure did. All a result of Bud Grant's obsession with timing. The coach never wanted to get to a stadium on game day too early. Only he hadn't figured on the horrendous traffic jam that always takes place at PonMet. So, by the time the Vikings' bus got to the stadium approach, traffic was so backed up, there was no way the bus was going to get there on time.

"Well," Hoffman was warming to his story, "the driver panicked. He figured everyone would think it was his fault the Vikings were late. So he opened his window and shouted to a traffic cop, 'Hey! I've got the Vikings!' And the cop yelled back, 'I've got the Lions and six!' ''

Al laughed uproariously. It was a funny story, although perhaps not that funny.

"Easy, Al," Hoffman cautioned, "we don't want to attract attention."

Instantly, Al reduced the volume of his laughter, but maintained an appreciative chuckle.

Experience had proven to Hoffman that one of the more perfect places for a clandestine meeting was this small restaurant almost across the street from The Building. Employees of The Company, at least those who worked in The Building, would never dream of eating here. There were too many satisfying places to eat housed in The Building.

And if one wanted to dine outside The Building, there were many quality restaurants nearby, among them Fisher 666 and Topinka's. No one from The Company ever ate here. Hoffman counted on this. He wanted no one from The Company to be aware of this meeting.

"By the way, Al," Hoffman said, after Al retrieved control of himself, "how are you fixed for tickets for Sunday's game?''

"We're sort of praying it will be a sellout and they'll televise it locally," Al replied with a touch of humility.

"Nonsense! Take mine."

"Oh, sir, I couldn't—"

"Of course you can. You'll like them. They're just beneath Billy Ford's box. I'll have my secretary get them to you later today."

"I don't know how to thank you, sir."

Hoffman could have been the author of the paraphrase, "There is no such thing as a free game." In fact, he was about to collect for it.

"Speaking of later today," Hoffman came to the point, "is everything set up for your meeting with Chase?"

"Yes, sir." Al appeared confident.

"What's the agenda?"

"The same two principal topics that will be considered at next week's general board meeting: the Lemon Laws and our prime demographic target."

"Good! And you've got the stats I sent you?"

"Yes, sir. I have those and a few supporting statistics I was able to dig up myself."

"Good man! Who else will be at the meeting?"

"Just my associate, Clem—"

"Are you sure you can keep him in line? We can't have anything—*any*thing—go wrong at this meeting. It will be hard enough to convince Chase to adopt this position even in the face of a united front. One dissenting voice, and—"

"You have absolutely nothing to be concerned about, sir." Al very seldom interrupted a superior but, he judged, this interruption would be both justified and appreciated. "Clem and I have worked together on similar projects before. And I've been over this with him exhaustively. He'll follow my lead. No doubt of it. Clem's a good Company man and he . . . uh . . . knows his place."

Hoffman smiled. "Good! Anybody who knows his place in The Company should live to see that place constantly upgraded."

Hoffman briefly contrasted the young man who had so rashly won a small victory in this morning's racquetball match and Al here, who seemed to have learned well the art of playing the proper supportive role. The latter was sure to follow Hoffman up the corporate ladder. While the former was likely to experience a stagnating career. No matter how much high pot he had exhibited to the recruiters.

"Anybody else scheduled for the meeting?"

Al hesitated. "Clem and I are all we really need. We'll have the stats, and together we should be able to handle any argument he might raise."

"I don't like it!"

In which case, Al didn't like it either.

"Chase may object that the two of you represent only one department. He may demand, in effect, a second opinion from someone other than your department."

"But sir, our department is the only one involved in the policy decisions of both those questions."

"No," Hoffman said thoughtfully, "we've got to anticipate that possibility. If we provide another—still supportive—opinion, that may just be the final nail in the coffin. But who . . . ?"

There followed a pregnant silence during which both men sipped at their coffee.

"How about someone from P.R.?" Al offered.

"No. It's too late to try to find just the right one. And almost anyone in P.R. is just as likely to raise objections as Chase is. No, that won't do."

Having failed once, Al decided he'd better retire from this game with only one strike. It was his preferred stratagem. Never chance striking out with a superior. If one try proved a failure, wait for word from the boss and then support that word for all you're worth.

"What about that guy from the ad agency? The one that services our Cheetah division?" Hoffman searched for a name. "You know: The guy who is such a complete horse's ass . . . the one who spends all his time with jocks."

Al brightened. "Zaleski! Ziggy Zaleski!"

"That's it! That's the one. No preparation needed with him. Just make sure you and Clem get the ball rolling."

"I know. I know. Once he sees the direction of the momentum," Al began to anticipate the sports jargon, "Ziggy will be sure to go with the flow."

They laughed.

"Just one final thought, sir." Al grew grave. "Do you think we have set this up sufficiently? I mean, this will be the most serious and far-reaching decision for Mr. Chase in his entire time with The Company so far. Do you think he trusts me well enough to follow my advice? I mean, this is going to be a big step for him to take."

"You've got nothing to worry about."

The waitress deposited the check for two coffees. Hoffman ignored it. It would be Al's privilege to once more clean up after Hoffman.

"You're top man in your department," Hoffman continued. "I made sure Chase saw your file when I recommended you to him. And since then, you have served him well and, in most instances, even though they were comparatively insignificant matters, given him good reliable advice. No doubt about it: He is set up for the sting.

"And you don't have to be concerned about covering your ass. When the shit hits the fan after next week's board meeting, I'll make sure none of it soils you."

Hoffman picked up his briefcase and slid out of the

booth. "After your meeting with Chase, be sure to report to me."

"Yes, sir." Al left a quarter tip and took the check to the cash register. He would wait till Hoffman was well inside The Building before following him.

As Hoffman crossed Grand Boulevard, he shivered. Damn! It was that blasted racquetball match followed by the chill he'd gotten driving to work. By God, if he came down with something, that young shit would pay a stiffer price than he already owed for beating his superior!

8.

"**Y**OU'RE NOT BUFFALO BILL, FOR CRISSAKES! You're not Chief Sitting Bull! You're not Frank Butler! And you're not Wild Bill Hickok! Hell, you're not even Charlie Davenport! Which is who you're supposed to be! So tell me, willya: Whatinhell are you doin' in *Annie Get Your Gun*?"

Nate Goodman, theatrical agent for, among others, Angie Mercury, was almost shouting.

"Calm down, Nate," said Mercury, "or you'll throw an embolism."

"What show is that from?"

"What?"

" 'Embolism'! What kind of word is that? That you should know from an embolism! It must have come from some show!"

Mercury smiled. " 'General Hospital.' I was on it a few years back. I was a doctor."

"A doctor, *maybe*. Charlie Davenport, *never*!"

They were in the ample auditorium of the Community House in Birmingham, one of Detroit's many affluent suburbs. There was a break in this early rehearsal of *Annie Get Your Gun*. Most of the cast was scattered about the auditorium, sipping coffee, smoking, silently

going over the script. Mercury was seated in the front
row. Nate, who had arrived only a short time before, was
at his side.

"It's work," Mercury said, almost apologetically.

"What, work! A hundred a performance and two
weekends open-ended? That's not work! That's a benefit!"

Mercury shook his head. "Nate, what makes you so
sore? That I got this gig myself, or that you're getting 15
percent of a hundred bucks?"

"Both! Plus, you are stooping to what is, in essence,
an amateur production!"

"C'mon, Nate. These kids are equity. You know as
well as I that I couldn't be in it if it weren't a professional
production."

"Professional! Look about you: These people are still
fighting acne!"

"Check their union cards, Nate: They're pros."

"I know what they look like, with or without their
cards. And so do the producers around town. Angie, this
is so bad I don't even want to see it in your file. Can't I
get it through that pancake makeup of yours that mere
work is not always good? In this business, you're either
going up or down. And *Annie Get Your Gun* in
Birmingham's Community House is not your stairway to
paradise!"

"You don't understand, Nate." How, thought Mercury, could he understand? "I have another source of income that hasn't got anything to do with this business.
But to get that dough, or to keep peace around the
house—or both, I don't know—I've got to keep working.
This money comes in, I got to be able to give chapter and
verse of what I'm in, what I'm rehearsing, and my fond
hopes for a rosy future. I don't do that and it's not so
much the money stops as there's just the devil to pay. Be-

lieve me, Nate, I've got to keep my hand in, accepting whatever comes along. I got no choice.''

Goodman slumped even further in his seat. ''All I know is you're not doing you, me, or your career any favors!''

The director reentered the auditorium. ''OK, gang! Let's take it from where we left off. And please, *please*, let's see if we can get through this alive!''

Mercury grinned and leaned toward Goodman. He spoke just loudly enough to be heard at close range. ''You wouldn't believe this rehearsal, Nate. Murphy's Law has been overactive.''

''I could believe it,'' Goodman said glumly.

''In one scene,'' Mercury went on in spite of, or perhaps because of, Goodman's dourness, ''Annie Oakley is supposed to perform a brand-new trick in Buffalo Bill's Wild West Show. It's all done offstage, of course. But she's supposed to ride around on a motorcycle balancing on her head and shooting eggs off poodles' heads.''

''I think I would prefer that onstage,'' Goodman said to no one.

''So, behind the flats, Buffalo Bill anounces this feat and yells, 'Annie Oakley, are you ready?' She yells back, 'Ready!'

'' 'Then, go!' yells Bill. The sound effects gal hits the tape switch—and we hear, 'Chug-a-chug-a-chug—wooh-wooh!' It's a train effect!'' Mercury doubled up with laughter.

Goodman's lip curled. ''I could give you a better example? You see, it's like I been telling you all along: amateurs!''

''OK, gang! We're going to start from where Annie's little brother and sisters are on stage.''

There was a scramble as three fully grown, but extremely young-looking adults clambered on stage. The man—boy—wore a scruffy shirt and jeans. The girls wore what appeared to be loose-fitting potato sacks.

"OK, now," the director instructed, "you're locking Annie's rifle case. The two girls try to keep the keys inside their dresses. When the keys fall to the floor the second time, Little Jake puts them in his pocket. And," he cued Little Jake, "you say: '*I'll* keep 'em. I got pockets.' "

Little Jake recited with little emotion.

"And then, they fall to the floor again . . . you *do* have a hole in your pocket, don't you, Little Jake?"

Little Jake, bored, nodded.

"And then, Dolly makes her entrance and sees the keys.

"Everybody ready?"

The three actors began to be busy working with an imaginary guncase with a real set of keys.

"I'll keep the keys!" declared the first girl, tossing them down the neckline of her potato sack dress. The keys fell noisily to the floor.

The second girl scooped up the fallen keys. "I'll keep 'em," she recited, "you're too flat-chested!" She tossed them into her décolletage.

And there they stayed.

Everyone but the director virtually collapsed in laughter.

The girl with the keys fixed firmly in her bosom performed a sort of wild disco dance until the keys finally dislodged and fell to the floor.

"That's what happens when you send a woman to do a girl's job," snickered Mercury.

The director threw up his hands in a helpless gesture. "Some days you can't make a nickel. This seems to be our day for coming up empty.

"OK, everybody, let's break for today. Be here at ten

tomorrow morning. And Shirley: See if you can flatten your chest overnight.''

Some of the cast left immediately; others milled about.

"Sound engineer doesn't know a bike from a train," Goodman groused. "Girl with keys stuck in her shelf! This isn't for you, Angie. You're an actor! You're a pro!''

"And as for you, Nate," Mercury said, in a rare show of assertiveness, "let's keep things straight: You're my agent! You work for me! I don't work for you! Your job is not to tell me where I can't work! Your job is to find me so many roles I'll have a hard time trying to decide which one to accept!''

"OK," Goodman responded after a slight pause during which he appeared to have been taken aback. "What's with the aggressive? It ain't you, Angie. You don't even play it good. Where'd you get it?''

Mercury smiled and shrugged. Found out again. "*West of Waco*—just a B western. '59, I think. I played the sheriff.''

"Angie," Goodman sighed, "I've seen actors and I've seen actors . . . but you take the cake. You're the only guy I know who lives his entire life as written by somebody else.

"But," he hitched up his trousers over a pronounced potbelly, "you've got a point. Nay, you have motivated me. I'll find you a better vehicle than *Annie Get Your Gun* or my name ain't Swifty Lazar!''

"That's the spirit, Swifty!" Mercury slapped Goodman on the rump after the fashion of a coach with a footballer entering the fray. "Get out there and win one for Charlie Davenport!''

Together, they walked across the street to the metered parking lot.

"Whatcha driving?" Goodman scanned the lot for his car.

"That Panther over there." Mercury gestured toward a sleek black sports coupe.

Goodman whistled. "Whatever 'other source of income' you got must be something! Since I get a slice of what you make in the business, I know if you bought a Panther with that income, you wouldn't eat the rest of the year!"

"Don't try to figure it, Nate. You'll only hurt your head." Mercury waved and trotted toward his car.

As he drove down Southfield toward Dearborn Heights, for a change—for a major change—Mercury did not turn on the radio. Instead, he became obsessed with the purposely lost racquetball games, the purposely lost card games, the generous check that came in each month, this damn luxury car.

Damn! That guy permeates my life. Cindy and I might just as well be on welfare—high class welfare, but the dole nonetheless. Frank Hoffman is the reason I have to drag myself out of bed any morning he wants and play racquetball—no, *lose* at racquetball—when I'd rather be going slowly through the paper and having several leisurely cups of coffee.

Hoffman is the reason I'm drivng a car so big I can barely afford gas for it. Hoffman is the reason I have to look for and accept any acting job I can get, instead of waiting for the right role. It's bad enough having to accept money from him without having to admit, under his regular scrutiny, that I haven't got any job at all.

He swung off the Southfield Freeway onto Ford Road. Only a few miles from home.

If it weren't for Cindy, I'd never do it. How I yearn to beat that bastard at racquetball; beat him at poker; tear that damn check into shreds and throw it in his face; get rid of this damn gas guzzler—wouldn't you know it had to be a product of The Company, and a none-too-gracious gift from Hoffman! A new car every year, always from The Company, courtesy of Frank Hoffman. A car we could never finance. A car so extravagant we couldn't even keep it in gas without that damnable check! How could a certified bastard like Frank Hoffman have a sister as sweet as Cindy?

Mercury pulled into his driveway. Cindy was raking leaves in the front yard.

Mercury had always thought his wife to be one of the most attractive women he'd ever known. And, in his business, he had met some of the most beautiful women in the world. Even after twenty years of marriage, his opinion had not changed. His opinion, of course, was not entirely unbiased. But most students of feminine beauty would have agreed with him.

Mercury had the relatively rare distinction in his field of never having been unfaithful to his wife. Undoubtedly if he had been, his brother-in-law probably would have had his legs broken. But that motivation was irrelevant and of no more importance than a further third-party annoyance. Mercury was faithful merely because he loved his wife and no one else in any comparable way. And he firmly believed that there had to be love or sex was meaningless.

He left the Panther in the drive and walked deliberately toward Cindy. She had on gray slacks and a loose-fitting wool sweater. He admired her figure as he approached from the rear.

Though the phrase meant nothing, hers was a figure that was classically described as "legs that don't quit." At five feet eight, she was only a couple of inches shorter than he. She maintained her trimness not by spa visits or exotic diets, but simply by eating abstemiously and getting a lot of healthy exercise in and around the house and lawn.

He slipped his arms around her waist from behind. She was not startled. She had seen him pull into the drive and had been aware of his approach. She half turned toward him with a smile. He'd always thought she had the profile of Grace Kelly.

"What brings you home so soon?" She rested the rake against herself.

"Bad rehearsal." His arms tightened about her.

"Bad rehearsal, good show. As you always say."

"Actually, it was because they sent a woman to do a child's job."

"What?"

He smiled. "What would happen if you were to toss a set of keys down the inside front of your dress?"

"Why would I do a silly thing like that?"

"Because you were keeping the keys for Annie Oakley."

"Annie Oakley!"

"What would happen," he slipped his hands beneath her sweater and ran them up her body until they cupped her breasts, "is that they would stick right there. Lucky keys."

She laughed softly, deep in her throat. "You ought to have bad rehearsals more often."

"You mean you're willing to leave your leaves?"

"The leaves we will have with us always." She gave the rake a push. It fell to the ground, scattering leaves on either side. "Who are you going to be today? Robert Redford? Humphrey Bogart?"

"I think . . . Errol Flynn." He scooped her up in his arms and swung her in a circle. Then, still carrying her, he sprinted toward the house with a whoop.

She shrieked and then called out, "Then I'll be Maureen O'Hara!"

Who cared if the neighbors were watching!

Later, Mercury toyed with a ham salad sandwich while Cindy prepared a small pot roast for dinner.

"Pam called from Western Michigan this morning," she said as she went about her culinary work.

"Oh?" He looked up, startled. "Anything wrong? She's not ill or anything, is she?" He was naturally concerned about their only child . . . though at nineteen, she was a child no longer.

"Oh, no. Nothing like that. She wants to take a course in medieval history. She wants to fill in a liberal arts curriculum . . ." Her voice trailed off.

"I suppose that means more money. Is it worth it?"

"Oh, yes, Angie, I think so. With a good liberal arts background, no matter what major she settles on, she'll be well prepared for almost anything. Plus it's just going to broaden her knowledge. Make her a better-informed person."

"But," he shut his eyes tightly, "where are we going to find the money?"

She left the roast, dried her hands on her apron, and touched his shoulders. "Don't worry. We'll find the money."

"Frank!" He fairly spat the name out.

She shut her eyes and massaged his shoulders. "Frank wants to help. Maybe he does it a little clumsily. Maybe he is a little arrogant. He isn't a saint. He never claimed to be. He just wants to help us."

"You."

"All right, *me*. But it works out to be us."

"He's taking my manhood. He makes me feel like a kid. He makes me feel like a beggar. He holds our lives by a string. Do you ever think of what would happen to us—to our entire way of life—if he ever turned off the faucet?"

"He'd never do that!" She backed away, shocked.

"Emma isn't nutty about his giving us all that money. What if she made him quit?"

"Em has nothing to do with it."

"She's his wife."

"It doesn't matter. It's *his* money."

He was silent. She returned to the roast.

"Medieval history," he said after a few moments. "Why in the world would anyone want to study medieval history?"

"She wants to be a German medievalist." It was said almost defensively.

"A German medievalist," he repeated in awe. Until that moment, he would have had a difficult time thinking of any profession other than his own that could almost guarantee regular unemployment. "A German medievalist! Well, that's great: If anybody ever needs one, she'll be there."

Cindy, chopping carrots, smiled.

"She could be Greer Garson," he continued, "doing 'Madame Curie Was a Closet German.' "

Cindy laughed. Angie may never have grown up—might indeed never grow up—but she remained head over heels in love with him. Even though he hardly ever got offstage.

Without reflection, she began to hum, "Can't help lovin' that man of mine."

It was catching.

9.

"**W**HAT BRINGS YOU HOME SO EARLY?"

Father Koesler looked up from transcribing a baptismal certificate as a figure passed his office door.

"I'm not home, exactly." Bishop Ratigan stuck his head through the door. "Sort of in transit. I'm meeting Frank Hoffman for lunch."

"It's all right for you to do that, you know. You don't have to check in with me before you go to the Orchard Lake C.C." Koesler had no trouble speaking with his tongue in his cheek.

Ratigan almost smiled. "I'm picking up something I want to give Frank. The reason I'm giving the appearance of 'checking in' with you is that you never leave home. Thus I simply can't avoid running into you."

"Easy there." Koesler waved a hand. "I ring my share of doorbells. Besides, I'm just about to go over for a penance service."

"The school kids?"

"Uh-huh."

"What grades?"

"Fifth and sixth."

"Good! You couldn't handle anything higher." He disappeared from the doorway.

Actually, thought Koesler, the bishop couldn't have been more wrong. It had been Koesler's experience that the younger the congregation, the more difficult time he had communicating.

"By the way," Koesler called after him, "can you see your way clear to taking early Mass again tomorrow?"

The bishop's face reappeared. "I guess so. What is it this time?"

"Got to take my car back for repair."

"Ha! I knew it! And you just had the weather stripping fixed, didn't you?"

"That's right. But while they were replacing the stripping, they noticed that one of the pillars was cracked."

"I've heard of planned obsolescence, but your car takes the cake."

Koesler completed transcribing the baptismal certificate. As he signed it, he recalled a similar transcription at a parish which, in its beginnings, had been heavily Italian. The first pastor had been Italian and had kept his records in a mishmash of Italian and Latin. One record Koesler had transcribed had been in Italian. He had transcribed it, faithfully, as was prescribed, in English. But between the names of the godparents, the old pastor had noted, in Latin, "nil dederunt." So, Koesler had dutifully noted on the transcribed certificate, between the godparents' names, the homey comment, "They gave nothing."

He carefully folded the certificate and placed it in the self-addressed stamped envelope that had accompanied the request. As he sealed the envelope, he heard the back door of the rectory close. The bishop was off to the country club.

Hoffman had never invited Koesler to the club. Koesler didn't mind. Ratigan and Hoffman were, after all, rather close. It was only natural they should socialize. Usually, it was better, Koesler believed, if the pastor was not all that socially familiar with his parishioners. It lacked professionalism and could prove a hindrance if the pastor ever felt it necessary to reprove someone who also happened to be a social companion.

Time for the penance service. Koesler adjusted his cassock, slipped into his cape, and walked the short distance to the church.

The children were already there, assembled into the first few pews. Their teachers having given up trying to keep them quiet, Koesler caught a distinct but unintelligible murmur as he entered the church. It did not cease as he walked by them and into the sacristy.

However, as he reentered the church, now in surplice and stole over his cassock, the children stood and sang the entrance hymn. All was in order.

Koesler proceeded to the rear of the church and entered his confessional.

He walked around the screened portion of the room, sat behind the screen, draped a narrow violet stole over his shoulders, and waited for the afternoon's first young penitent.

He gazed about the light, airy room. It is different than it was, he reflected. In fact, this type of confessional denoted one of the most decided and stark changes in the Church to flow from the Second Vatican Council of the early sixties. And today's children—the ones who would be entering here in the upcoming minutes—would have no concept of what the experience of confession had been for centuries before.

For the vast majority of Koesler's priesthood, he had been squeezed into one grossly uncomfortable confessional after another. Appropriately termed "the box," the traditional confessional space had consisted of three compartments. The priest-confessor sat in the central compartment. On either side of him was, usually, a sliding door. If no penitent was in either of the outer compartments, both doors were left open. Once a penitent was in either compartment, the priest would slide the opposite door shut.

Even then, the confessor was separated from the penitent by a screen and a curtain. While there was no "standard size" for these compartments, the usual dimensions made it necessary for skinny priests to do a good bit of sliding back and forth in order to hear the whispered sins. Whereas a corpulent confessor had less room than that afforded by the average coffin.

Koesler recalled one priest with an aversion to blondes that stemmed from an incident that had taken place one Saturday afternoon as he sat in his confessional. There he was, peacefully minding his own business, when suddenly a small blonde girl raised the curtain on the door, peered in at him, then shouted to the church at large, "Mommie! There's a man in here sitting on the pottie!"

In order to inform waiting penitents that one or another of the compartments was already occupied, some long-gone genius had installed small electric lights over each compartment. A green light went on when the confessor sat down, red when a penitent knelt.

Koesler had a clerical friend who would occasionally place a brick on each kneeler, triggering the red lights. Then he would slip into his compartment and have himself a nice little nap.

But now, in most churches, the old confessionals, along with their associated jokes, existed only in the memories of those old enough to have experienced them. Confession had segued into the sacrament of reconciliation.

It was much, much more than a change in name only.

Now, many, if not most, confessionals were outfitted in much the same manner as Koesler's. His was a room divided more or less in half by a large, opaque screen with a kneeler in front for those who preferred confession in the old style, or who always or occasionally desired anonymity.

Or one could—and many did—walk around the screen and occupy a chair facing the confessor. Confession under such circumstance tended to be less formal, as did the penances imposed by the confessor.

Penances, a form of "punishment" meted out for sins confessed, also had changed—at least for those who chose to confess face to face.

In ancient times, penances often were both public and extreme. Public begging for a year, for instance.

In modern times, penances generally had consisted of prayers to be offered privately. Due in large part to the anonymity of the confessional, most confessors doled out a certain number of Our Fathers and Hail Marys as penances—the thinking being that while the priest would not know who the penitent might be, he could be reasonably sure that all Catholics knew the Lord's Prayer and the Hail Mary.

Since almost all penances, or "punishments," consisted of the Lord's Prayer and/or the Hail Mary, numbers became important to differentiate between serious and not-so-serious sins. A penance might consist of three Our Fathers and three Hail Marys. Or perhaps the most popular of all, five Our Fathers and five Hail Marys. For sins the priest considered "deliberate violations of serious matters," perhaps ten Our Fathers and ten Hail Marys, or, if the confessor felt adventurous, the recitation of the Rosary.

It was only natural that humorous, sometimes apocryphal, stories sprang up to illustrate this moral foray into crime and punishment. Koesler had heard—and told—the story of a series of young men going to confession one after the other. Each had confessed a fairly innocuous series of sins, such as being tardy for Mass, talking in church, being disrespectful to elders. And each had concluded his recitation of sins with, "and I played the fiddle." The priest never having heard of a sin called "playing the fiddle" decided not to inquire into the exact nature of this crime. One tended not to inquire too deeply into such matters in direct proportion to the number of years one had been hearing confessions.

In any case, the priest dismissed the first three penitents with the standard five Our Fathers and five Hail Marys. But when the fourth consecutive penitent concluded with ". . . and I played the fiddle several times," the priest lost the battle with his curiosity and asked, "Just what is it you mean by 'playing the fiddle'?"

"Fornication," responded the young man.

Considering the mild penances he'd been handing out for one of Catholicism's traditionally most grievous sins, the priest leaned out of the confessional door and called out, "Will the first violin section please come back in here?"

The question of anonymity, even in the Good Old Days, was not as uniformly guaranteed as it was intended to be.

It is true the confessor could not see the penitent in the traditional confessional. It is also true that confessor and penitent communicated in whispers. But even then, sometimes there were peculiarities that to one extent or another shredded secrecy.

Some penitents, for instance, spoke softly rather than whispered, thus communicating the distinctive qualities of their voices. And even though the confessor might be uninterested in the penitent's identity, perhaps even to the point of preferring not to know, sometimes in such circumstance there was simply no mistaking the identity.

Then there were those who, while whispering, had a peculiarity of speech that while it might not have revealed their identity, yet would identify them as having been there before. Sometimes it was a specific introductory formula. Koesler recalled a man who always began his confession, "Bless me, Father, for I have sinned. I confess to Almighty God and to thee, my Ghostly Father . . ." While Koesler never knew the man's identity, the formula identified a frequent visitor who was scrupulous.

Finally, there were those who simply identified themselves. For whatever reason, they wanted the confessor to know who they were. There were not many of these.

All this Father Koesler reflected on while he awaited the arrival of the first of the day's young penitents. Nowadays, fifth and sixth graders were eligible to go to confession. Fourth graders and younger no longer were granted this sacrament. They were warming up on the sidelines. Nor would *all* the fifth and sixth graders go to confession today. Only those who felt the need of reform.

This, too, was a far far cry from the routine of only a few years before, a time when children in the second grade and up had begun to go to confession. Koesler had often thought that there was no more cruel torture devised by man for man than what used to take place in a Catholic school setting on the Thursday before First Friday. Spurred on by promises alleged to have been made by the Blessed Mother to St. Margaret Mary, many Catholics made a special effort to receive communion on the First Friday of each month. The promises required only nine consecutive First Fridays, but once the habit was begun, most Catholics simply couldn't turn it off.

The best time to begin this habit, many thought, was while one had the captive audience of parochial school children. And since it was a holy and wholesome thought to receive communion on First Friday, it also seemed to someone a good idea for everyone to go to confession the day before.

And so, on the Thursdays before First Fridays, at

about 9:00 A.M., the good sisters would begin lining up the entire second grade for confessions. They were immediately followed by the third, fourth, fifth, sixth, seventh, and eighth grades. Break for lunch. Back to the box for high school freshmen, sophomores, juniors, and seniors.

Koesler's mind ached at the memory. An exercise like today's with individual members of a mere two grades choosing to confess was literally child's play compared with the Good Old Days.

His musings were interrupted when a small blonde girl stepped around the screen and sat opposite him.

"Hi." He greeted her with somewhat less formality than the rubrics suggested.

"Hi, Father," she said brightly. And then in a more serious attitude, "I've been thinking, and I guess I haven't been as good to my mother as I should."

"No?"

"No. She wants me to help around the house but I almost never do. And she's so old now, she probably won't be around much longer."

"Oh? How old is she?"

"Thirty-six!"

Koesler controlled an urge to smile.

"So, I think I'll help her more. At least I'll make my bed in the morning. And that's all," she announced with a satisfied nod.

"I think that's a good resolution, Sally. Why don't we make your penance just making your bed tomorrow?"

Again she nodded.

Koesler raised his right arm and intoned, "God, the Father of mercies, through the death and resurrection of His Son, has reconciled the world to Himself and sent the Holy Spirit among us for the forgiveness of sins. Through the ministry of the Church may God give you pardon and peace, and I absolve you from your sins," he traced the sign of the cross in the air, "in the name of the Father and of the Son and of the Holy Spirit."

"Amen," said Sally. And, smiling, she exited.

After a few moments, Koesler heard the familiar sound of knees hitting wood. For whatever reason, the next child was going to use the screen.

"All right," Koesler said, as he leaned head and shoulders toward the plastic-latticed screen.

"Bless me, Father, for I have sinned. My last confession was about a month ago."

Koesler guessed what was going on. The whisper sounded as if it belonged to a boy. In any case, it was probably the youngster's parents who had countermanded the training he'd received in school and had taught their child to confess in the manner they had been taught. If Koesler was correct, this formula would be followed by the old-fashioned "laundry list" of sins.

"And since then," the child proceeded, "I disobeyed my mother ten times. I disobeyed my father about five times. I swore six times. I talked in church four times. I used God's name in vain once. I lied twice. I fought with another boy once. And I stole a nickel from my little sister. I am sorry for these and all the sins of my past life, especially for adultery."

Koesler did not bat an eyelash. This was by no means the first time a child had demonstrated ignorance concerning the nature of things sexual. But Koesler, in confessional matters, lived by two rules: Don't interrupt a child's laundry list of sins—the list is probably memorized and if it is interrupted one may reap prolonged silence. Followed by a starting over. And secondly, don't use the confessional for teaching.

To these, the priest had recently added a third rule, occasioned by experiences such as this: If parents insist that their child grow up in the same manner they did, let it be.

The only bad thing was that the young person would

probably never mature out of this childish approach to confession, just as the parents had never shed their own penitential adolescence. But parents had prime responsibility for their children—let them look to it.

"OK," he said to the screen, "for your penance, say three Our Fathers and three Hail Marys—and try to return the nickel to your sister."

"Yes, Father."

Koesler gave absolution, after which the child departed.

He was followed by an extremely small girl who fairly skipped around the screen and lifted herself onto the chair. Seated, her feet did not reach the ground. Koesler recalled that barbarians sometimes used such as a position of torture, and he resolved to have a smaller chair added to the confessional furnishings in the near future.

"Hi," he greeted the new penitent.

"Hi, Father, I've been thinking about all my faults, and I think the worst one is I bug my brother. I'm going to try not to bug him so much."

"Good idea, Andrea. I'm sure Tommy will appreciate that. For your penance, try to do something nice for Tommy tonight."

He absolved her and she departed.

A few moments later, he heard the sound of small knees hitting the kneeler on the other side of the screen.

"All right," Koesler said, letting the penitent know that all was ready.

After a few moments, came a small boy's voice: "Hell, damn, shit, son-of-a-bitch, fuck it, fuck it in a bucket." Then, silence.

Silence also from Koesler's side of the screen. He had almost said, "What was that!" but he didn't need reiteration. He recalled with all too great clarity what the boy had said. The question was *why* he had said it.

Suddenly it was clear. Instead of confessing he had

used bad language, he had given Koesler an itemized account of just exactly what he had said.

"Is that all?" Koesler asked at length.

"Yes, Father."

"Then say five Hail Marys for your penance.

"And by the way: If this happens again, you don't need to tell the priest precisely what you said. Just say you used vulgar language."

"OK, Father."

There may be more exclusive clubs in the Detroit area, but not many, thought Bishop Ratigan, as he pulled into the circular area where valet parking was available.

Orchard Lake Country Club was nestled among a string of small lakes, not the least of which was Orchard Lake itself, quite possibly the most beautiful of them all.

Ratigan's car rocked as he braked abruptly in front of the attendants' station. A uniformed young man sprinted to the car so quickly he was there before Ratigan had climbed out.

"Hi, Bishop!" The young man's uninhibited smile beamed. Not only was Ratigan well known at OLCC, he was also known to be a generous tipper.

"Hi, Johnny." Ratigan smiled more with his eyes than his lips The crow's-feet deepened but the rest of his face remained nearly immobile. The phenomenon was indicative of his reserve. "Be careful with this heap of tin. There's not much life left in it."

Johnny just laughed as he swung himself into the car, adjusted the seat forward, slipped it into gear, and eased it into the parking space. Actually, the late model Olds Ninety-eight would be right at home with the other luxury cars in the lot. All the attendants were acquainted with Ratigan's penchant for self-deprecation. It was as if he knew that clergymen should exist on a less opulent level than his. But, rather than live poverty, he talked it.

"I'm meeting Mr. Hoffman for lunch," Ratigan announced to the desk attendant.

"Right, Bishop. Mr. Hoffman is expecting you. He's downstairs."

Ratigan made his way down the stairs, ignoring wall plaques commemorating past officers of the club. Once on the threshold of the sunny downstairs dining room, he easily spotted his host sitting alone studying the menu.

"Been waiting long?" Ratigan seated himself across from Hoffman.

Hoffman consulted his watch. "No, just a few minutes."

"Here's the relic you wanted." Ratigan pushed a small golden reliquary across the table. The he handed Hoffman a folded parchment. "And here is its certification. Notice the words typed in, 'Vera Crux.' But," he leaned back, "you didn't tell my why you wanted a relic of the true cross."

"It's not for me. It's for my sister Cindy. She likes this sort of thing. Send the bill to my secretary, Mike."

"Already have."

Ratigan barely had time to adjust his napkin before the waiter arrived to take drink orders. Hoffman ordered a perfect Rob Roy, Ratigan an extra dry Beefeater martini.

"I thought we'd just have something light, if you don't mind," said Hoffman. "I've got some things I'd like to talk to you about."

"Perfectly all right."

"Shrimp salad?"

"Fine." Actually, Ratigan would have preferred a far more substantial lunch. But while he normally was an assertive person, he generally deferred to Hoffman.

The waiter returned with the drinks, took the salad order, and left.

Hoffman took a sip of his drink, hurriedly set it down, and was just able to produce his handkerchief and cover his nose and mouth before sneezing violently.

"Bless you!" said Ratigan. "Coming down with something?"

"Blasted cold, I suppose. This day did not begin well. And, while it's improving by the hour, I got a chill this morning that seems to be developing into something nasty."

"Better take care of it. Bad time of year to come down with something. Just going into winter and all."

"You're right. I think I'll stop in and see the doctor on the way back."

They sipped in silence. Both gazed out the window. The trees, still multicolored, were beginning to lose their leaves. Ratigan noticed that a single leaf, tinted gold and red by the season, had been placed in the table vase usually reserved for a fresh flower. A nice touch.

Salad was served. Hoffman ordered another drink for each of them.

"A nice time to be alive," Ratigan commented. The martini was cold, delicious, and soothing. Any hint of winter's coming severity was muted by the longer autumn.

"A nice time to be in Rome," Hoffman said.

"Eh? Oh, I suppose. You going?"

"Not me. Not now. Frank Martin."

Ratigan rolled his eyes as he placed a forkful of shrimp salad in his mouth. "When?"

"Next month."

"Still be nice then." Ratigan sensed that something to do with Frank Martin's impending Roman holiday was the reason for this luncheon.

"I'd like to arrange something nice for him while he's there."

"Oh?" Had this been a poker hand, Ratigan felt he now would be raking in the chips.

"What would you suggest?"

"A papal audience, I suppose. After all, the Pope is Rome's most important product."

"I know. But there are audiences and then there are audiences."

"Indeed." Ratigan enjoyed cat and mouse as much as Hoffman did.

"So, what sort would you suggest?" As Hoffman finished the last of his salad, the waiter was there to remove the plate. Hoffman ordered another drink. Ratigan declined.

"How would it be," Ratigan leaned forward, "if you were to go into Frank Martin's office and tell him you'd arranged for a private audience for him with the Pope?"

Hoffman smiled. "Not the sort where the Pope goes around a circle meeting individuals in a group?"

"No." Ratigan's crow's-feet crinkled. "More the sort that heads of state receive. Mr. and Mrs. Frank Martin, His Holiness, and maybe an aide, in the throne room."

Hoffman slapped the table top. "Just what the doctor ordered, Mike. Can you pull it off?"

Ratigan nodded curtly. "Give me a few days."

He had arranged for many varied meetings, tête-à-têtes, what-have-yous in his day. But he'd never tried for a private audience with a Pope. He would have to call in virtually his every marker. But with the president and chairman of the board of The Company, one of the most influential and wealthiest Catholics in Detroit, even a private audience might be possible. Ratigan was certain he could elicit the cooperation of Mark Boyle, Archbishop of Detroit. And, since Boyle was a Cardinal, his support would carry the added weight of the red hat.

Ratigan, as was the case with most priests, seldom, if ever, played a game of quid pro quo with favors for or from the laity. Such a game would have been hopelessly uneven from its inception. Priests, most of them shameless do-gooders, genuinely enjoyed doing favors for people. Ratigan was no exception.

But most priests could not compete with the laity in this sort of venture. Over the years, dentist and doctor friends would build up untoppable advantages just in uncharged fees. And priests, unless they dined alone or with fellow clergymen, very rarely picked up a dinner check or even contributed to its payment. In time, if anyone were keeping score, most priests fell heavily in debt to their lay friends. But, of course, generally, no tab was kept.

So, Ratigan would do his best to secure the honor of a private papal audience for Hoffman's employer. He would do so gladly. But between this papal audience and the next favor Ratigan would render Hoffman, the auto executive would pick up many a tab, host many a luxurious trip, buy many an expensive gift for his friend the bishop.

"How're you set for time, Mike?"

Ratigan consulted his watch. "OK. I've got nothing on till three."

Hoffman pushed his chair back from the table. "Then how about a short stroll?" He sneezed again.

"Bless you! OK. But you'd better put something on. Almost November and you're coming down with something."

"You're probably right."

They stopped at the unattended cloakroom where Ratigan retrieved his hat and coat and Hoffman slipped into his topcoat.

"No hat?" Ratigan donned his hat and coat.

"Never wear one. You know that."

"Yeah."

Up the stairs, past the main dining room, and out the

double doors. They were on the veranda overlooking Orchard Lake.

"Did it ever occur to you, Mike, that if you hadn't become a bishop, we would never have become friends?"

Ratigan mulled this over. "Oh, I don't know. Any number of ways we might have met. We could have been on some committee together. Or, I easily might have been pastor of your parish."

"I said *friends*." They walked briskly along the perimeter of the veranda. "Father Koesler is my pastor but we're not friends. Have you ever given much thought to *our* friendship? Do you know why you and I are friends?"

"Can't say that I have. We like a lot of the same things: golf, concerts, poker, good cars, good food . . . it's natural, I would think."

"That's not it."

"What, then?"

"We're cut of the same cloth."

Ratigan stopped dead in his tracks. Hoffman stopped one step ahead. Ratigan's amazement was impossible to conceal. Hoffman smiled. "Surprised?"

They recommenced their walk.

Ratigan was more than surprised. He was shocked. He knew something of Hoffman's business dealings, some of his method of operation at work. And, in all honesty, he could not approve of all he knew. In addition, Ratigan was aware that what he knew of Hoffman's business practices was only a tip of the iceberg. Normally, Ratigan preferred not to think about it.

"Think about it sometime, Mike. We are upwardly mobile. We have high pot, as they say in my industry. And you didn't become a bishop by choosing the lowest place at the table as in the Gospel story."

"Now, wait a minute—"

"I know what you're going to say. And I know there

are people who actually make the Gospels work for them. There's Mother Theresa of Calcutta and there's Dom Helder Camera of Recife. There are exceptions in my field too. Every once in a long while you may run across a genuinely nice guy who's made it. But we both know that's the exception, not the rule.

"Mostly, it's guys like you and me. We know which strings have to be pulled, which backs need to be scratched, which side the butter's on, who to get papal audiences for. . . ." Hoffman glanced at Ratigan, who seemed to wince slightly.

"We know where the power is. We know the path to power and we take it. I don't know where the skeletons are in your closet—I don't want to know—but I know where the bodies are buried in my past, and I don't regret one of them. I'd guess neither do you regret yours. If I hadn't pulled the rug out from under some of the people who stood in my way, I'd still be on the bottom looking up."

"But . . . but . . . deliberately undermining some-body else's career . . . why, that's immoral. It's a sin!" Ratigan felt as if he should be hearing Hoffman's confession rather than listening to an *apologia pro vita sua*.

"Sin! How could the only sure road to success be a sin! The Beatitudes may work in a monastery or a con-vent. But they don't work at The Company. They don't even work all that well among the people who preach them."

"Must say I can't agree with you, Frank. No, not at all!"

"Your problem, Mike, is that you haven't thought about it enough. I know—"

Ratigan seemed about to speak again, but Hoffman's raised hand cut him off.

"I know," Hoffman continued, "because you've done it before, that you're about to quote St. Paul about

how if a man desires the office of bishop, he desires a
good work.

"Well, I've never heard Frank Martin say it in so
many words, but I can assure you that he has similar
thoughts to those of St. Paul. 'Any employee of The
Company,' Frank might say, 'who desires a management
position—and the higher in management the better—
desires a good thing.'

"God bless us, we in management know damn well
that we've got a good thing. We'd be too stupid to get
where we are if we didn't know we're billions of times
better off than the suckers on the line. And the higher we
go, the better off we are. So, now, let me paraphrase St.
Paul: 'We who desire to be chairman of the board of The
Company desire the best damn thing available.'

"Sure, it's a good thing to desire to be a bishop.
You've got it better than any priest in a parish or monastery. Your perks go up in direct proportion to the height
of your position.

"It just comes down to this, Mike: Some of us will do
anything we have to do to get to this 'good office' that we
desire."

"I can't agree with your reasoning, Frank." They
were standing at the shoreline of Orchard Lake. In another couple of months, this large lake would be frozen
over, and instead of swimmers, rowboats, and fisher-
men, it would be dotted with fishing shacks, iceboats,
and skaters.

"It may be true," Ratigan said, "that there are some
ancillary advantages to being a bishop, but along with
that are greater responsibilities and obligations."

"Of course there are, Mike. They go with the territory. It's lots easier tightening bolts on passing chassis all
day than making multimillion-dollar educated guesses
about where the auto market will be several years down
the road.

"But then, the blue-collar guy works in a pit, makes a slightly better-than-average wage, and lives in Detroit. While we have plush offices, private secretaries, investment counselors, and live in Dearborn, the Pointes, or Bloomfield Hills. It goes with the territory.

"And sure it's easier filling out records, saying Mass, and bestowing sacraments than it is being responsible for personnel placement, purchasing sites for future parishes, and fielding problems too complex for a mere pastor. But priests' lives fit into square boxes a few miles wide called parishes, and they do the same dull things every day of their lives. Whereas you bishops have as many offices as you want, live virtually where you want, at whatever level you want. And when you deign to visit a parish, it's like the Second Coming of Christ: They throw down every red carpet they can find for you. And the perks go on, we all know it. It goes with the territory.

"We're both of us in middle management, Mike. I'm living for the day I'll be president and chairman of the board of The Company. And you can't wait to get your own diocese. And," he glanced briefly but significantly at the bishop, "it is just possible we can help each other get where we want to go."

Silence.

Ratigan felt as if he'd been hit with buckshot. There was both truth and fallacy to Hoffman's charges. But distinguishing one from the other was comparable to trying to pry little pellets from one's body after a buckshot blast. Furthermore, what had Hoffman meant by "helping each other"?

Hoffman glanced at his watch. Time to go.

They turned and moved toward the clubhouse.

"More than anything, Michael, we are cut from the same Company cloth. We are Company Men."

Ratigan wanted to hear no more. But there seemed no way he could prevent Hoffman from continuing.

"From time to time, I've seen those questionnaires they send to Very Important Catholics when they're looking for nominations to the episcopacy. You've seen them, of course."

"Of course."

"Add up the desired answers to those questions and what have you got?"

Ratigan shrugged.

"A Company Man. Orthodox in theology, faithful to Church law, obedient to superiors, and above all—above everything—loyal to the Pope. A Company Man! And why not? You don't need or want a rebel in the hierarchy. And what is really convenient is that new members of the hierarchy are selected by the existing hierarchy."

"Now wait a minute, Frank. That's not true. We've had bishops demonstrating against war, disagreeing publicly with positions taken by the National Conference . . . even some that left and got married. Hardly Company Men!"

"No one's perfect, Mike. Even the Church blows one now and then. But, by and large, you are all Company Men. And so am I.

"Know why I'm wearing a blue three-piece pinstripe suit? Because that's what Frank Martin wears. The same response answers such other pertinent questions as why my reading glasses are gold-rimmed, what time I get to work, and when I leave. People like Iacocca and DeLorean were our exceptions to the rule that people who succeed, especially in the auto industry, are Company Men. We're all colorless clones of top management. To borrow from the Gospels once more, we must decrease while The Company increases.

"You could do it, Mike, but ask someone else—ask your friend Father Koesler if he can name the president and/or the chairman of the board of Ford, GM, Chrysler, AMC. Chances are, even though he's lived in Detroit

virtually all his life, he can't do it. We're colorless,
Mike. We disappear into the corporate fabric of The
Company.

"And look at you! Look at your daily uniform!"

Ratigan found himself briefly examining his attire, as
if he'd forgotten what he had put on this morning. The
lines around his eyes crinkled, but his mouth remained
firm. "What did you expect, a green and coral zoot
suit?"

"Hardly. But look again. A very plain black suit, navy
blue Aquascutum, simple black fedora, and a plain silver
ring."

"So?"

"It's not *you*, Mike. No more than this blue pinstripe
is me. Left to your own devices, you'd be wearing a
black suit, yes—but a three-or four-hundred-dollar silk, a
Burberry, and a splashy jeweled ring. But: Who dresses
the way you do? Mark Boyle. Cardinal Mark Boyle.
Your clerical equivalent of my Frank Martin. You're a
clone of Mark Boyle. A Company Man in simple black."

They had reached the large double door of the clubhouse. They paused on the threshold.

"Don't get me wrong, Mike; I'm not disparaging the
Company Man. Hell, I freely admit I'm one. Neither The
Company nor the Church could function without people
like us. It's just a good idea to know yourself. And,"
Hoffman locked eyes meaningfully with Ratigan, "to
know we are very much alike.

"In keeping with that thought," he continued as their
eyes remained locked, "earlier this week I revised my
will. I've named you executor."

"Frank, I—"

"Let me finish. I've left a substantial sum for both you
and the archdiocese."

"Now, wait a minute, Frank—"

"If I should go before you, not only will you be well

fixed; you'll also be able to bring a handsome gift to the Church. Which should endear you to the powers that be. Just as that private audience with the Pope is going to endear me to Frank Martin. You see, just about everything in life is a quid pro quo. And so it should be, especially between Company Men.''

They walked in silence past the main dining room, where a big luncheon party was beginning to break up.

As they went through the front door, Ratigan noticed there were quite a few people waiting for cars. He also noticed that Johnny recognized Frank Hoffman the moment he appeared in the doorway. Obviously skipping over several of those waiting, Johnny dashed off to retrieve Hoffman's car.

They parted with a simple handshake. Ratigan felt he should say something. Something between a protest and an expression of gratitude. But there was no time. Nor did anything come to mind.

Ratigan stood under the awning watching Hoffman drive away. As usual, he had mixed emotions regarding Hoffman. Now, those emotions were more confused than ever.

He was happier when their relationship ran on a lighter level. He knew there was a distinctly dark side to Frank Hoffman. For his own peace of mind, Ratigan tried not to focus on the Mr. Hyde who was The Company Hoffman. But it had been Hoffman who had focused Ratigan's attention on his other self. Worse, he had suggested that Ratigan was the ecclesiastical equivalent of Hoffman and that The Company and the Church were not all that dissimilar.

Ratigan felt somehow soiled. As if he had been invited not to an exclusive country club but to a sandbox where they had dabbled in mudpies.

An oft abandoned resolution again presented itself to Ratigan: He would break off this friendship. It demeaned him. The relationship was almost antithetic to a good spiritual life.

But there was no getting away from it: He enjoyed golf at Hilton Head, first class flights to exotic vacations as a sort of personal chaplain to the Hoffmans, parties with Detroit's elite, casual invitations to lunch at the country club.

He enjoyed these and all the other lagniappes that were part of a close relationship with Frank Hoffman.

He wished he were stronger, but knew in truth that he was not. At this moment, he hated himself for his lack of integrity. And, along with self-hatred, he despised Hoffman for dragging him down.

As Hoffman's car disappeared around the bend, Ratigan mused that someone like Hoffman should not go around letting others know that they would profit from his death. The concept might prove too tempting to someone who could bear to contemplate murder.

10.

He PATTED HIS PAUNCH AS HE LOOKED IN THE mirror. It was not a significant bulge, merely the combination of gravity and years causing a shifting of weight.

Charlie, he said to himself, you're too old for this nonsense!

But he was in "this nonsense" up to his ears. He'd dived in when his old friend and golfing buddy Frank Martin had persuaded him to join The Company. Had it been a mistake? Had Charlie Chase blundered in leaving behind what he'd built?

It was one thing to own one's own business and quite another to become a cog, albeit a very important cog, in a gigantic corporation.

He and Louise had known hard times, without doubt. But by dedicated hard work and, here and there, a little luck, he'd built his auto supply company into a business that was successful by anyone's standard. He'd grown comfortable in the familiar surroundings and routines. Then had come Martin's offer.

Perhaps the chief reason that had motivated Chase to chance the traumatic move was the apparent stability of The Company. Should the auto industry fall upon bad times for an extensive period—and that certainly had happened often enough in the past—it was always the smaller feeder companies, the suppliers, the ancillary industries that suffered most. As the owner of such a concern, such a catastrophe could have spelled financial ruin for him. In such an event, he could envision himself pouring his life savings into his business in a desperate attempt to keep it afloat.

It was very possible—probable—he could have lost everything.

But nothing like that was likely to happen to him now, surrounded and shielded as he was by The Company. Recessions might come and go, small companies might founder; hourly and even some of the lower echelon salaried employees might lose their jobs, possibly forever; but nothing short of a total breakdown in business nationwide would affect his present position. And certainly not before he could retire in comfort and security.

So, he had traded his baby, the business he had created and which he knew and understood inside and out, for The Company, in which he was less sure of himself, less knowledgeable, but—theoretically—more secure.

There were some obvious and immediate advantages to his move. He was looking at one of them now. His office space was generous, comfortable, and attractive, as well as functional.

The room he was in now adjoined his main office. It was, in effect, an efficiency with a kitchenette with full refrigerator, a sofabed, wet bar, table and several chairs, and a full bathroom attached.

The office proper was divided into two large sections. One held an executive desk with straightback chairs around it and a swivel chair behind. The other section was less formal, embracing a large coffee table. Spaced against three walls were couches and upholstered chairs. The fourth wall comprised large picture windows that displayed an impressive view southward toward the downtown skyline highlighted by the Renaissance Center.

Between the office and the corridor a reception area provided more than adequate facilities for his secretary, Brenda McNamara.

Brenda was a prize that Chase had been able to bring with him from his company. She had been with him nearly twenty years, fifteen of them as his private secretary. In the time he'd been with The Company, she had been his one oasis of familiarity and dependability in a desert of unpredictability and strangeness.

Chase could not quite put his finger on why he should have these lingering feelings of uncertainty relieved almost solely by the presence of his old faithful secretary. His responsibilities in The Company were not that new to him. The corporate structure was, of course, a vastly different way of conducting business than that which he had been used to when he had been independently responsible for an entire company. But there was something else; some element that seemed to elude him—that seemed to be keeping him off balance.

He had not yet identified it. But he would.

There was a quiet knock at his office door. From his adjoining suite he could scarcely hear it. He slipped into the office at the same moment Brenda entered from the reception area.

"Mr. Chase, there are three men to see you." She had never addressed him on a first name basis. Nor he her. "It's about next week's board meeting."

"Three?" Mild surprise. "I was expecting two . . . just Kirkus and Keely."

"I know. That's what the log shows. But there's a Mr. Zaleski with them. He's from the ad agency that handles the Cheetah account."

"Hmmmm. All right; send them in."

"Uh . . ."

"Yes, Mrs. McNamara?"

"It's probably nothing." She hesitated. "It's just that from the beginning, I've had a feeling about those two. They seem to be somehow different while they're waiting in my office than they are when they come in here."

"Oh? Can you be more specific?"

"They always strike me as being . . . oh, somehow conspiratorial—at least while they're waiting. I'm afraid I can't really be more specific. It's just something I feel. But," she looked at him earnestly, "it's a very strong feeling."

"That's interesting, Mrs. McNamara." He seemed to be thinking. "I've gotten no bad advice from either Kirkus or Keely . . . that I know of. But," he smiled reassuringly, "we'll have to keep our eyes open, won't we?"

"Yes, sir."

"Very well, then; let's not keep them waiting. Show them in."

"Yes, sir." She left the office.

He circled behind his desk and sat in the upholstered swivel chair. His three visitors would use the straight-back chairs. He would keep this meeting on a formal basis.

As he waited, he briefly considered his secretary's suspicions. While he valued her efficiency and professionalism greatly, he was less influenced by her perceptions. Being a nuts-and-bolts type, he put no stock whatever in intuition. Which was the category in which he slotted her opinion of Al Kirkus, Clem Keely, and any hypothetical conspiracy.

As he was dismissing her speculation, his visitors entered. Kirkus introduced Ziggy Zaleski. The three were then seated across the desk from Chase.

"We've got the presentation for the board meeting pretty well mapped out, Mr. Chase." Kirkus took the lead. "What we want to do now is to submit our research and approach for your consideration and approval. If you approve of our approach—and I think you will," he smiled and glanced confidently at his two companions, "then we'll get to work on the draft for your presentation."

"Very well." Chase propped his elbows on the arms of the chair and made a steeple of his fingers, which he rested against his lips. His face was expressionless. The ball was in their court. And they would have to be convincing.

"The first item on next week's meeting will be the new Lemon Laws that are up for congressional action this session," said Kirkus.

Both Kirkus and Keely began arranging documents, pads, and charts at the edge of the desk nearest to them. It was a delicate and deliberate arrangement. Each man used no more desk space than he minimally needed. None of the piles came close to infringing on any area that Chase might want to use. They were so to speak, polite piles.

Zaleski watched the building of the piles with passive interest. He had brought nothing to this meeting except his effervescent self.

"This is, of course, by no means the first time Congress has considered Lemon Law legislation," Kirkus proceeded. "As you know, the bills presently before both houses would call for a full refund of the full purchase price of any vehicle if, after three attempts, a problem cannot be solved, or if the vehicle is out of service for a total of at least thirty days during one calendar year."

"Yes," added Keely, "a full refund or a replacement vehicle, whichever the owner prefers."

"That's right," Kirkus confirmed.

"I know all that," Chase observed.

"Yes, sir. So," Kirkus continued, "the question before the board next week will concern just what approach The Company should take on this proposed legislation." He paused for effect. "We think The Company should take a public position of backing the legislation."

Chase's right eyebrow arched; his steepled fingers slipped down and became entwined.

"That position may come as a surprise to you," Kirkus correctly analyzed, "but it is the result of a study of the voting records of some pivotal Congressional leaders, plus an analysis of the information our Washington lobbyists are feeding us."

"What it comes down to, Mr. Chase," Keely picked up the cue, "is that the forces proposing this legislation simply haven't got the votes. There is no way in hell they can possibly get this legislation through either body, given the makeup of the current Congress. Our friends in the House outnumber our enemies by a two-to-one margin. In the Senate, it's three-to-one."

"So you see, sir," said Kirkus, "this gives us a marvelous opportunity for a public relations coup. We, as one of the Big Five, come out in favor of something that is undeniably consumer legislation. In effect, we are making ourselves liable for in the neighborhood of billions in refunds or replacements.

"Now this would appear to be a form of corporate suicide . . . an absolutely unique stand on the part of any industry: sacrificing our company in favor of our customers. I don't think, sir, you could find such an example since the industrial revolution of any corporation comparable in size and importance willing to combine confidence in our product with respect and care for our customers.

"In effect, sir, we will appear to favor legislation which would force us to guarantee our customers complete satisfaction."

"Meanwhile," Keely picked up the theme, "we know the legislation we appear to be supporting can't pass. We're in an all-win, no-lose position."

"We stutterstep, we give the opposition a leg and then we take it away!" Ziggy Zaleski, gesturing orotundly, was picking up the mood created by Kirkus and Keely. "We send out the word that we've come to play. The opposition is just going through the motions while we've come to play. We are giving 120 percent."

Chase's eyes moved slowly in the direction of Zaleski. Without turning his head, Chase contemplated this creature afflicted with an apparently terminal case of sportsspeak.

"What of the other major auto firms?" Chase asked, after a moment. "Do we have any indication regarding their stand in this matter?"

"Yes, we do, sir." Keely shuffled through several documents until he found the one he wanted. "Ford, GM, Chrysler, and AMC—all of them have their lobbyists working overtime, trying, in effect, to save the saved. They're so scared that this idiocy will become law, they keep going back over ground all of us have covered.

"As we said, sir, we've got the votes. There is no doubt about that. But the others apparently can't believe it. They keep lobbying not only the few who may vote against us, but the rest—the majority we know will be with us."

"In other words," said Zaleski, "we've got the momentum and our opponents don't know it. Our penetration is good. We've got them on the run. They're in a prevent defense. They're going to let us have the short ones. And we'll take 'em while we eat up the clock. It's a two-minute drill and we've got the momentum. Yes, sir; we've got the momentum!"

Chase was able to ignore the verbal yardmarkers and go on.

"In the event we do decide to adopt this position—and as of this moment I cannot commit my support to it—when would you propose this position should be made public?"

Keely deferred to Kirkus. "You've hit on the most important point of all, sir," said Kirkus. "The timing has to be perfect if we're going to have maximum impact. We considered this question in great detail and we would suggest a delay of no more than a month. Congress is scheduled to debate these bills the end of November, beginning of December at the latest. Just before that happens, the other automakers are sure to voice their opposition in the strongest terms possible. Then we take our stand in favor of the legislation and sit back and watch as the bills go down to defeat. And The Company reaps a public relations bonanza!"

"We realize," Keely added, "that on the surface this might appear to be a dangerous, even a foolhardy gamble. But we assure you, sir, nothing could be further from the truth. This, sir, goes beyond the proverbial lead pipe cinch. If there were a risk of any sort whatsoever, sir, we certainly would point it out. But, frankly, there isn't. This is just a golden opportunity for The Company to score an unprecedented public relations coup. And, if I may be so bold, sir, it would certainly be a feather in your cap. It's no secret that you're new to The Company. This will be, in effect , your first major meeting presentation. If I may be so bold as to suggest, sir, this could be a once-in-a-lifetime opportunity for you as well as for The Company."

"And," Kirkus gestured toward Zaleski, "the bottom line would fall to advertising. Once we are identified through the predictable media blitz as the consumers' best friend, we will profit nicely in advertising correlation."

"First in world class quality!" Zaleski's voice was almost a shout. "First in design and performance! And first in the hearts of the consumer market! We're number one! We're number one! We're number one!"

His cheers proved non-infectious.

The three looked expectantly at Chase, who seemed to be pondering the proposal.

Finally, he spoke. "We'll see." But a slight smile played about the corners of his mouth.

The three knew that they had sold and that Chase, indeed, had bought.

"Next on the agenda," said Kirkus, inserting a stack of papers into his briefcase and shifting others to the top of the pile on the desk, "will be establishing and planning for our prime demographic target two years down the line. This is of critical importance, sir, because we will be committing the vast majority of The Company's resources to whatever demographic target we establish."

"I understand all that." And, indeed, Chase did understand the literally vital risk involved in this planning. A faulty projection could cost The Company that share of the market necessary for survival.

"Of course, sir." Al waxed appropriately apologetic. "And I know you're well acquainted with the traditional categorization of the buying public, divided into urban men thirty-four to fifty-five; upscale working women eighteen to thirty-four; and housewives eighteen to fifty-four."

Chase nodded.

"Well, sir," Kirkus continued, "I'd just like Clem to update you on a more recent and more reliable curve of buyer statistics, grouped under the acronym VALS."

"VALS?"

"VALS," replied Keely, "stands for Values and Life-

Styles. It divides the buying public into more revealing categories.

"First, at 33 percent, are the Belongers—buyers who tend to be more stable, content, and traditional."

"Like your middle linebacker," offered Zaleski.

"Then, at 25 percent, you have your Achievers—middle-aged and materialistically oriented."

"Like your tight end."

"Then, at 10 percent, are the Emulators—generally ambitious young adults just breaking into the system."

"Like your halfback."

"At 9 percent"—Keely's voice tightened; Zaleski's clarifications were beginning to irk—"are the Societally Conscious. Those are attracted to causes; they're mission oriented."

"Something like the wide receiver."

"At 7 percent are the Experiential. They're people—oriented—directed toward inner growth."

"Like the center. The offensive center, naturally."

"Also at 7 percent are the Sustainers. They're having a hard time making ends meet and they're damn resentful about it."

"Like a second-string quarterback."

For the first time during this presentation, Chase glanced at Zaleski. Chase seemed ready to believe that Zaleski was not real.

"The I-Am-Me group makes up only 5 percent of the buying public—the impulsive young adults. They're narcissistic and unconventional."

"Just like some quarterbacks." Zaleski rubbed his hands together.

"The least of the buying groups at only 4 percent are the Survivors. They're the poor, old people with little hope for the future."

"The over-the-hill lineman." Zaleski's voice held a touch of sadness.

"Well, sir," Kirkus had tried to speak quickly enough to cut Zaleski off at the pass but had been unsuccessful, "that's the way it is. VALS identifies today's buyers. By the way, Clem, thanks for a concise presentation." No mention of Zaleski's antiphonal contributions.

"So you see, sir," Kirkus continued, "the interesting thing about this categorization is who we find at the top and who at the bottom of this scale. We might suppose that today's youth—impulsive young adults, ambitious young adults, young men and women just making their mark in the business world—would be among the highest percentage of buyers. But VALS makes it clear they are not. Such young men and women make up a mere 15 percent of the buying market.

"On the other hand, while we might not anticipate it, we find by far the majority of today's buyers to be that old reliable group of middle-aged, stable, content, traditional men and women. A whopping 58 percent."

"I guess there's no doubt which market we're aiming at," Keely broke in. "The guys and gals we'll be aiming at are the middle-of-the-roaders—the ones who demand economy and value; straight, old-fashioned American virtues. They won't want to throw their hard-earned money down a drain marked 'Flashy and Sporty.' No, sir; they're going to demand the kind of cars they've been buying over the past several years. The fuel-efficient compacts. The kind of car that vaulted the Cheetah into world class competition."

At mention of the Cheetah, Zaleski moved forward in his chair. "It's like they always say: The best defense is a good offense. We pick up our market and we go with the flow. Remember: We're giving 120 percent and we've come to play. But we've got to play in the right ballpark."

"And the right ballpark for us, sir," Kirkus slid in smoothly, "is the park we've been in for the past several years. We would be foolish to abandon what has contributed to our latest and most conspicuous success."

Again there was a moment of silence while the three men tired to gauge the effect of their presentation.

"I'm going to have to check those VALS findings," said Chase finally.

He would find them to be precisely as Keely had presented them. "Then, I'll want to work them out myself."

Kirkus and Keely quickly assembled a packet of graphs and documents. Kirkus offered the packet to Chase, who accepted it. "I'll take these with me over the weekend, and give you my answer Monday. Now, if there's nothing else—"

"There is one thing more, sir, if you don't mind."

Keely and Zaleski looked at Kirkus with genuine surprise. They were unaware of anything further on the agenda.

Chase nodded at Kirkus and settled back in his swivel chair.

"Actually, sir, it's a rather delicate matter."

Keely and Zaleski leaned forward.

"It has to do with our operation in Mexico. And the production of the Cheetah in Mexico.

"Now, as you know, The Company has its own glass division. We and Ford are the only ones who make their own glass. And, as you know, our glass division is based entirely in this country. Well—and it is not that difficult to trace this—the Cheetahs manufactured in Mexico arrive in this country complete with glass."

He paused to let this fact have its effect.

"You mean to say," Chase inquired, "that our Mexican operation is buying the glass for the Cheetah from a competing Mexican glass company?"

"That's it, sir: We have no opportunity to provide our own glass for our own cars because those same cars are being outfitted with glass while they are still in Mexico. Before they're shipped back to the States!''

Chase reacted with authentic indignation. ''But what's the meaning of this? What's behind it?''

Kirkus shrugged. ''The usual, I suppose, sir: Kick-backs, money on the side, bribes—*la mordida.* It's been going on for years—known only to middle to lower levels of management. But high time the board knows of it, sir. In a way, I'm taking a chance even bringing it up now, sir. But I thought you ought to know. I thought I ought to tell you—''

''You did well to do so.'' Chase's indignation remained pronounced. ''Document this as fully as you can and get it to me first thing Monday. The Company clearly is being bled. You're absolutely correct: The board must know of this.''

''Imagine!'' said Zaleski, sharing a bit of the indignation, ''those spiks red-dogging us! Shooting the gap! We've got to pick up their stunts or it's the old ball-game!''

''First thing Monday!'' Chase emphasized to Kirkus. And so the meeting was concluded.

''God bless you, sir!'' Kirkus' concern was evident. ''Shouldn't you be in bed? That sounds like a dreadful cold. Maybe the flu!''

''It's OK, Al,'' said Frank Hoffman. ''Don't worry. Just run that by me again!''

''Certainly, sir.

''As I was saying, things were going so well that I threw the Mexican import-export business into the pot. And he bought it, sir. Mr. Chase was absolutely indignant that The Company was being bled by some of its own people.''

''That was nervy of you, Al. We hadn't planned on

that, you know." Hoffman's tone held a hint of disapproval.

"I took the liberty, sir," Kirkus explained. "Things were going so well I was really sure of him, and, of course there was no immediate opportunity to consult with you. But there was almost no chance that an outsider—and Mr. Chase certainly qualifies as an outsider—there was no chance that an outsider would understand our Mexican operation."

"And he bought the demographic projection and Lemon Laws stance?"

"He didn't say so in so many words, sir. But he gave every indication he did. I'd stake my life on it, sir."

Though he didn't say so, Hoffman thought that at the very least Kirkus was staking his job on the way he had carried off that meeting.

"OK, Al. So far so good. Make sure you give him the documentation he needs for the Mexican scam. If that comes off the way it should, it will be the final nail in Chase's coffin."

"Yes, sir."

"Oh, and Al: Did my girl get those Lions tickets to you?"

"Yes, sir."

"Enjoy the game." Hoffman was coughing as he hung up.

"Yes, sir." Al would not take in the football game. He would be working to make the documentation perfect and perfectly enticing. A football game was a small enough sacrifice for the advancement of his career.

11.

IT WAS AS IF A GIGANTIC INVISIBLE HAND WERE writing the words over and over across the top of the side of the building. One after another, the script letters lit up: C-A-N-A-D-I-A-N pause C-L-U-B. Then a repeat performance of the scriptwriting, followed by the two words simultaneously flashing on in their entirety: CANADIAN CLUB. Over and over.

A girl could get mesmerized.

She stood at the window wall, gazing somewhat absently at the familiar scene.

This was one of the very few buildings in Detroit known only by its address: 1300 Lafayette. A posh highrise condo at the eastern edge of downtown, almost in the shadow of the Ren Cen. Within easy walking distance of Bricktown, Greektown, theaters, restaurants, hospitals, a shopping center, the Collegiate Club, a surprising number of churches—most of them Catholic—police headquarters, and, by no means least, the morgue.

Only a few short blocks separated 1300 Lafayette from the Detroit River. And across the river was Windsor, Ontario, Canada. By a geographical oddity, Detroit is the only city in the United States from which one reaches Canada by going south.

Shortly she would not be able to discern even this gigantic bright sign. An ever more dense fog was building. It was not uncommon for Detroit at this time of year. In late October, early November, the weather within this hub of the Great Lakes traditionally vacillated between fall, winter, and spring, frequently resulting in a late-evening to early-morning fog. Already the streets lights immediately below were a dull blur.

Life seemed to be closing in in more ways than one.

It was almost contradictory. Her apartment was more than ample. It was bright and luxuriously appointed and furnished. It was situated in one of Detroit's more lively and vibrant areas—convenient to nearly everything she could want or need. At thirty, she was still young and in good health.

Even if her tastes and lifestyle were not quite modest—which they were—she could easily afford to live on an even grander scale. Yet, withal, she felt trapped. And the thickening fog that seemed to slowly obliterate the outside world and seal her into her apartment merely intensified this feeling. Almost as if she were slowly being buried alive.

It was not alone the fog nor her isolation that contributed to this trapped feeling.

Jacqueline LeBlanc was a kept woman.

By no means was she alone in this profession. Nor was she by any means the only mistress in Detroit. But, as far as she was concerned, she must have been among the least likely women to have become a mistress. Yet she was. And the fact that she had come to exist for and at the good pleasure of a man now made her feel trapped, enslaved.

Jacqueline was born in Fall River, Massachusetts, where her family had lived determinedly within the city's French Catholic community. Which is the same as saying that they did not live within the Irish Catholic community. Jackie grew up in Fall River during a time of transition. While she was a child, Fall River Catholics were still recovering from their notion that a mixed marriage was one between a French Catholic and an Irish Catholic.

Jacqueline had attended the local Catholic school. That was during the late 1950s. She had learned from the traditional Baltimore Catechism, under one form or another, the basic tenets of the Catholic faith, over and over. She had memorized the Commandments, the sacraments, the six Church laws that most commonly affected Catholics.

She had learned moral laws that had taken centuries to formulate. Mostly about how much better it was to be over- than underdressed. And about what boys had in mind (girls). And, concomitantly, what girls had to keep in mind (how to avoid the glances and advances of boys).

Jacqueline had learned how to go to confession. That all mortal sins were to be confessed according to their kind and number. And that a mortal sin was a deliberate violation of a serious command. Venial sins were to be confessed, again, according to nature and number. On Saturday afternoon, at least once a month, young Jacqueline would examine her conscience and come up with a list of sins she had committed, memorize the list and the numbers, wait her turn, then whisper them to the priest from within a musty dark box of a room. Usually, month after month, year after year, her sins would be the same sins, differing only in the number of times committed.

Young Jacqueline had been a good student. She was proud of getting good grades consistently. She would have preferred to be known as a good student. But she was far more famous as the prettiest little girl in Ste. Jeanne d'Arc Elementary School.

Young Jacqueline attended Immaculate Heart of Mary High School at about the same time that the Catholic Church was celebrating—or agonizing over, depending on one's liberal or traditional bent—the Second Vatican Council. Jacqueline found herself relearning most of the eternal truths she had mastered in elementary school days. But she relearned them well. She yearned to be known as the student with one of the sharpest minds in school. Instead, most of the girls envied her mature body while most of the boys lusted after it. And not just quietly in their hearts.

Ms. Jacqueline LeBlanc attended Boston College. She watched, sympathized with, but seldom participated in protest rallies and marches against the war in Vietnam. The Church now was sharply divided between conservatives and liberals. The faculty of Boston College was largely liberal. And largely due to that, Jacqueline began to slip in her fidelity to Mass attendance. She selected a well-rounded liberal arts curriculum and majored in theater and dance.

In her senior year, she portrayed Adelaide in B.C.'s production of Frank Loesser's *Guys and Dolls*. She was a major hit. She desired to have her mental powers and talents recognized. But the consensus was solid that she was the most beautiful girl in school. Maybe the most beautiful girl in any school. She was no longer a virgin.

After graduation, and after many bitter arguments with her parents, Jacqueline took what little money she'd saved, put together her amateur theater portfolio, and went off alone and unattended to make it big in the Big Apple.

There she learned that agents were not desperate for clients; that lots of very pretty girls were looking for work; that there were comparatively few jobs in the entertainment field; that a small savings account was soon exhausted, especially in New York City, and that the casting couch frequently was the sole gate to even a minimal paying job in a nightclub chorus.

It was while singing and dancing in just such a chorus

that she had caught the eye of Frank Hoffman, and he hers.

Hoffman was in Manhattan on one of his frequent business trips. Alone that night, he had gone to the Pink Erotica, a sleazy club that ordinarily he would have avoided. But a New York rep had urged him to check it out with the promise that the Erotica featured a few exotics whose acts were worth catching.

He hadn't thought all that much of the strippers. Very ordinary, untalented broads whose only virtue was an ability to remove their clothing while writhing.

But that blonde in the chorus: She was something else. Hoffman could recognize class when he saw it, even in a twenty-five-cent costume in a nickel-and-dime chorus line.

They met. Close up, she was one of the most breath-takingly beautiful girls he had ever known. He was one of the most handsome, exciting, and wealthy men she had ever known. They made love—off and on—as often as business brought him to Manhattan.

Eventually, he had set up house for her in a twenty-first-floor luxury apartment in 1300 and she had become his full-time mistress. The rest, as they say, was history.

A key turned in the lock. She would have been alarmed but for the cough. The cough was unexpected, but it came from the voice box that was unmistakably Frank Hoffman's. All unforeseen, her master had arrived.

"That you, honey?"

"It better be, or you're in a lot of trouble."

She went quickly to the hallway. Hoffman had hung his coat in the closet and was draping his silk scarf over a hanger.

"You didn't tell me you were coming tonight." It was neither complaint nor protest, merely a statement.

"Didn't know till this evening that I would be here.

The day started horribly, but it got better as it went on. So, I decided to reward myself.''

She took that as a compliment and smiled. As always, there was a glitter to her eyes. She reached up and threw her arms around his neck. He lifted her from the floor and kissed her. But then, as quickly, he lowered her, turned slightly, and sneezed.

"God bless you. Where did you get that? It sounds ugly.''

"This morning, I think. The upshot of a score yet to be settled. But it will be.''

"I've got some aspirin . . .''

"No. No, I stopped at the doc's this afternoon and got this prescription.'' He fished a pill bottle from his pocket. "Been eating them like candy. Should do some good.''

Her brow knit. "You shouldn't overdo that.'' She smiled. "You probably need some food in you. How 'bout I whip you up some steak and salad?''

"No, that's OK. I stopped for a bite on the way over. Why don't you just make me a drink. I just want to relax for a bit.''

Now that they were in the living room there was a little more light. He looked at her more critically. "Why are you wearing that rag?'' he said harshly. "I told you I didn't like it!''

She clutched her old faithful housecoat about her. "I feel comfy in it. It's warm. Besides, I didn't know you were coming.''

"Well, take it off! And get rid of it—I'm sick of it!''

She turned abruptly and disappeared into the bedroom. He settled into a reclining chair near the window and marveled at the fog that blotted out the river. All he could make out was the Canadian Club sign.

Jacqueline had known her share of drinkers. However, none but Frank drank a perfect Rob Roy. With talent born of long practice, she mixed one. Two small ice cubes in a large glass. Dewar's Scotch nearly filled the glass. A bit of dry vermouth, a bit more of sweet vermouth. She no longer measured, merely blended to the proper color. Then a dash of bitters and a maraschino cherry.

She returned to the living room carrying the drink. As she entered the room, she felt a chill. She had replaced her cozy housecoat with a revealing peignoir Frank had given her last Christmas.

He took the glass wordlessly, popped a pill in his mouth, and swallowed it with a sip of the drink. She almost warned him that pills and booze were a dangerous combination. But she did not.

She sat on the arm of his chair. He had removed his jacket and tie, rolled up the sleeves of his monogrammed white shirt, and unbuttoned his collar. Her arm dropped familiarly and she began to massage his shoulders. "Remember how it used to be, Frank?"

"When?" He sipped his drink.

"In the beginning."

"No. God, that was . . . what? . . . five, six years ago."

"It used to be different, Frank. You used to talk to me. We hardly ever talk anymore. About your problems at work . . . about your work at all."

"You wouldn't understand."

You'd be surprised, she thought. She was growing desperate for him to discover her mind. All he ever groped for now was her body.

"What's the official reason you didn't go home tonight? It *is* Friday."

"Had to put in some extra work. And then decided to stay downtown. Which," he laughed, "come to think of it, is true."

"Maybe it's because we never go anywhere, Frank. Maybe that's why we don't talk much anymore."

"That's ridiculous! What difference would going anywhere make?"

"I never see you outside these walls. You never see me outside of them. We never have anybody in for dinner or drinks or anything. There isn't anybody outside of ourselves to add a dimension to our relationship."

"Don't try to pull that! You knew how it would be when you moved in here. You know I can't be seen with you. I aim to reach the top at The Company. Which means I've got to maintain a good measure of invisibility. And that's a long way from the image of a swinger. Besides, a scandal with you would be all my wife would need for a divorce wherein I would get the diving board and she would get the pool and everything else. I don't need that and neither do you!"

During the lengthy silence that followed, he gazed out at the rising fog while her fingers toyed with the back of his head.

"Look at it this way. . . ." His voice softened. "I'm about a quarter of a century older than you. Plus, women are supposed to be more long-lived than men. And I've taken excellent care of you in my will—"

"Frank! Don't talk that way! You make me feel like a vulture just waiting for you to die so I can pick your bones! Besides: You're a healthy and fairly young man!"

He looked up at her and smiled. "Well, let's find out how young and healthy I really am."

They made love. At least he thought they did. She was forced to call on the skills she had learned so well as a thespian. As usual, she passed the test with flying colors.

If all he considered her to be was a body, that's all she could find it in herself to be to him. Quite beyond her control, the emotions needed to participate in the act of love were held in check. Besides, she thought, he obviously doesn't give a damn whether he's giving me his cold.

He lay back, smiling. He was warm, relaxed, satisfied, and pleased that once again he had proven his manhood.

After a while, she propped herself on one elbow. "I've been wondering . . ."

"There you go, thinking again. I told you you weren't supposed to try that."

". . . why do you do it? I mean, why do you need it?" she persisted. "Why do you need more than one woman? What's the matter with your wife?"

"Variety, my dear girl; variety. I don't think women will ever understand the male need for variety."

Variety! Somewhere out there there must be men who didn't need variety . . . even if she had never had the good fortune to meet one.

They lay side by side silently. Hoffman was almost asleep.

"Frank," she said softly, without moving. "Frank?"

"Mmmm?"

"I have a confession."

"It's not my field. I build cars. You'd better find yourself a priest."

"Don't make fun, Frank. I've got a confession that involves you, Frank." She paused. "Frank, I saw her."

His eyes opened in premonition. "You saw whom?"

"Your wife. I saw Em."

"Where?"

"At Madame Tirana's. You said she had a weekly appointment there. I phoned and got an appointment at the same time."

"When?" His anger was evident.

"The other day." She grew defensive. "I didn't talk to her or anything, Frank. She was with another woman. I'm sure she didn't notice me."

"Didn't notice you!" Furious, he sat bolt upright. "Do you think she is goddamn blind? Everybody's nude in there! Tell me she didn't notice your goddamn perfect body! Don't make me laugh! And you're not, you know!"

"Frank, she's gorgeous. OK, so she's fifty, but she's obviously kept in good shape. She looks like Susan Hayward. I mean, after I saw her, I couldn't help wondering why you need me. I couldn't help wondering," she spoke more slowly and deliberately, "how long you would continue to need or want me."

"Until this moment, I never had cause to consider that. But now, I wonder too!

"First you case the woman; next, you'll probably invite her up here for tea!" He got out bed and began to dress, jerkily, furiously. "I can save you some time. Don't bother asking her to share the bed with us. Her tastes do not run to the ménage à trois scene. She's never been a chorus girl or been through the casting couch routine with every agent and producer in New York!"

He was trying to hurt her by throwing back her confidences at her. He was succeeding all too well.

"Frank! Where are you going? Please don't be angry—"

"For your information, I'm going to spend the rest of this night at the Collegiate Club. I tell you that just in case you want to call Em and keep her informed as to my whereabouts."

"Frank, don't go! Please don't go angry!"

"I'm going! And I'm going angry! And you can just think about that while you're wondering—and with damn good reason now—how long I will continue to need or want you!" He slammed the door as he left.

She stood staring unseeing at the closed door until she heard the elevator begin its descent. Her eyes filled with tears; they flowed freely down her cheeks.

She turned and went to the window. Even the Canadian Club sign had disappeared in the fog. Her prison walls had closed in. She was buried alive.

One day soon she would be forced to break out of this prison, and she feared the only avenue of escape might involve an act of violence. She didn't care for the prospect—but one did what one had to.

After all, she hadn't spent years living on the underworld fringe of Manhattan without learning a few tricks of the trade.

12.

"**B**UILDING A NUCLEAR WEAPON?"

"Huh?"

"This sign . . ." Father Koesler read aloud from the warning hung on the greenhouse door: " 'Extreme danger! Keep out until further notice.' Not only did you hang this rather ominous warning, you bolted the door."

"That's because I meant it," said Bishop Ratigan. "Having a bit of a problem with aphids. Actually, a bit of an infestation. So last night I lit a nicotine bomb."

"Will that get rid of the nasty bugs?"

"Them and anything else that goes in there before I ventilate it . . . which I will be doing in just a few minutes."

Koesler reflected. "Sounds sort of powerful. Isn't it dangerous?"

"You betcha. So dangerous you can't get the product on the retail market."

"Then, how—"

"How did I get it if you can't get it? Nurseries, garden shops, professional horticulturalists can get it. Which includes Sharps, the landscapers for whom I used to work while you were being God's gift to little campers."

"Oh . . . so they'll still sell it to you for old times' sake?"

"How many of their summer helpers grew up to be a bishop? Besides, they know I know how to use it."

"We've got a little time till January first, but I'm going to anticipate and make one resolution right now."

"What's that?"

"From now on, I'm going to pay attention to your signs."

The lines around Ratigan's eyes crinkled. "You'll live longer."

"By the way," Koesler's tone indicated a change of subject, "speaking of January first, tomorrow happens to be November first."

Ratigan checked his calendar watch. "You're right. So?"

"Just that they both used to be holy days of obligation, and today is Saturday and old habits die hard . . ."

"So?"

"So, there may be a few more confessions than usual. Any chance you could give me some help either this afternoon or evening?"

"Sorry; I've got a meeting with the Cardinal this afternoon. Won't even be here for dinner."

"OK; just wondered. Will you be back later this evening?"

"Why?" Ratigan, after almost being trapped into hearing confessions, was wary.

"We could go together to the Mercury's party. About eight? Easier that way. And we can cut out early if we want to."

"OK; but if I'm not back by the time you want to leave, why don't you just go ahead, and I'll see you there later."

"Right." Koesler left to see whether the janitor had

removed the rice that had been thrown at last evening's wedding.

Ratigan busied himself venting his greenhouse. Hear confessions, indeed! He had no meeting scheduled this afternoon. But he'd find something to occupy him outside the parish. Obviously, he thought, Bob Koesler doesn't understand that, generally speaking, bishops retire from hearing confessions by the very fact that they become bishops. That was the good news.

The bad news was that bishops had to confirm virtually every child in the diocese. He knew one auxiliary bishop in Minneapolis who publicly announced that the reason he had been made a bishop was because he had a car rugged enough to get him around for confirmations during a typical Minnesota winter.

Hear confessions, indeed!

Ratigan recalled learning in seminary moral theology class that according to the Church law of the time, Cardinals, among the many, many ecclesiastical perks they enjoyed, had automatic faculties, or permission, to hear anyone's confession anywhere in the world without being deputized by the appropriate bishop. The only thing overlooked by the canonist who wrote that law was that it had been so long since any Cardinal had heard a confession that no Cardinal could remember the formula for absolution.

He could see no one on the course as he drove down Golf View Drive. But the pins were still upright in the greens. There was life in the old Dearborn Country Club yet.

Frank Hoffman had once belonged to the D.C.C. But no more. He had moved on to the Orchard Lake Country Club. It was all part of his plan, his timetable, his upward mobility.

He turned up Hawthorne, then quickly onto Lawrence.

Take his present home, for instance. A good house, a good substantial Dearborn address. As nice a house as any in Bloomfield Hills. Just not as prestigious. But that would come as he climbed The Company ladder.

When they had bought their present home on Lawrence, they had been in Dearborn's Sacred Heart parish. Among West Dearbornites, it had been known as The Parish, which seemed appropriate to Hoffman since he worked for The Company. Then, St. Anselm's parish had been formed in Dearborn Heights, and the Hoffman home had been just within the cut by three blocks. But he'd been a good sport and had gone along with the redistricting. It had become a bit of a joke among some of the other Catholics at The Company: how, inevitably, one day the Hoffmans would belong to St. Hugo of the Hills—nicknamed St. Hugo of the Wheels—in Bloomfield Hills.

As he drove down Lawrence, Hoffman was conscious of the trees that lined the pavement and sidewalks. Stately old maples, oaks, sycamores, and firs. A tribute to the neighborhood's age. No recent suburban spread this, with newly planted infant trees. Most of the leaves gone now. Oaks still holding on. Well, after all, it was, what . . . the end of October.

The end of October . . . Damn: Halloween! And they were scheduled to attend the Mercurys' dinner party tonight. He'd have to check with Em and make sure their maid would house-sit this evening, and that she'd be well supplied with candy for the little beggars. Beggars . . . Dearborn beggars; almost a contradiction in terms.

And if this was Halloween, tomorrow must be All Saints. What the hell, if he found time today, he might just go to confession. For old times' sake, if nothing else.

He left the car in the driveway and entered the house through the back door. He had to give Em credit: She certainly kept a neat house. Of course she had help: a maid who came in six days a week, seven if needed. And two cleaning women twice a week. And no kids to mess it up. Their three, Mark, Claudia, and Charles, were married and living in other states.

He rambled through the downstairs. It seemed no one was at home. Not a sound. He climbed the stairs to the second floor. The master bedroom door was closed. He opened it.

Em was seated at the vanity, back to the door. She wore only a bra and half-slip. She was applying makeup. She could see his reflection clearly in the mirror. But his entrance had startled her. Even though she recognized him, her back had stiffened.

"I didn't hear you come in. I didn't know you were home." She spoke to the mirror.

"Just." He was tired. He hadn't slept well at the Club, and he hadn't had a change of clothing. And despite all the pills, that chill he'd gotten seemed to be waging a winning war. That plus his spat with Jackie had not created a euphoric mood this morning. But here was an attractive woman in a state of dishabille. Never mind that she happened to be his wife. Hoffman considered the scene a challenge to his manhood. What should he think of himself if he were to leave a half-naked woman alone!

He walked up behind her and unsnapped her bra. She stiffened further, but was not surprised. From long experience, she had known from the moment he entered the room that she was headed back to bed. Just her luck! A few minutes more and she would have been dressed and he would not have felt impelled to action.

They went to bed. A repeat performance of the previous night's encounter. Except that Em didn't bother trying to be the actress that Jackie was. And so, since he apparently had not satisfied his wife, Frank was not as pleased as he might have been.

After a few moments of lying motionless, Em swung her feet over the side of the bed and retrieved the bra and petticoat that had been tossed to the floor in one-half of an act of lust.

"You really ought to see someone, Em. Maybe a psychologist. It's been a really long time since you've gotten anything out of lovemaking—at least on a regular basis. You're really missing something." Hoffman remained in bed.

"Maybe you're right. Maybe I ought to see someone." Again in bra and half-slip, she had returned to the vanity to repair her makeup. "Maybe I ought to see your doxy. Maybe she could tell me how you arouse her passion. We could compare notes. Maybe you're just doing something wrong by the time you get around to me."

"Hey! What's this all about?"

" 'Sorry, Em; have to work late tonight. I'm going to stay downtown. Get a good night's sleep now.' " It was both an imitation and a parody of his phone call to her the previous night.

"It just so happens that I did stay at the Collegiate Club last night. You may feel free to call and check it out."

"Oh, never mind. If you bothered to tell me specifically where you slept, you probably slept there. So what happened—she go home to visit Mommy? Or did you two have a falling out? Trouble in paradise, hmmm?"

"Where did you ever get the notion that there's another woman? You haven't a shred of proof. It's an unfair accusation, you know, and I resent it!" He hoped—almost prayed—that Em had not identified Jackie at the spa.

"You wouldn't understand, Frank. A woman knows.

"For one thing, if you were not having satisfactory sex with some woman—and by satisfactory, I mean that you'd experienced her orgasm—you'd be plenty worried about yourself. I know you, Frank. God, how I know you. I don't come, yet you stay serene and relaxed. That's not you, Frank. That's not Frank Hoffman, the over-achiever, Frank Hoffman, the smashing success, Frank Hoffman, the macho man, Frank Hoffman, God's gift to womankind.

"No, Frank: You know there's nothing wrong with you because there's at least one woman somewhere else who is moaning and groaning and coming due to your manly ministrations."

Hoffman began to protest, but Emma interrupted him. "No, Frank, just this once let it be my show. We both know I know the truth." She continued dressing, not for tonight's party, but for the balance of the day.

"The point is," she continued calmly, "that, as the man said, Frankly, Frank, I don't give a damn. We're not in love anymore. But we make a good couple. We look good together. So we can show each other off at concerts, parties, weddings, nights on the town, at Company shindigs, and for the benefit of your pal Bishop Ratigan. And if you feel the need, as you apparently did a few minutes ago, I'll study the ceiling for the duration. It just doesn't matter.

"And we won't get a divorce," she continued as he sat up and stared open-mouthed at her. "I have no present reason for seeking one, and you can't afford one: It would ruin your carefully constructed reputation as a good Catholic and a good family man—and that would hurt you at The Company.

"On top of everything else, you would never settle for even half of our property—and I would never walk away from you without much more than that.

"So hang on to your mistress, Frank. But just one thing: I don't ever want to meet her. I mean that! If I ever

even see her, all that I've just said may very well go right
out the window."

Fully dressed, she left the room.

A bravura performance. He was not totally surprised.
She always had been a strong-willed, impulsive woman. But the intensity of her attack had brought him up short.

Gradually, he became aware that he was still naked,
sitting upright on the bed. He might just as well begin the
day again with a shower.

As he showered, he considered again all she had said.

She was right, of course, about the divorce; it was out
of the question—for more reasons than she had enumer-
ated. With that in mind, and knowing now how she felt
about him, the future did not look all that bright.

In situations such as this, it was not Frank Hoffman's
habit to sit still and allow fate to have its way with him.

The more he considered his future, both immediate
and distant, the more life with Jackie at his side seemed
the ideal solution. At least better. They turned each other
on. Jackie was Catholic, too, even though she would be
more accurately described as lapsed. Still, there was no
previous marriage, no legal impediment to her return to
the Church. And even if there were some problem, he
was sure Mike Ratigan could solve it. And they would
look good together. Better even than he and Em.

Yes, it seemed right. However, all that did not come
close to altering the fact that divorce was out of the question.

But what other way could he possibly get Em out of his
life? He pondered that problem as he stood still and let
the hot water massage him.

Since no one would be at the rectory tonight, Father
Koesler had not bothered to shop for treats for the kiddies. An empty parish rectory on Halloween undoubtedly

would result in soaped windows. There was no help for it. Today's schedule had him available for confessions from 4:00 till 5:00 this afternoon, offering the 5:30 Mass; then, after a light supper, he would offer the 7:00 Mass, after which he would again be available for confessions for approximately an hour. And Ratigan would not return until later this evening.

He glanced at his watch. 4:30. In half an hour he would leave the confessional and begin preparation for the afternoon Mass, another comparatively recent innovation in Catholic life. Before the Second Vatican Council, Church law had obliged Catholics to attend Mass on Sundays. Now, the obligation remained the same, but the time span had been expanded to include any Mass offered after 4:00 P.M. on Saturdays.

Koesler breathed a sigh of gratitude that Ratigan had been unable to help with confessions today. Koesler's anticipated crowd of penitents had not materialized. He had thought that the combination of Halloween, the Feast of All Saints, and Sunday might beckon multitudes to the box. But so far, it hadn't happened.

There had been a few more adults than usual—people who remembered the good old days when plenary indulgences that could free souls sentenced to purgatory could be easily gained on November 2, the Feast of All Souls. Since plenary indulgences could be gained only by those who were free from serious sin, confession was very popular as these feasts approached. The Feast of All Souls still followed All Saints, but indulgences had pretty well fallen into desuetude. Still, some Catholics had formed the habit of confessing before All Saints' Day. And for some, the habit was hard to break.

But Koesler had badly misgauged the number of habit-ridden Catholics.

He heard the shuffling sound peculiar to someone entering the confessional room. He looked to see who might appear coming around the screened area. Instead, the person knelt on the other side of the screen. Silence. No way for Koesler to know whether the penitent was collecting his or her thoughts or whether he or she was waiting for some sign from the priest to begin.

"All right." He got the ball rolling.

"Oh!" came the startled whisper, as if the penitent were surprised there was actually a priest on the other side of the screen. "Oh . . . bless me, Father, for I have sinned. It's been, uh . . . maybe six months since my last confession."

Koesler didn't recognize the voice. But then he never tried to.

"I've lied a few times. Lost my temper around the house. Got angry at the kids. And missed Mass once— but I had a bad cold. And that's about it, Father. I'm sorry for these and all the sins of my past life, especially for disobedience."

It was a man's voice. That was clear even through the whisper. And it was not a chronologically elderly man. But, in terms of sacramental and moral theology, this was an old-timer of the first water.

He had no serious sin to confess. Yet, instead of concentrating on one fault and trying to do something to correct it, he was still bringing in the old laundry list of sins. He felt the need to confess missing Mass even though he had a perfectly legitimate excusing reason. And, finally, after all these years, he still concluded his confession in the very same way he had as a young boy, even to the specification of disobedience as the most serious fault of his lifetime.

This was the type of penitent who used to confess monthly on a regular basis. After Vatican II, he'd heard that Catholics might consider going to confession less frequently, perhaps, but more penitently, more resolved to reform. However, he, and many like him, elected to cut back on the quantity while changing nothing else about the quality of their confessions.

As was his wont, Koesler, at this point, would deliver a brief fervorino. Whether the penitent paid any attention to it or not, he would expect it.

"Maybe on your way home from work," Koesler suggested, "you could give a little thought to the difficulties your wife and children have faced that day. Then, if you can try to forget the problems you experienced at work and concentrate rather on how tired and frustrated those at home might be, maybe you will be able to be more thoughtful and considerate to them."

"Yes, Father."

It was an automatic response. Koesler had expected nothing more.

"For your penance, say three Our Fathers and three Hail Marys."

Koesler began the absolution in English, but, instead of silently listening to the words, the penitent began reciting the traditional act of contrition. An old-timer to the very end.

What the hell, thought Koesler, if this guy isn't going to listen to words he can understand, I'll just slip into the old Latin formula.

After Koesler completed the absolution in the ancient language, the penitent rose and departed.

Koesler felt great. Just like the good old days when everything was automatic. The penitent puts sins in "the box" and the confessor wiped them out with an absolution which the penitent could not have understood even if he had been listening. He was not listening because he was mouthing a prayer of contrition by rote. It didn't make a great deal of sense now any more than it had then. But an occasional nostalgic return to the past could be fun now and again.

The next penitent entered. Business was picking up.

Once again, the penitent knelt on the other side of the screen. "Bless me, Father, for I have sinned. It's been . . . uh . . . oh, it's been quite a few months since my previous confession."

Frank Hoffman. Koesler couldn't help recognizing the voice, which was pitched softly but not whispering. Besides, Hoffman was the only penitent in Koesler's experience who correctly referred to his previous confession as "previous" instead of the grammatically incorrect "last" confession. As usual, Koesler had not tried to identify the unseen penitent; he simply couldn't help knowing who it was.

"During this time since my latest confession I have been angry many times, frequently with my wife. I have taken God's name in vain several times. I was tardy for Sunday Mass a few times." He paused.

Koesler knew Hoffman to be a very wealthy and important executive. This recitation of a series of mundane peccadilloes caused Koesler to wonder again, as he had many times before, at the lack of "business sins" confessed. In all his years of hearing confessions, he would not have to go beyond the fingers of both hands to count the number of times he had heard anyone confess sins relating to business life. Were Catholics sinless from nine to five? He did not think that possible.

"And," Hoffman continued, "I committed adultery many times. Too often to bother counting."

Koesler recalled that in his previous confession, Hoffman had confessed to adultery. Yet he could not treat Hoffman as a recidivist, since by kneeling on the other side of the screen, the man had consciously chosen to remain anonymous. He had not been successful in achieving anonymity only because Koesler had recognized a specific speech pattern. Yet for the priest to indicate that he was aware of Hoffman's identity by bringing up a detail from a previous confession would violate Hoffman's

right to his choice of at least a semblance of anonymity.
The rule was that a confessor was not to do anything relating to confession that would be odious to the penitent.
On the other hand, based even on this confession alone,
Koesler thought he ought to say something about a sin
which by Hoffman's own admission was not only serious
but habitual.

After Hoffman had concluded his confession, Koesler
said, "You are a married man, since you confessed being
angry with your wife. And the person with whom you are
sinning sexually, she is married or unmarried?"

"She's . . . uh . . . never been married, Father."

"I see." Koesler paused momentarily.

"The problem, I fear, is that, no matter how this relationship began, by now you are merely using this
woman. Perhaps you are using each other. But it is not
likely a healthy or productive dalliance.

"Worse, since you are married, it has nowhere to go.
And I think a continuation of this relationship may be
particularly unfair to the woman. Don't you think you
ought to do something about this situation?"

There was a slight pause. Then, rather brightly, "You
know, that's funny: I was thinking along those very same
lines earlier today. I think I have an idea that just may
solve this problem. Your advice, in a way, just brought
my thinking to a head." He did not add that Father Koesler might well not approve of his plan if all the details
were revealed. That might be a matter to be handled in
some future confession.

"Very good!" Seldom had the priest's advice been so
quickly effective. He felt very good about that. "For
your penance, suppose you try to do something particularly nice for your wife."

I tried to do that earlier today, thought Hoffman, but
she didn't care for it.

Koesler absolved Hoffman, who then departed.

There followed nearly twenty minutes during which Koesler alone occupied the confessional. Once again, he was grateful Bishop Ratigan had been unable to help out. It would have been a long spell before Ratigan would have allowed Koesler to live down the confessional jam that didn't gel.

His line of thought was interrupted by a teenager, who hurried around the screen and plopped in the chair opposite Koesler.

"Hi, Freddie."

"Hi, Father." Freddie settled into the chair as if this were going to be an extended visit. That was seldom the case with fourteen-year-old boys, and it would not be the case with Freddie. "It's been a couple of months since I was to confession, Father. I really got on my mother's nerves this time, Father. She's been on my case for most of the two months. But it finally come to me: It's my fault. My dad says it's a phase I'm going through. I hope to hell it is . . . oh, excuse me, Father. But anyway, it was getting so bad I thought I'd try to turn it around and go to confession. And that's just about it, Father."

"What could you do for your mother this evening, Freddie?"

"Everything! Take out the garbage, clean my room, practice the piano, do my homework, not bug her to go out trick or treatin', go to bed on time." Freddie appeared frustrated. "And that's not the half of it, Father."

"Well, every trip begins with the first step, Freddie. So, why don't you clean up your room for your penance."

"Neat!"

Koesler absolved Freddie and he was gone.

No one followed him. Koesler glanced at his watch. A quarter to five—fifteen minutes to go.

Just above his watch, Koesler noticed a speck of dust on the sleeve of his cassock and brushed it off. It brought to mind the old Holy Cross priest who, years back, had been an institution within an institution at Notre Dame. One of the stories about him had it that the Notre Dame boys would go up to the old priest's room for confession. As each boy knelt by the priest's chair to confess, he, now having trouble with his memory, would make little chalk marks on the sleeve of his cassock to aid him in remembering what sins had been confessed so he could assess and impose a proper penance.

One Saturday afternoon, so the story went, a boy arrived at the priest's room and began confessing violent acts bordering on mayhem. The priest nearly covered his sleeve with chalk marks. "How did you manage to do all this damage?" the priest asked when the student had completed his confession.

"Playin' football."

"Oh? And who were you playin'?"

"Southern Methodist."

"Oh, well," said the priest, brushing away all the chalk marks, "boys will be boys!"

Koesler again glanced at his watch. Ten to five. Ten more minutes.

Koesler reflected upon his habit of checking the time more frequently as the end of any event neared. He decided this would be a good time to review quickly the outline, which existed only in his mind, of the homily he would preach at Masses this weekend.

However, he was distracted soon after beginning his review by someone entering the confessional. Instinctively, and throughout his years as a priest, Koesler had never come to terms with the last-minute penitent. Especially when most of the hour went by unused by anyone, why did people wait till the last minute? He considered it a thoughtless act. He had never considered that what to him was the last minute was to some penitent his or her only available moment.

This penitent happened to be Cindy Mercury, well
known to Koesler. She stepped around the screen and
took the seat opposite him. She was wearing a blue cloth
coat with a small artificial fur collar. It seemed an inex-
pensive garment for one of her station in life.

Her hair, covered by a silk scarf, was in curlers. To
Koesler, a woman whose hair was in curlers was simply
stating that she was soon to be somewhere more important than where she was right now.

Cindy's husband was an actor. So, unlike the auto executives of the parish, there was little way anyone could
estimate Angie Mercury's income. But Angie and Cindy
appeared with some regularity on the lifestyle pages of
local newspapers and magazines. And their donations to
the Church were substantial. Not as much as Charles
Chase or Cindy's brother, Frank Hoffman, but well
above average, nonetheless.

Koesler considered Cindy perhaps the most attractive
of many attractive women in the parish. Her abundant
blonde hair seemed naturally wavy, and she had a model's profile, reminiscent of the late Grace Kelly.

Koesler picked up the Bible from the small table next
to his chair. In the new form of the sacrament of reconciliation, the first rubric was the reading of a passage from
the Bible. A rubric that Koesler dispensed with in the
confessions of children.

"If you don't mind, Father, can we skip the scripture
reading? It's kind of late—and I'm sorry about that—but
neither of us has much time." She seemed upset. About
what, Koesler guessed he would be informed shortly.

He nodded and returned the book to the table. He
waited. She fidgeted.

"I'm beginning to think I'm a failure as a wife."

Not many things surprised Koesler anymore, but her
statement did. Koesler had always considered the Mercurys among the more stable couples in the parish, and

Cindy one of the more efficient and dedicated homemakers. On the other hand, he had had similar thoughts about other couples who eventually had become divorce statistics.

"Why would you think that?" he asked at length.

"My management—or rather, mismanagement—of our budget." She paused, then looked at him ingenuously. "Do you suppose having a deficit budget could be a sin?"

He could not suppress laughter, even though her question was undoubtedly sincere. "If it is, then this entire country is headed for hell in a handbasket."

She smiled briefly, then appeared concerned again. "There are times, Father, when everything seems to be closing in on me. The bills keep piling up and I'm constantly shifting money from one account to another. Then I have to separate the creditors who charge interest on unpaid accounts and try to pay them first. Then come the hounding letters and phone calls. Eventually, I begin to feel guilty about it. And, I guess, that's why I'm here."

In a way, Koesler was not surprised; yet in another way he was. He had spent much of his adult life amazed at people who, foolishly, he thought, lived above their means. So, it did not surprise him that the Mercurys were living over their heads. It did surprise him that the Mercurys could not afford to live at a level that was relatively modest compared with many in his parish.

"I can understand why you might begin to feel guilty about this. And I suppose that a lot of those creditors try their best to make you feel guilty. But I really doubt that you're committing any sin. Especially if you are not the one who's running up those bills. Are you?"

"Well, no, not really, Father. It's Angie." She said it with a sense of fatality. "But it's not all his fault," she added quickly. "It's just that when you're in show business, you're never offstage. The world really is, as

Shakepeare said, a stage—at least for performers. Whether they're working or, as they say, between shows, they have to act as if all is well.

"Angie feels compelled to pick up the tab, get the expensive theater tickets, pay the taxi, throw the party . . . that sort of thing. If he doesn't, everybody will know he's between shows, or, worse, that he is working and making peanuts.

"And the truth of it is, Father, that's the way it is: He keeps working, but he might just as well be doing benefits."

"I'm afraid I don't understand." Koesler knew he could not offer advice unless he understood the problem. "Why should your husband think he has to create an affluent impression when he can't afford to? It's been my experience that when people fall upon bad times, they try to reduce their lifestyle, tighten the belt, that sort of thing. We all understand that. It's just part of life for most people."

"Not with show biz people, Father. I know. I've been there. Right after we were married, I had a brief theatrical fling with Angie under the theory that two actors can eat better if both are working. For a few years, we did just about everything in show biz. And we were just barely getting by. I know how he feels now. If you don't act as if you're on top, the word goes out that you're cold, that you're not a good property, not a good casting risk. And it becomes a self-fulfilling prophecy."

"Why did you quit?" Koesler had long been interested in the theater but had no behind-the-scenes knowledge of it.

"Well, a baby came along . . . and Angie's luck began to improve. But if you can have good luck, you can also have bad luck. And that's what we've had for longer than I care to remember. I'd join him on stage again, but there's no future in that. I'd be more a hindrance now than a help. He wouldn't even get the parts he gets now if I were in the package."

"If you don't mind my asking," Koesler sensed he'd grasped only the tip of this problem, "how do you manage to carry things off as well as you do?"

Cindy lowered her head in evident shame. "My brother Frank." She looked up in anxiety. "This mustn't get out!"

Koesler shook his head. "You're in confession. What you say here isn't going anywhere else."

"Oh, that's right. I'm sorry, Father, I forgot. Sometimes when I just sit here and talk to you, I forget I'm going to confession."

The priest smiled.

"Well, anyway," she went on, "for years now, my brother has given us—me—a very generous check just about every month.

"You see, Frank and I are very close. We always have been. He can't help himself, Father. He couldn't let anything bad happen to me. He's very generous. All the money he's given . . . well, it's not deductible or anything. It's down the drain as far as he's concerned.

"But that brings up another problem, Father. As badly as we need Frank's help, Angie resents it . . . resents it bitterly. He gets so angry that I try not to let him know whenever I get a check. But he knows of course that Frank is helping."

"Yes," Koesler nodded, "St. Vincent de Paul had a lot to say about the 'proud poor' and how delicate the approach to them must be."

"That's just it, Father: Frank is hardly delicate about his help, especially where Angie is concerned. Frank looks down on Angie and Angie's theatrical career. So, here I am, in the middle between my husband and my brother, the two men I love most in the world. And they hate each other." Her lips trembled. "Sometimes I get to feeling it's my fault. There must be a way I can make those two be friends. If I could get a job . . . but I've looked, and there's nothing. And if anything happened to cut off that money Frank gives us . . . well, I just don't know what I'd do.'' She pulled a handkerchief from her purse, covered her face, and began to sob quietly. ''Sometimes I feel as if I'm cracking up, Father,'' she managed to get out between sobs.

Few things in life made Koesler feel more helpless than being in the presence of someone, particularly a woman, who was crying. There was so little he could do. There was little anyone could do except perhaps offer a shoulder on which to cry. Probably there were priests who could carry off such physical closeness and maintain their position. Koesler did not believe he was among them.

On top of that, in a few minutes, he would be late for Saturday afternoon Mass. For the past several minutes, he'd been aware of the sound of the gathering crowd in the church. He glanced at his watch. Twenty past five. Ten minutes to go.

''This much you must know and believe,'' Koesler said, with as much reassurance as he could muster, ''what's going on is not your fault. I know there are lots of forces conspiring to make you feel guilty, but you have no guilt. All I can tell you at this moment is to pray. I know that sounds like a cop-out, but you're dealing with forces and relationships that are really quite beyond your ability to control. It's just that in situations like this we must turn to God with confidence. I think it was Lincoln who said something about how there are times when man has no other direction open to him than down on his knees.

''And, too, why don't you come back—maybe some-time next week—to the rectory so we can talk about this at greater length. Maybe between the two of us we can come up with something to help this situation."

At the moment, Koesler did not have the faintest clue as to what to do about Cindy's problem. For now, he resolved to do a bit of praying over this problem himself.

Cindy was drying her eyes. She seemed a bit more composed.

"Now, if you'll excuse me," Koesler rose, "I've got to begin Mass in just a few minutes. Why don't you remain here till you feel better? And since you didn't have any sins to confess, there's no need for any absolution. I'll just give you my blessing." He traced the sign of the cross in the air over her.

She crossed herself. "I'm all right now, Father; really I am. Thanks. And," she even managed a smile, "I'll see you at the party tonight."

"What? Oh, yes: the dinner party. Yes, I'll see you then." Koesler hurried to vest for Mass. In concentrating on Cindy Mercury's problem, it had completely slipped his mind that he had been invited to her house that evening.

It could be awkward attending the party, now that he knew so much more about the hosts and one of their guests than he had just a few minutes ago. He hadn't known anything of her brief theatrical background. Nor of their financial plight and its completely unnecessary—as far as he was concerned—cause. Nor of the pressure on Cindy as a result of the friction between her husband and her brother.

Tonight's party would be one of those many occasions when Koesler would have to virtually forget his intimate knowledge of what had been told him as a secret—or, at least act as if he had forgotten. Strictly speaking, Cindy had not gone to confession to him. But she had placed herself in a confessional situation. And Koesler's responsibility would have to be the same as if all she had told

him were protected by the fabled seal of confession. Yet
it was, or could be, an awkward situation. Except that
Koesler had lived through so many similar situations that
keeping secrets was second nature to him.

The 5:30 Mass was completed without incident. Although he experienced many a distraction as his subcon-
scious led him down many blind alleys searching for
some solution to Cindy Mercury's problem.

After Mass, in the rectory, Koesler searched the refrigerator, finding half a carton of ham salad, more than
enough for a sandwich. Which, in turn, was enough to
carry him through to tonight's dinner.

The seven o'clock Mass was taken care of in due order. As usual, it was very sparsely attended. He had tried
several times to get the parish council to drop that Mass
from the schedule. But he had not yet been successful. If
the members of the council had to repeat the same lit-
urgy, along with the same homily, over and over each
weekend, they might not feel so strongly about retaining
a Mass that had practically nothing else going for it except a rather long history.

After the evening Mass, as was his custom, he locked
the collection in the sacristy safe and turned out most of
the lights, leaving on only those few that illuminated the
area near his confessional. He also turned off the heat.
More than likely, he would be the only one in the church
for the next approximate hour that he would sit in the
confessional. No point in heating the whole church for
one person.

He turned on the light in his side of the confessional
and turned the collar of his topcoat up around his neck.
He'd have to look into the purchase of a space heater.
There might not be any good reason to heat the whole
church for one. On the other hand there was no good reason why that one should freeze.

He took a book from the nearby table. *Twelve and*

One-Half Keys, by Father Edward Hays, like Koesler, a diocesan priest. Hays was a contemplative and an artist who had written a series of books of prayer deeply valued by Koesler and often recommended by him.

His hand began to shake from the cold. Koesler resolved he'd have to get a space heater, and soon.

13.

I‍T WAS WITH MIXED EMOTIONS THAT KOESLER faced this evening's dinner party. It wasn't that he didn't enjoy such gatherings. On the contrary, especially with his peers, he was known on occasion to be the life of the party. But so recently supplied with the background of conflict that Cindy Mercury had imparted earlier, Koesler would be seeing some of the partygoers in a new light. And he was not at all happy about that.

When he and Ratigan arrived at the Mercury house, one car was already in the driveway. Ratigan recognized it as the Hoffmans'. The Chases hadn't yet arrived. Ratigan parked at the curb. He didn't want to chance being hemmed in. He anticipated that he and Koesler probably would be the first to leave.

Cindy Mercury greeted them at the door, and took their coats and hats. She was wearing a black evening gown with a deep "V" fore and aft. She looked every inch the professional dancer she once had been. Ratigan and Koesler appreciated the view. Both belonged to the look-but-don't-touch school of the chaste clergy.

Next they were greeted by Angie Mercury, then by the Hoffmans. Mercury was sporty in a maroon jacket, with tan slacks and a white open-collared shirt. Hoffman wore

134

a dark blue business suit, while his wife was in a white suit, which, while it covered her amply, revealed that all of her curves were still in the right places.

Before the clergy's arrival, all had been seated in the living room. Now they resumed their places. Ratigan and Koesler found chairs at opposite sides of the large room.

No sooner was Koesler seated than a waiter approached and inquired as to his drink preference. Koesler asked for a bourbon manhattan—yes, on the rocks and, as a matter of fact, lots of ice.

Koesler noted that, across the room, a waitress was taking Ratigan's drink order. But before she did that, she had removed an empty cocktail glass from the table before Hoffman and replaced it with a full one. He also noticed that Hoffman popped a pill into his mouth and washed it down with a swallow of his drink.

From what Cindy had told him this afternoon, he marveled that this party was being catered. He'd seen the waiter and waitress and, judging by sounds from the kitchen, there must be at least one cook on hand. Despite Cindy's "No one must know!" he wondered how many people present did know that, for all practical purposes, Hoffman was picking up the tab for this display of affluence. Possibly everyone but Ratigan.

Then again, considering their close relationship, perhaps Ratigan, too, was in on the secret. Koesler smiled mentally as he considered that probably as far as the others were concerned, he was the only one who did not know. And, without Cindy's confession today, that would have been true.

Looking about the room, he reflected that, of the other five here, two of them had been to confession to him today. In this era of most infrequent confession, that was a bit of a coincidence.

As usual, in gatherings such as this, the conversation became fragmented. The breakup began when Hoffman and Ratigan started the conversational ball rolling with today's trends in big business. First to lose interest were the women. Cindy had leaned toward Emma and they began talking quietly between themselves. That left Mercury and Koesler, neither of whom was interested in either multinationals or women's fashions.

"From time to time," Koesler opened the third topic, "I've wondered about your name. I don't think I've ever known anyone else named Mercury. If I'm not being too personal, what nationality is it?"

Angie smiled. "Try Angelo DeMercurio, Father. Does that give you a clue?"

"Italian, of course. But how—?"

"Show business, Father. Angelo DeMercurio might look OK on an old-time fight bill, but, believe me, it doesn't play on a marquee."

Koesler rattled his manhattan in an attempt to melt more ice. He wondered how may questions about his host's life and lifestyle could be answered with the words "show business."

"Well, then, how long have you been Angie Mercury?"

"So long I've almost forgotten Angelo DeMercurio. I was Angie Mercury before I married Cindy. So, she may not have won any prize, but," he laughed engagingly, "she can't claim she wasn't warned."

Koesler made an embarrassed gesture as one tends to do when someone makes a self-deprecatory statement. "So you've been in show business that long. . . ."

"Some kids want to grow up to be doctors, some lawyers, some cowboys," Mercury looked meaningfully at Koesler, "some priests. Me, I always wanted to be an actor."

"Now that you mention it, most Catholic boys at least consider the possibility of becoming a priest. At least they used to. Didn't the thought ever cross your mind?"

"Oh, yeah, sure, Father. But it wasn't that I wanted to be a priest: I wanted to be an actor in a priest's suit. Meaning no disrespect, but when you get all vested for Mass, that's not all that different from getting into a costume. And, especially when you preach, among other things, I suppose, you're trying to hold a crowd. And, I must say," he raised his glass to Koesler, "you're pretty good at it. But," he took a sip of his drink, "you know right away, don't you, whether you've got them or you've lost them?"

Koesler nodded.

"Well, that's not all that removed from what an actor tries to do with an audience. So, in that sense I gave a few thoughts to becoming a priest. But, in the end, I would never have been satisfied with only one role, one stage, one audience. And besides, it was just about that time that I discovered that girls could be fun. And I wanted one of my own. And," he looked across the room and smiled at his wife, "I got one!"

There was such evident love flowing from him to her that Koesler was moved. These days, it was indeed rare to find a married couple who had so completely preserved the love affair with which they had begun.

On second thought, Koesler decided that he had rarely encountered such a strong love at any time.

"She is such a trouper, Father. I mean, show business is my life. Cindy likes it and enjoys it, yes, but I know she could easily live without it. And still, to help me and so we could be together, she joined me in forming an act after we got married. She already had training as a dancer, so we didn't have to work on that. But everything else, I taught her. And was she a great pupil! We did the whole bit, Father." He was growing excited in relating the experience, and the pride he felt for his wife was evident.

"We played the Catskills, nightclubs, dinner theaters, the legitimate stage, the whole shot. We used to do those bits you still see on TV every so often. . .you know, where you get some volunteers from the audience and hypnotize them and give them a post-hypnotic suggestion and then they do silly things like clucking like a chicken. Or the one where one member of the team is blindfolded and the other goes out and holds up articles belonging to members of the audience and the blindfolded one identifies what the partner is holding. We got so good at it—and so bored with it —we used to reverse roles.

"Then we did most of the world's great musicals— *Annie Get Your Gun, South Pacific, The Sound of Music, Oklahoma!*—like that. Funny thing . . ." he seemed momentarily lost in thought, "when it came to the musicals, she was always better than I was."

"Better?"

"Yeah. Like she was a better Annie than I was a Frank Butler. She was a better Julie Jordan that I was a Billy Bigelow. A better Maria than I was a Baron Von Trapp. Come to think of it, when she was Nellie Forbush, I was just a gob in the chorus. Isn't that funny, Father? There's a whole segment of show biz—musical comedy—that she does better than I do.

"But she was so . . . oh, I don't know . . . self-effacing, maybe . . . so sweet about it that she never let on. And, would you believe it, Father: It never dawned on me till just this minute—she didn't want me to feel bad because she was better at musical comedy than I was, so she never let on! All these years . . . I ask you Father, is that some kind of girl!"

The doorbell rang. The Chases had arrived.

Cindy went to the door. As a cold blast of air entered the room, Koesler noticed that Hoffman shivered, then blew his nose. It occurred to the priest that if anyone should feel the cold, it ought to be Cindy. She certainly was wearing less than anyone else. No doubt about it: She was some kind of girl!

There was the usual confusion and profusion of greetings between those at the door and those in the living room. Charles Chase wore a blue suit almost identical to that worn by Hoffman, only slightly darker and more severe in cut. Louise Chase's floor length gown was full enough to mask the blemishes of time, yet revealing enough to state that she was still an attractive albeit matronly woman.

The two newcomers circled the room, the men shaking hands, the women leaving lip pecks on cheeks and in the air. Finally, as if cued by musical chairs, all were seated. Waiter and waitress took drink orders from the Chases.

Peripherally, Koesler had noticed that of those present, the Hoffmans' glasses were being refilled far more often than anyone else's. Emma was drinking what appeared to be martinis. Frank's was an amber liquid that Koesler took to be the renowned perfect Rob Roy.

In short order, the conversation again broke down into at least temporarily homogeneous groups. Ratigan and Hoffman were now joined by Chase in sorting out the pressing problems of Big Business. Emma and Cindy discussed the coming winter's effect on the greenhouse occupants. Mercury had disappeared, presumably in the kitchen checking on dinner preparations.

Koesler found himself seated next to Louise Chase. Ready or not, they were about to open conversation.

Throughout his years at St. Anselm's, Koesler had always thought he would like Mrs. Chase. He could not be certain, because their relationship had always been on a professional pastor-parishioner basis. And even then not on a frequent basis. She seemed to have a good sense of humor without having discovered much to laugh about. She wore that seemingly bored visage common to very wealthy women. But her countenance seemed relieved by a private joke she was sharing with no one.

Louise leaned toward Koesler, who turned his chair slightly to face her. "I don't suppose you are interested either in horticulture or the vagaries of foreign trade, Father?"

"I'm afraid not." Koesler felt himself almost redden. As if he should be interested, but, in truth, was not.

"Well," she said in a philosophical tone, "there are other things in life. I think we noticed you at the symphony the other night."

"It's very possible. Bishop Ratigan was kind enough to take me."

"What did you think of it?"

"To be frank, about the only reason I went was for the Brahms Fourth. But I was truly surprised by their opener. It's almost as if once you've heard the Tchaikovsky First Piano Concerto, you've heard it no matter who plays it. But Thursday, with Andre Watts at the piano, it was almost as if I had never heard it before!"

Louise turned full attention on him. It was a rarity these days to find a music lover with whom one might be in total agreement. "And I suppose you were one of those boisterous aficionados on your feet and shouting when the concerto was concluded?"

"Yes, I was," Koesler admitted.

"So was I!"

They continued their discussion on classical music, discovering to their mutual delight that they shared much the same taste: Almost nothing could excel the great romantics; they could neither understand nor abide anything by Schoenberg or any of his disciples, especially Bartok; John Cage should be deported; Gershwin and Copeland belonged with the immortals.

While they conversed lightly and amicably, Koesler became growingly aware of a subtle change in the atmosphere.

He had been vaguely aware that as he had been refusing refills, Emma Hoffman had been taking advantage of each new opportunity to add to her martini intake. He had not noticed her eating anything, just drinking. And, as the martinis had been going down, her voice had been rising. He also noticed that as Emma's voice became more strident, across the room her husband had been increasing his Rob Roy intake. Somewhere down the line, Koesler feared, a commotion was about to take place.

Koesler was by no means alone in taking notice of Emma Hoffman's escalating manifestation. In his clique, Bishop Ratigan had slightly raised his volume in an attempt to distract the others from Emma's vociferousness. And Koesler's tête-à-tête with Louise had become a monologue as she ranged from topic to topic in another attempted diversion from the one who was quickly becoming the focal point of this gathering.

"I must admit," said Louise, a bit more forcefully than necessary, "that I was surprised when Charles and Frank began working together so well. I would have expected there to be more friction, more competition at The Company . . . especially with a newcomer on the scene."

Koesler became aware that, for the first time this eve-

ning, Louise was not maintaining eye contact. She was, in
fact, looking just over his shoulder. He, in turn, glanced
over her shoulder and saw that Emma was nibbling on an
hors d'oeuvre. Getting some food into her system to off-
set all that liquor was a step in the right direction. But he
feared it might be too late.

"Mmmm," Emma popped the remainder of the hors
d'oeuvre in her mouth. "My dear," she said to Cindy in
a tone devoid of sincerity, "this is delicious! What is it?
It tastes like a combination of crabmeat and shrimp. You
must let me see your recipe. But it must be terribly, terribly *expensive*!"

She went out of her way to emphasize the final
word. It was but one in a series of sarcastic remarks
she had been making. Koesler noticed that Cindy's
face had reddened.

"It is probably the result of what can happen when
good Christian men get together to do a job," Louise
continued almost mechanically. "Their relationship
must be a source of edification to the rest of the executives at The Company."

Koesler suspected that Louise did not fully know what
she was saying, but was making conversation from embarrassment.

The waitress brought Emma still another martini.
And, on her way out of the room, she deposited
another perfect Rob Roy before an obviously angry
Frank Hoffman.

Koesler winced as Emma immediately downed nearly
half her drink in a single gulp.

"Oh, yes." Emma looked directly and argumenta-
tively at her husband, while ostensibly addressing her
comments to Cindy. "Oh, yes! These hors d'oeuvres are
outstanding. What's this one? Caviar? Caviar and something. My dear, how do you afford such delicacies?

Angie must be doing fabulously! Strange; I haven't seen any notices in the papers.''

"Why, Frank has even given—yes, given, for all pratical purposes—a couple of his closest advisors to Charles." From her tone it seemed clear that even Louise knew no one was paying any attention to her. "My guess would be that you'd have to search far and wide to find such a generous spirit of cooperation, especially in a major industry."

Angie Mercury popped into the archway in much the same manner as an effervescent KoKo might make his entrance in *The Mikado*.

"Ladies and gentlemen," he announced, "dinner is served." Then a frown crossed his face. He had perceived that Cindy looked beleaguered. He did not know why and there was no time to discover the reason.

The guests filed silently and ill at ease into the adjoining dining room.

Mercury directed his guests to their places. He and Cindy sat at opposite ends of the table. The Hoffmans sat across from each other at mid-table. Both had quaffed their latest drinks before entering the dining room.

All took their seats in silence.

Easily qualifying as the ranking clergyman, Bishop Ratigan was delegated to lead the grace.

"Bless us, O Lord, and these Thy gifts," Ratigan traced the sign of the cross over the table, "which we are about to receive from Thy bounty. Through Christ, Our Lord, Amen."

Although he was rather proficient at extemporaneous prayer, Ratigan was at a loss for an ad lib sentiment that would not be a mockery in this situation. Invisible waves of anger were flowing across the dinner table. Thus, the bishop had fallen back on the most traditional Catholic formula for grace before meals.

Ordinarily, Mercury would have begun to roll the conversational ball. But he was preoccupied with whatever it was that was troubling his wife. He kept looking over the long expanse of table for some sign or signal from her. But Cindy kept her eyes down. Her cheeks were still flushed.

Bishop Ratigan broke the heavy silence. "Anybody notice in the paper last Sunday, they're predicting a long, hard winter?" Weather he considered to be neutral.

"Oh, yes," Louise Chase quickly responded, "I couldn't more agree. Have you noticed the bushes are just almost overburdened with berries? And judging from the animals I've seen, their fur seems a lot thicker."

The waiter and waitress began serving the soup course.

"Hell of a lot more acorns on the ground, now that you mention it," Charles Chase agreed.

"What an exquisite pattern," Emma Hoffman remarked, fingering the soup dish. "Someone's inheritance, is it?" She directed question and gaze at Mercury.

"Are you kidding, Em? You know we may have a skeleton or two in the closet, but neither of us had any rich relatives." Unaware of Emma's intent, or what had gone before, Mercury answered straightforwardly.

"You do now," Emma purred.

"What? What are you talking about, Em?" Mercury missed her meaning since he had not been searching for it.

Most of the others knew what she was driving at and grew more ill at ease.

Koesler foresaw an explosion and wondered only at what point it would come. Seated next to Emma, he looked across at Hoffman, who placed a tablet or pill of some sort in his mouth and downed it with water. Hoffman was obviously angry with his wife, but his complexion was ashen, which Koesler considered odd. People usually flush when angered.

"The way I see it," said Ratigan, "it can't be a long, hard winter. We're not ready for it. They haven't repaired last winter's potholes yet. Why, Outer Drive looks as if it's been through a war." Ratigan toyed with his soup. It was delicious. But, since it was vichyssoise, he didn't have to worry about its getting cold.

"No atheists in potholes, eh, bishop?" Mercury quipped.

The ensuing laughter sounded forced.

"Where are you performing now, Angie?" Emma feigned ignorance. "I haven't noticed your name in any of the theater ads."

"Oh, just some dinner theater, some community theater, Em. Not much." Mercury was beginning to wonder why his sister-in-law was zeroing in on him. Ordinarily, she paid him little or no attention.

"Just the same, it must pay well," said Emma. "I mean, a catered meal and all . . ." Her speech was beginning to slur noticeably as the martinis assaulted her system.

Koesler fervently wished she would eat something. If he could, he would gladly have literally spoon-fed her the soup.

"How about Bloomfield Hills, Charlie?" said Ratigan. "I don't suppose you're plagued by potholes out there. Probably against the law." His eyes danced around at the others. Sort of a visual jab in the ribs.

"Well, no," Chase was almost apologetic about the absence of potholes. "But then we live in one of the newer developments. The pavement hasn't been there long enough to wear out and break up."

"Really, Angie," Emma wore that silly smile that

sometimes marks the inebriated, "I don't know how you can afford all this luxury. You must save a lot from the milk money!"

Her implication finally reached Mercury. He clenched his jaw and dropped his spoon to the table.

"For God's sake, Em, will you shut up! You're drunk!" Hoffman was furious. His wife's blatant, snide verbal assault on Mercury had created the very situation Hoffman had hoped to avoid. He had intended to pass this evening colorlessly, just as he did at The Company. Now, due to his wife's petty spite, he could no longer avoid becoming the center of attention. "One more word, and I'm taking you home!"

"One more word, is it, my lord and master?" She turned on him as if all along he had been the one she really wished to rip into and only now had he given her the opportunity. "So, you're going to take the little woman home, are you, big man? And then what? Then it's off to the mistress for the night, is it?"

She was now almost shouting. The waiter had half entered the dining room but when he caught the tone of her voice, he thought better of it and returned to the kitchen.

Cindy Mercury began sobbing uncontrollably. She covered her face with her napkin and rushed from the table down the hallway to the bedroom.

Mercury sprang to his feet, knocking over his chair. He threw his napkin to the table. "Damn it, Em! Now look what you've done!"

Hoffman, too, rose from his chair. "You bitch!" He spat the words. "If you could, you'd ruin everything. I could throttle you!"

Suddenly, Hoffman doubled over as if he'd been pole-axed, then fell to the floor. For a moment, his body shuddered violently. Then he lay still. Very still.

"Oh, my God," Louise Chase shrieked, "he's dead!"

Emma Hoffman seemed to experience instant sobriety.

14.

"**H**E'S CERTAINLY NOT DEAD," PRONOUNCED Dr. Rambeau, as he closed the door to the guest bedroom behind him. "Now, let's see if we can find out what happened."

Frank Hoffman's collapse had been followed by several minutes of panic occasionally relieved by chaos.

Louise Chase had screamed her premature obituary. Emma Hoffman became demonstrably sick at her stomach several times on her way to the bathroom and several more times inside the bathroom. Angie Mercury had loosened Hoffman's clothing—one of the few positive steps taken. Cindy Mercury, startled by the commotion, had run from the bedroom to the dining room, where she had fainted. Bishop Michael Ratigan had tried very hard to remember the formula for absolution. Charles Chase had applied a cold towel to Hoffman's brow, another positive step. And Father Koesler had phoned Dr. Rambeau, yet another positive step.

Rambeau was by no means the only doctor in St. Anselm's parish. But he was the one Father Koesler called on in emergencies. First, because Rambeau always came, and second, he always did something. In his professional life, Dr. Rambeau had been an internist, a surgeon, and also a pathologist. Thus, he embodied the aphorism that an internist knows everything but does nothing, a surgeon knows nothing and does everything, while the pathologist knows everything and does everything but it's too late. In addition, Dr. Rambeau was getting on in years, refused to stop smoking, and did not expect to live much longer—and so couldn't have cared less about malpractice suits.

Now, Louise Chase was assisting Emma Hoffman from the bathroom. Emma appeared very pale and slightly unsteady. She had paid a stiff price for all that gin and vermouth undiluted by food.

Introductions were unnecessary. All were members of St. Anselm's and the doctor had at least a nodding acquaintance with each of them. He addressed Emma.

"Your husband's vital signs are strong, Mrs. Hoffman. His blood pressure is satisfactory and his reactions are adequate. That is, in the context of—at least for the moment—a very sick man, you must remember. His nostrils are irritated. Has he had a cold?"

"Oh, yes, doctor." Emma said weakly. "A bad one for the past couple of days."

"Is he on medication?"

"There's this." Angie presented a small container to the doctor. "It fell out of his pocket when he collapsed."

The doctor tilted his head back to allow the bottom section of his bifocals to focus on the container's label. "Hmmm: Dynatab. A prescription drug and powerful. He was taking these?"

"He was eating them like candy." Emma seemed to be regaining vigor.

People!" The doctor shook his head. "They think a doctor's prescription is meant for lesser beings. How about alcohol? Had he been drinking, especially before dinner?"

An embarrassed silence. Everyone was acutely aware

that both Hoffman and Emma had been imbibing heavily.

"He had quite a few drinks, doctor," Ratigan at length volunteered. "I was sitting with him before dinner."

"What did he have?"

"Rob Roys . . . uh . . . perfect Rob Roys."

Rambeau whistled softly. "Pure booze! On top of a probable overdose of Dynatab! How about pressure? Has he been under any stress?" The question was directed at Emma, but the answer came from Angie. "Plenty!" he blurted, as he glared at her.

"Well, that does it." said Rambeau. "Too many pills, too much booze, too little food, and plenty of stress! Mrs. Hoffman, my guess is that your husband has the constitution of a bull moose. Otherwise, he might well be dead now.

"I'm going to call an ambulance and have him taken to Oakwood for observation."

"How long do you think he'll have to be hospitalized, doctor?" There was a sense of urgency in Chase's usually bland voice. "I mean," he adjusted back to his normal unanimated tone, "there's a very important meeting at The Company Wednesday. Do you think he'll be able to make it?"

Rambeau shrugged. "It's just impossible to tell at this point, Mr. Chase. But, if I had to guess," Rambeau was one of the few doctors who allowed himself a public guess, "I would guess we won't be keeping him long. Despite the damage to his physical and psychic health, he appears in relatively good condition. But, it's best to be on the safe side. We'll get him into the hospital so we can monitor him. Actually, the next few hours are the critical ones."

Rambeau offered Emma a ride to the hospital. Passively, she accepted.

Cindy Mercury, since she had been revived, had been

sitting on one of the dining room chairs, numbly absorbing all that was going on.

Angie Mercury began gathering and presenting coats and hats. "I'm sorry about the party, folks," he said to all in general. "God, am I sorry about this party!"

The cook, assisted by the waiter and waitress, was packing away a virtually untouched dinner. Most of it was being stored in the refrigerator. There were not many dishes to wash, mainly cocktail glasses and soup bowls.

"What the hell are we going to do with all this food?" Angie, slightly disheveled, was feeling considerably depressed.

"You know the one-hundred-and-one things to do with hamburger? Well, you're going to see a like number of things done with pheasant." Cindy had almost completely recovered not only her consciousness but her natural ebullience.

She seemed to improve the moment it was known that her brother was not in any danger and that, in all probability, he would fully and quickly recover. Her improvement continued as Emma Hoffman apologized profusely for her drunkenly abrasive behavior. An apology that Cindy accepted with good grace. Angie had not matched Cindy's open spirit of forgiveness and, in fact, was nursing a grudge.

The two now sat at the dinner table, which was being cleared quietly and efficiently.

Angie slouched in his chair. "This was NOT a real fine clambake. And we did NOT have a real good time." It was a parody of a song from *Carousel*.

"It happens." Cindy shrugged. "I've never found a good way of turning off the booze for a guest. By the time I realized that Em was drinking too much and eating too little, she was already over the edge. But once she recovered, she did apologize."

"Fat lot of good that does. The damage was done."

"I know it was embarrassing for you, honey, but she didn't actually say anything. It was all innuendo. Her sarcasm would have been wasted on the Chases and the priests. As far as I know, none of them knows about what Frank gives us." She thought it pointless to mention that just that afternoon she had told Father Koesler about the monthly check. That had been in the confessional, a world apart.

"Actually," he looked directly at her, "I wasn't as sore at her for what she said to me as I was at what she must have said to you in the living room beforehand. When I came in to announce dinner, I saw that you were close to tears. But I didn't know why, and there was no time to find out. And then when Em started in on me, I remembered that she'd been sitting right next to you before dinner—and it all fell into place. That's the main reason I was teed off. If Frank hadn't collapsed, I'm afraid my Italian fuse was about to burn down."

"People make mistakes; that's all there is to it. Try to look at it that way. Em made a mistake and afterwards she was sorry about it. And I don't think there was as much damage done as you suspect. Besides, there was a good side to it." Cindy was renowned for her ability to find silver linings. "We were able to get a doctor for Frank right away. And after what happened to him tonight, Frank isn't likely to do anything foolish like that again."

She rose and began folding the tablecloth. "It's getting late, honey. Why don't you go on to bed? I'll make sure everything is taken care of and be with you shortly."

Angie affectionately kissed her cheek and patted her bottom, then started down the hall to the bedroom. God, he thought, how I love that lady!

But, try as he might, he could not extend any such positive feeling toward her brother. In fact, when Frank toppled over and Louise had screamed that he was dead, Angie had had the fleeting thought that all his problems were solved.

The way Frank felt about Cindy, she almost certainly would be well taken care of in his will. With Frank dead, Angie and Cindy undoubtedly would be able to live very well on the interest from what Frank would leave her.

No more monthly checks, no more insults, putdowns, games deliberately lost, groveling.

But then, Frank hadn't died.

It put Angie in mind of the story he told on those rare occasions when he had to entertain children. It was about a little boy whose pet turtle died. For a while, he was inconsolable. Then, his father, in an attempt to cheer him, took him on his knee and told him about the grand funeral they could have for the turtle.

"We'll have a procession," the father said, "and all your little friends can be in it. We'll sing hymns and march out to the back yard. We'll dig a little hole in the ground and we'll put the turtle in a little box. We'll put the box in the hole and cover it up and put a cross and some flowers over it, just like in real cemeteries. Then we'll come back in the house and have a party."

All the while the father was talking, the boy's eyes got bigger and bigger. "Can we have ice cream and candy?"

"Sure," answered his father.

"And we can play games and sing songs and have fun?"

"Yup!"

At that very moment, the turtle, who had been presumed dead, woke up, stretched its legs, and wiggled.

As he realized his grandiose plans for the gala had just gone down the drain, the lad's face filled with dismay.

Then, slowly, he looked up at his dad. "Let's kill the turtle!"

Let's kill Frank!

No, of course he shouldn't even think of a thing like that.

And yet . . . and yet . . .

He couldn't erase the memory of Frank flat out and presumed dead.

It was approximately eighteen miles from Dearborn Heights to their home in Bloomfield Hills, but the traffic flow and the generally favorable green lights of Telegraph Road made the trip seem far shorter than the actual distance. Then, too, the Chases had been making the weekly trip from home to St. Anselm's for so many years that familiarity added to the sense of proximity.

Since leaving the Mercury house several minutes before, neither Charles nor Louise had said a word. WQRS-FM, Detroit's classical music radio station, was broadcasting a recording of a Boston Pops concert. Gershwin's "Rhapsody in Blue" emanated from the quadraphonic system.

The Chases were one of those couples who were comfortable with each other in silence. They had been together so many years and had shared so much that they frequently found a common ability to sense what the other was thinking and actually to communicate in silence. They fully intended to grow old together.

"Somehow," Louise broke the silence, "I feel as if I just stepped out of a soap opera."

Charles grunted. "Pretty awful, wasn't it?"

"Tasteless. You'd think a woman with Em's background would know better—instinctively—than to drink like that and then run off at the mouth. I mean, she *is* Old Money!"

"Probably under a lot of stress. It's the only thing I can think of to explain it. Though where the stress comes from, I confess I'm at a loss to know. She's got everything money can buy. Always did."

"What about this mistress bit she brought up?" Louise turned down the radio. "I'd say a mistress could cause a lot of stress."

Charles shrugged. "Don't know."

"There's no talk of it at The Company?"

"There's talk of everything at The Company. The rumor mill is as active there as it is at any large concern. But it may be no more than talk. I just don't know."

"Would you be surprised if the Hoffmans broke up?"

He thought for a few moments. "Nothing should surprise any of us anymore. But, yes, that would surprise me."

"I don't think I would be all that surprised." Louise shifted so she could more nearly face her husband. "But if they were to divorce, I think they would follow the familiar pattern. I think Frank would initiate the proceedings. After all, Em's getting to an age when life settles into a more or less comfortable rut, but a rut nonetheless. She wouldn't be interested in playing the boy-girl games that are a part of dating and courtship. She's probably comfortable having the escort service Frank provides, no matter how she feels about him personally.

"Frank, on the other hand, gives every indication of having the roving eye of many men his age. He's good looking and, despite what we saw tonight, he's in excellent health. Just the type who'd want to turn in an older model for some young thing."

"So far so good, but you're forgetting a couple of important things: Em, even with all her own money, would never let him get away unbloodied. And Frank would never give up what he's worked so hard to get.

"And then there's The Company. Frank has his eye on the top. That's obvious. And he'll likely get it if he bides his time and wins his struggle to stay invisible. A Hoffman divorce would be a red flag to the local, maybe even national, media. And no one who gets involved in garish headlines is going to be chairman of the board of The Company.

"No, I'm afraid they are doomed to remain together until death does them part."

"And, speaking of death, Frank's collapse tonight was kind of scary."

"Yes. But you know, when I saw him on the floor, all I could think of was that I needed him for next Wednesday's meeting and, almost for that reason alone, I wanted him to live. How selfish of me!"

"Don't be so hard on yourself. That meeting means a lot to you and, from all you've told me, Frank has helped a lot."

"He has. He's been almost selfless." He paused. "Well, of course no one is selfless. But I'm sure Frank knows that I surely wouldn't forget him should I succeed in reaching the top."

"And so you will.

"I must confess, I had my reservations about Frank until you told me how much he was helping you. Now I think I could forgive him anything, even a mistress. Unless, of course, I were married to him, a possibility I don't even want to think about—why are you pulling in here?"

"Jacques! In case you've forgotten, all we've had tonight was a bowl of soup—and not all of that."

"Aren't you taking a bit of a chance? Jacques on a Saturday night without a reservation?"

He smiled as he handed his keys to the parking valet. "Oh, I think Claude will dig up something for us."

⊛

"I can't believe I just ate dinner at a Wendy's!" Bishop Ratigan said in good-natured disgust.

"You should have tried the salad bar; it was great," Father Koesler was gustatorially satisfied.

"There wasn't anything special about that place. I should have asked for chapter and verse when you claimed there was something special about that particular Wendy's. The last time you took me in like that, we saw *Ice Station Zebra* because you told me it was a historical movie about the ice age."

"Some people never learn."

Ratigan started his Olds and drove out of the restaurant's parking area. "I'll bet I'm the first bishop to eat at a Wendy's."

Koesler could tell Ratigan was not soon going to forget this episode—or let him forget it. "You are probably the first bishop to eat at Wendy's while wearing his pectoral cross. Of course Gump has probably eaten in any number of fast food places. But he was probably in mufti or dressed as a simple and humble parish priest." Pause. "Like me."

"There are any number of things Bishop Gumbleton does that I'm not about to do. One of them is staying at a YMCA during a bishop's meeting. Another is ever again eating at a fast food emporium."

"Admit it now: The hamburger was good."

"Kiss my ring!"

Ratigan drove on in silence for a few minutes. Then, "By the way, we haven't yet discussed what occasioned our eating out tonight."

Koesler sighed. "It sort of makes one grateful to be celibate."

"What?"

"Frank Hoffman's wife done him in tonight. Of course the pills and the booze didn't help. But I doubt he would have drunk as much if he hadn't tried to match his wife drink for drink. Then she spent the evening needling him. And finally, there was that bit about a mistress. His wife helped make him what he was tonight—a near fatality. And a wife is a relative you and I don't have."

"It's a sacrifice we make. Doing without a wife and family."

They fell silent again.

The bishop's thoughts returned to the luncheon he'd had just the other day with Frank Hoffman at Orchard Lake Country Club. Ratigan had thought more than once about their conversation. It had been, on the whole, an unpleasant experience. Sure, there were political considerations attached to becoming a member of the hierarchy and then continuing to climb the ladder of authority. But that was true of any career. Besides, he didn't like anyone to focus attention on the more venal aspects of improving one's station in life.

And thinking of the word venal, Ratigan recalled that when he saw Frank Hoffman lying on the floor and he was under the momentary impression that he had died, close to the first thought that crossed his mind was the money Frank had promised to will Ratigan and the archdiocese. Not only would that have made Ratigan a wealthy man; he would have, as Frank had pointed out, been able to bring a substantial gift to the archdiocese. Not an inconsiderable reason for Archbishop Boyle to advance Ratigan's chances at getting his own diocese.

He recalled feeling sharply resentful on learning that Frank would live. An unworthy thought. But one he felt almost compelled to return to. He had to come to some decisions. Decisions that were likely to be crucial for him and his future. It was as Frank had suggested: If you just wait for something to happen, it very likely won't happen. If you want something badly enough, make it happen.

They turned in on the street that led to St. Anselm's church and rectory.

"Damn!" said Koesler, with some fervor. "The Pumpkin Fiend has struck again!"

"Huh?"

"Look! St. Anselm!"

The statue of the parish's patron saint stood on its pedestal in the middle of the large grassy park between the church and Outer Drive. St. Anselm was outlined by the street lights. A hollowed-out pumpkin had been placed over his head. The pumpkin rested on Anselm's shoulders and covered his head. Only the tip of his pointed miter could be seen above the pumpkin.

"Every Halloween," said Koesler, "some fiend fits a pumpkin on Anselm's head. Damn! I'm going to catch whoever's doing this if I have to put Anselm under surveillance all night some Halloween! And then I'll turn him over to somebody. The Sacred Inquisition, probably."

Crime and punishment. Something else Ratigan decided he would have to think about.

15.

Bright and early Wednesday, The Company's top executives began filing into the board room, which was centrally located on the Fisher Building's thirteenth floor.

Most of the executives seemed to share an air of quiet camaraderie. Most of them had been with The Company for many years and had grown up and older as they climbed the corporate ladder. A glaring exception to this span was Charles Chase, an outsider, but one upon whom Frank Martin had smiled. And because the chairman of the board had smiled at Chase, so did everyone else smile and accept him. Though the natives deplored the notion of an outsider rising above them to The Company's top position, there was little they could do to stop Chase. So, realistically, since Chase would one day undoubtedly be their boss, it made sense for the others to treat Chase with kid gloves. It would be wise to be in his favor long before he entered his kingdom.

Although Chase was an outsider, he didn't appear to be one. He was wearing a conservative, three-piece business suit just as, with varying shades and cuts, was everyone else. As they filed into the board room, conversing quietly in small groups, they almost, but not quite, resembled clones.

Inside the board room, an executive pecking order was clearly established through the judicious placement of chairs.

At the far end of the room, against the wall, four chairs, significantly larger than the others, stood behind a large table on a low dais. Facing these chairs was a series of semicircular rows of chairs, each with its own small desk-table.

The four large chairs were reserved for the chairman of the board and chief executive officer, the president and chief operations officer, the vice-chairman of the board, and the executive vice president and chief financial officer. Charles Chase's place was at the center of the first row of chairs. Frank Hoffman was almost immediately behind Chase in the second row.

All quickly took their places. Frank Martin rapped the table once with his gavel. He did not call for silence; he already had that. The gavel merely marked the opening of the meeting.

While executive papers were shuffled, providing a soft background sound, the secretary read the minutes of the previous meeting, which were approved. Old business was called for, discussed, and disposed of.

Chairman Martin announced new business, then launched into an elaborate introduction of Charles Chase. The introduction certainly was not needed for the benefit of anyone in this room. The few who had not known Chase personally before he joined The Company certainly had read all about him when the move was announced. It had been one of the major business events of that year.

Martin's introduction was, and everyone understood it to be, a sort of benediction. It was the corporate equivalent of the clouds parting with a disembodied voice declaring, "This is my beloved employee; hear him!"

Actually, Chase was somewhat embarrassed by the rather lavish tribute Martin paid him. And Chase would not have confessed to anyone but Louise that he was more than a little nervous. This was his first major presentation to the executive board and his fellow executives. Although he had, with Kirkus and Keely's contributions and assistance, prepared this presentation most carefully, Chase had butterflies in his stomach. All in all, he thought, the tension he felt was a good thing. Something akin to that felt by even the most experienced actors. Something that aided them in giving good performances.

Introduction complete, Chase adjusted his bifocals and began his report. He addressed, in detail, each of the two items on the agenda: the forthcoming congressional debate and vote on a "lemon" bill, and The Company's future demographic target.

First, he explained why The Company should take the unexpected position of supporting legislation which, if passed, could cripple not only The Company but the entire automotive industry. Lobbyists for The Company had ascertained that the legislation stood no chance of passage. Thus, by taking this harmless stand, The Company would be hailed by consumer groups throughout the country, possibly the world.

As he progressed, Chase could feel something strange taking place. He couldn't put his finger on it, but something was happening. He could get no hint from the faces of the officers before him. He could not turn to scrutinize the faces of those seated behind him. He could only press on.

He proceeded to present the Values and Life-Styles demographic theory as it had been projected to the car buyers of the immediate future. He explained why 58 percent of their targeted market would be that steady group of middle-aged, stable, content men and women who would demand the kind of cars they had been buying over the past several years. Going for the fuel-efficient compacts and continuing that phenomenon of an "Escort Family" or a "Cheetah Family." The sons and daughters buying the same kind of cars their parents had.

Again, Chase fought off the disquieting feeling that something was wrong. Still, no emotion on the faces of the men before him. But something was up, no doubt about it . . . something with which he was unfamiliar.

Teachers, professors, preachers, those who frequently speak in public, could have explained the phenomenón. He was losing his audience. Often the audience or congregation lets the speaker know he's wasting his time—sometimes by coughing, sometimes by shifting in their seats, sometimes by barely audible sounds of distraction. But always, even if undeliberately, one's audience lets the speaker know.

Chase proceeded with his revelation of the "Mexican scam," along with his recommendations to cure the problem. He concluded his presentation to the sounds of shuffling and throat-clearing. An uncomfortable silence followed.

Finally, Chairman Martin asked for comment. More papers were shuffled. Almost anyone there could have made a comment. Even though the report had been convincingly and unequivocally delivered, most of those present felt there was something wrong with one or another of the points Chase had made. But where were the facts and statistics to refute them?

In addition, the other executives were well aware that Chase had been personally selected for his prestigious and promising position by the chairman of the board himself. One did not attack the boss' favorite without being loaded for bear.

After a short, awkward pause, a hand was raised in the

second row. Chariman Martin recognized Frank Hoffman.

"Mr. Chairman, Mr. President; ladies and gentlemen . . ." Hoffman had almost completely recovered from his cold. The slight nasal quality of his voice, the final vestige of his illness, merely lent his tone a more impressive resonance. No one at The Company, other than Charlie Chase, knew about the tumultuous events in which he'd been involved the previous Saturday evening, nor of his hospitalization, brief as it was. Only Chase could have revealed these events, and gossip was not his style.

"With all due respect to our general manager," Hoffman proceeded, "I must beg to differ with him on one or two points he has made so well. And I do so, of course, only with the good of The Company in mind."

Nervy! was the consensus. Hoffman was, in effect, putting his future with The Company on the line in publicly challenging the chairman's fair-haired boy. No one, however, was particularly surprised that it was Hoffman who had flung down the gauntlet.

"In the matter of the so-called Lemon Laws, we are all well aware, ladies and gentlemen, that Congress has been flirting with this sort of bill for many years. A few states have similar restrictions on us as local legislation. Obviously, everyone in this room, everyone in The Company, every fair-minded citizen opposes such laws. Our public support of this legislation, as proposed by Mr. Chase, would be a bold and utterly unpredictable move that would indeed capture the attention of the world, let alone the media. And it would seem, as Mr. Chase has so convincingly presented, that, in its present form and with nothing else intervening, the legislation hasn't a chance. Thus, our support of this presently doomed legislation would appear to be a major public relations coup.

"However, there is another side of this question with

which Mr. Chase appears unfamiliar. Undoubtedly, it is no fault of his, since this information has come to light only in the past couple of days.''

Hoffman's attempt at exculpating Chase, as everyone, including Hoffman, knew, was spurious. It was Chase's responsibility to know of important events no matter how recently they might have occurred.

"Our lobbyists," Hoffman continued, "went back for another straw vote of both houses asking what the outcome of a vote on the Lemon Laws would be *if* The Company first endorsed this legislation. The surprising thing they discovered was that such a move on our part would turn the vote around. Our friends in Congress have a tough enough time suppressing this sort of legislation, with the considerable pressure they get from their constituents. Only a completely united front can hope to keep these ridiculous laws off the books. Were we, one of the major automotive firms, to even create the impression of endorsing these bills, the ball game would be over.

"By actual count, were we to make the move Mr. Chase has recommended, our advantage in the House would slip from two-to-one against the legislation to three-to-one in favor; and in the Senate from three-to-one against to four-to-one in favor.

"In short, we would be solely responsible for the first national passage of Lemon Laws. Laws that would not only virtually hamstring us but also the entire automotive industry.''

Hoffman paused. A murmur spread through the room. Something akin to the sound probably made by the judges at Inquisition trials.

Charles Chase was devastated. He could feel the blood rising to the surface of his face as Hoffman began his refutation. And the longer Hoffman went on, and the more inevitable became his conclusion, the worse Chase felt. He was in no position to say anything. All he could do was sit there and take it. And the end, he felt, was no-where in sight.

"Secondly," Hoffman resumed, "we come to the matter of our future demographic targets. Mr. Chase's citation of the VALS conclusions presents an interesting series of speculative statistics. But, I'm afraid, ladies and gentlemen, that's all they are: speculative statistics.

"Out there in the real world of car sales, in recent years, the average age of a person who buys a car from The Company has been nearly fifty. Whereas the average age of those who buy cars from our major competitors and especially foreign cars, is about thirty-five.

"I submit, ladies and gentlemen, that's our demographic target: the younger buyers. And they want the European look, the high performance version of the basic family car. A very reliable source at GM tells me their defined principal target market is going to be the affluent twenty-five- to forty-four-year-old customer. They expect this market to account for over 50 percent of all new car purchases over the next few years.

"We must face the facts, ladies and gentlemen: What we're looking for is the incremental dollar. And that can't be found in the compact or subcompact models. The incremental buck lies in the limited-production, high-performance cars with fat price tags and substantial profit margins.

"Once upon a time," Hoffman glanced significantly at Chase as if to identify him with a fairy tale of the past, "young people traditionally drove the kind of car their parents favored. There were such things as 'Chevy Families.' That doesn't happen anymore. The son no longer automatically buys what his father drove. And keep this old made-in-Detroit adage in mind, ladies and gentlemen: You can sell an older man a young man's car, but you can't sell a young man an old man's car.

"The younger buyer is our prime demographic target

market. The young buyer is going to want the car that will return us to Detroit's essence. The big car that is going to mean big profit margins. And that's where The Company has to be.''

Again, Hoffman paused to indicate that he had finished his second argument but that he had not completed his rebuttal. He gathered his sheaf of papers and placed them at the upper right corner of his table.

Once again, there was the soft murmur of voices. Never had these executives witnessed anything like this. Never had a junior executive shredded a major presentation of a senior executive. But what would become known as the Wednesday Morning Massacre was not yet over. Almost all present could now predict what was to follow.

"Finally, Mr. Chairman, Mr. President; ladies and gentlemen," Hoffman swung into his peroration: "I feel certain that Mr. Chase's *charge*," he gave the word a sarcastic inflection, "that there is some hanky-panky at work in our Mexican imports is due to nothing more than our esteemed colleague's newness to The Company. Most of us are well aware that there is no 'scam' going on. But, for the benefit of those," again a significant glance at the back of Chase's head, where the bulging and reddening of his neck told its own story, "who are unfamiliar with the peculiar and tight import-export laws of Mexico, I'll explain. Briefly!

"We are not permitted to import any more from Mexico than we export to Mexico. In effect, we are hurting because of that limitation on our exporting materials that our factories down there need in order to build our cars with cost efficiency. So, the idea is to load up the cars made in Mexico that we import for sale in the States. The more we can build up the Mexican content of those cars, the greater the import credits we achieve, and the added export value they will have when we import them—and the more we are able to export.

"Therefore, while we buy Mexican glass for our cars instead of using our own glass, the benefit in the added value of the cars imported far surpasses the slight savings in expense were we to import the lower-valued cars from Mexico for the sole purpose of outfitting them here in the States.

"Thus," an expansive gesture, "no collusion, no conspiracy, no crime—just good heads-up business."

At no time in his life, not even while undergoing the tortures of adolescence, had Charles Chase felt a like embarrassment. What could he say? Explanation was neither possible nor expected. There was no doubt in anyone's mind that he had been the victim of some outrageously bad advice. But part of the responsibility of a top executive is to ensure against the possibility of receiving faulty information or having poor advisers.

There was no doubting where the buck stopped when it came to a person whose position was general manager of The Company.

Chase could not bring himself to glance up at Frank Martin. Chase could imagine the chairman did not feel all that much better than he himself did at this very moment.

He was correct. Ordinarily, Martin did not allow himself much emotional demonstration. But there was no doubt that his face was crinkled into a definite scowl. Instead of conducting the remainder of the business and closing the meeting, Martin quietly requested the president to carry on.

As the meeting wound to a merciful conclusion, Martin shrugged. Too bad. It was a damn pity. But the die had been cast. This was hardball, and, by damn, to the victor go the spoils. Chase would never be effective in

The Company after this morning's humiliation. His fate was sealed.

On the other hand, there was Hoffman. Martin had had his eye on Hoffman for some time. He had shown promise. Definitely high pot. And this morning's showing put him up a couple more rungs on the ladder. If Charlie can't make it, maybe Hoffman can. The Company would go on. The king is dead; long live the king.

Martin's thoughts were not far different from those of the other executives as they closed briefcases, mingled a bit while ignoring Chase, then filed out.

There is a scene near the end of the musical comedy *How to Succeed in Business Without Really Trying*, when the blame for a catastrophe at World Wide Wickets is shifted back and forth between two executives. As the blame falls upon the shoulders of one, the entire cast moves to the opposite side of the stage. And vice versa.

In a metaphorical sense that was now happening at The Company.

Before the meeting, Chase had been not only a very important person; he'd also been a very popular person. Everyone knew that his presentation was on today's agenda as well as the fact that he was the chairman's personal selection to be his own successor. Many executives had stopped to pat Chase on the back or merely offer a word of greeting or encouragement.

Now, it was as if Chase had suddenly contracted a communicable disease.

It wasn't that he'd been forgotten. On the contrary, everyone was talking about him or about Hoffman's destruction of him. However, no one was talking *to* him.

It was just as well. Chase wouldn't have heard. His chagrin was so intense that he was physically affected. His heart rate was up. He was certain his blood pressure must be sky-high. His stomach was acidic. His face was flushed. And the pounding in his ears would have made it impossible for him to hear a normal speaking tone. He was forced to try deliberately to maintain his equilibrium and not faint outright.

Returning to his office, he was unaware of seeing anyone or hearing anything. He concentrated on putting one foot after the other in order to find some sanctuary somewhere.

"Of course I don't like to see his blood pressure this high. But he's got a good strong constitution and that should help." The Chases' family physician was speaking to Louise. They stood just outside the bedroom door. The doctor did not normally make house calls. But for the Chases he would.

"Get these prescriptions filled, Louise. The Lasix is a diuretic. Have him take just one a day. The Slow K will replace the potassium he'll lose from the extra urination caused by the diuretic. Two Slow K twice a day, after meals. And Louise: No alcohol while he's on Lasix . . . might cause the pressure to go too far the other way.

"If there are any other problems, be sure and call me."

Louise thanked him and saw him to the door. She gave the prescriptions and the car keys to the maid and returned to Charles.

Wearing flannel pajamas, he was propped by several pillows. A bright sun streaming through the windows reminded him, if he needed a reminder, that he was not well. Why else would one go to bed in the daytime except when one is ill?

"How are you feeling, dear?" She sat on the edge of the bed.

"Tired. But better."

"Do you want to talk about it?"

He turned to look out the window. He was wearing his

glasses although he did not intend to read—or even to see anything, for that matter. "Not much more to say. After Frank Hoffman refuted every point I made, all the senators gave the thumbs-down sign."

"I don't understand. What went wrong? Was all the advice those two gave you incorrect?"

"Kirku and Keely? Not incorrect so much as deliberate untruths. They're Hoffman's men. I knew that all along and was a bit leery about them from the start. But everything they advised me on up to now has not only been correct, it's been insightful, brilliant advice. So I had no reason to suspect or doubt them in this." He shook his head. "I should have listened to my secretary. She told me she thought there was something ersatz about those two. And she was right. It was all a set-up. They were setting me up for the kill. All that they told me in preparation for today's meeting made sense—as far as it went. And insofar as I was able to check it out, it appeared to be right on target."

"Those horrid men! What will happen to them now?" She knew what she would like to have happen to them . . . something involving boiling oil.

He smiled sardonically. "They were waiting for me when I returned to my office after the meeting. I was so angry and felt so rotten I couldn't bring myself to say a word to them. Kirkus said he'd heard what happened and he wanted to apologize; that they had given me the best advice they could. But I could see in his eyes he didn't mean a word of it."

"Isn't there some way of punishing them?"

"They won't be reporting to me anymore—if you can call that a punishment. But they'll end up on their feet. They'll go back to Hoffman, unless I miss my guess. They were in his camp all along anyway."

"Frank Martin would know! He'd understand!" Louise thought she had stumbled on a solution. "If he doesn't know yet . . . if he hasn't figured it out—you can tell him: It was all a plot to undermine your position!''

Chase shook his head sadly. ''You don't understand, Lou. It doesn't matter whether Frank knows or not. To allow myself to be put in a position like I was in is the unforgivable sin. Not why I got into it. It's like . . . like . . . well, it's like war: Once you lose, it doesn't matter how or why you lost—except maybe to historians. As far as The Company is concerned, the reason I lost is of speculative interest at best.''

After a brief discouraged silence, Louise resumed. ''I guess my final question has to be why . . . why did they do it? That Kirkus and Keely, they were already working for the man who would one day become chairman of the board. What did they have to gain by sabotaging you? They were already on the winning team. Why would they do something to make it the losing team?''

Chase shrugged wearily. ''I don't know. But it's a good question. Whatever it was, it must have been pretty compelling.

''Maybe they were just unwilling to put their money on me. Maybe Hoffman promised them something special in the deal. Maybe they just thought Hoffman would beat me out. Maybe,'' he shook his head, ''maybe after what happened today they're right.''

''The bastard!''

Ordinarily, Louise did not use such epithets. ''If I ever see that hypocrite in church again, I'll be physically ill! At least we'll never have to see him socially again.''

''Afraid we will, Lou—at least one more time.''

She placed a finger against her lips and carefully considered their schedule. She could see their social calendar in her mind's eye. But she couldn't find on it an event they would have to share with the Hoffmans.

''It happened rather suddenly the other day . . . and I

forgot to tell you about it. The Company is hosting a combination birthday and bon voyage party for Frank Martin at the Collegiate Club Monday evening. Our calendar was open on that date,'' he hastened to add, ''and I accepted.''

Her memory affirmed that the date was, indeed, open. ''Oh, Frank . . . must we?''

''Afraid so. It will be a rather wide open party. I've invited Bishop Ratigan and Father Koesler. And—while we were still speaking—Hoffman told me he had invited his sister and brother-in-law. I'm afraid our absence would be noted. And not only would our absence be noted, it would be a tacit admission of something I am not yet willing to admit—that I'm through. It looks bad now—very, very bad. But at least I know who the enemy is . . . finally. And I'm going to do my damndest to come back from this.''

Louise silently resolved that she would be there. She would remain at her husband's side, proudly, no matter what.

''Well, well,'' she said, finally, ''the whole cast will be there. The clergy, the Hoffmans, the Mercurys, and the Chases. There should be enough friction to start a pretty good fire.

All in all, he thought he would get along very well with Father Dowling.

Koesler had only recently chanced upon the Father Dowling series of murder mysteries. One by one, he had checked them out of the public library. He enjoyed them so much, his only fear was that their author, Ralph McInerny, would run out of either ideas or patience. In Koesler's opinion, with the exception of J.F. Powers and those authors who were or had been priests, McInerny was the only creator of a fictional priest who truly captured what it was like to be a priest.

Koesler was about the same age and disposition as the fictional Father Dowling. Both were in their mid-fifties; neither cared for canon law; both got along ably in the modern Church, but both thought the good old days really were the good old days more than less, and neither understood the very young new Roman Catholic clergy.

Of course, since Father Dowling existed only in fictional murder mysteries, he was, naturally, McInerny's sleuth. At the denouement of each book, it was always Father Dowling who solved the mystery.

But, oddly, Father Koesler himself had become involved in several murder investigations in the Detroit area. Investigations that had comprised a strong Catholic element. As a result, Koesler had come to know not a few Detroit homicide detectives. Not the least of these was Inspector Walter Koznicki, the head of the homicide division. Over the years, Koesler and Koznicki had become fast friends.

And that, in turn, was interesting. Because the fictional Father Dowling's best friend was named Keegan. And he was chief of detectives in the Chicago suburb that was the setting for their mysteries. Life, thought Father Koesler, imitates art.

At present, Father Dowling and friends were keeping Koesler company while he sat in his confessional with plenty of time to read. If the numbers coming to confession were not what they used to be—and they weren't—Saturday night was about the slowest time of all.

From time to time, Koesler considered discontinuing Saturday evening confessions. But then he would think of the lonely soul, perhaps someone who'd been away so long he or she didn't know there were no more long lines of penitents. Such a person deserved an opportunity to go to confession while the inclination was there. Not infrequently, with the small numbers at daily Mass, at Lenten devotions, at convert classes, Koesler was forced to renew his faith in the value of just one immortal soul.

Seated in the confessional, thinking of one immortal soul brought to mind an incident that had occurred in his first parochial assignment at St. David's. The hour of 9:00 P.M. had been approaching and even though those had been the good old days of wall-to-wall penitents, none remained that particular Saturday evening. At exactly 9:00, Koesler had stepped out of his confessional to discover he was alone in the church.

He had stopped at the communion railing to pray for a few moments. When all of a sudden he had heard such a clatter in the rear vestibule! Head still bowed, but no longer in prayer, he had attempted to figure out what was going on.

They were young boys and they were apparently trying with vigor to get one of their number to go to confession. Just in case they might succeed, Koesler thought it well for him to return to his confessional.

All the way down the side aisle they struggled and shouted. The shouts were muted for the benefit of church decorum, but they were shouts nonetheless.

"Come on, Louie, get in there! It ain't gonna hurt ya!"

"Whaddya mean, it ain't gonna hurt me? If it don't hurt, YOU go!"

"I went!"

After much of the same, plus evident attempts by Louie to escape, at long last a small body came hurtling through the curtain at one side of Koesler's confessional. The body hit the wall and collapsed appropriately on the kneeler.

"Do you want to go to confession?" Koesler asked.

"I guess so."

Koesler had long considered the incident a prime example of Catholic action.

His reverie was interrupted by someone entering the confessional. Koesler was startled. He hadn't heard anyone enter the church. He decided he must have been deeply lost in thought. Whoever had come in knelt on the other side of the screen. Koesler turned out the light on his side.

"Bless me, Father, for I have sinned. It's been two months since my last confession."

This was a no-nonsense lady and, in all probability, an old-timer.

"I lost my temper with my husband, oh, four to five times. He's retired, you see, and he's always underfoot. I wish he'd go out once in a while. He could get a part-time job, maybe do volunteer work. But all he does is sit around the house making one mess after another. He just sits around and watches TV—soap operas—and smokes one cigar after another. God, how that house stinks after all those cigars."

She went on for several minutes enumerating her husband's sins. It had been a long time since Koesler had heard this type of "confession," although at one time it had been quite common. Experience had taught him there was no correcting her method of "confessing." There was really nothing to do but listen, give a penance, and absolve.

"And," she concluded, "we practiced birth control seven times. That's because he's home all the time with nothing to do."

Koesler almost laughed aloud. She must be well beyond menopause. Birth control for them must be no more than a habit describing their sex lives.

He said a few words, very few, calling her attention to the necessity of evaluating her own relationship to God rather then her husband's peccadilloes, gave her a penance of five Our Fathers and five Hail Marys, and absolved her.

After she left, he recalled her confessing birth control and was reminded of the story of the very elderly couple planning to be married. As they sat in the rectory, making arrangements, the priest asked where they intended to live. Looking lovingly at each other they said they weren't sure but wherever they would go they agreed they had to live close to an elementary school. Whereupon the priest told them that while they might be heir minded, they probably were not heir conditioned.

Koesler flipped on the light again and resumed his Father Dowling mystery. It was titled, *Second Vespers*. Odd title. So few would know what it meant . . . certainly very few of the younger clergy. Put a breviary in their hands and they wouldn't know what to do with it. Much less would they be familiar with the hour of prayer called Vespers, still less the recondite Second Vespers.

As far as Koesler knew, only a few of the older clergy still prayed, or "read" their breviaries. Basically a monastic choir prayer, the breviary was a prayer book that divided each day into canonical hours, eight in all, from morning until evening.

Following a gradual evolvement over centuries, Pope Saint Pius V had carried out the will of the Council of Trent and in 1568, he had obligated the daily recitation of the breviary for all the clergy in major orders in the Western Church.

And that was pretty much the way Koesler had found things when he received his first major order, the subdeaconate, in June of 1953.

It was one of the stereotypes. Catholics ate fish on Friday, went to Mass on Sunday, and priests read their breviaries every day. Usually, the priest could be found, breviary in hand, pacing back and forth, lips moving rapidly and noiselessly—it was one of the rules: Lips must move.

One of the jokes that emerged from this practice involved two priests returning from a day off and realizing at 11:30 P.M. that neither had finished reading the day's breviary. So the driver stopped the car on the highway shoulder and left the headlights burning. Each priest took his breviary and, each sitting in front of one headlight, began to read. At which point, a passing trucker leaned out of his cab window and shouted, ''That must be one hell of a book!''

Koesler continued to read his breviary daily, even though most other priests used a scaled-down vernacular version, or had long since quit . . . or had never begun. He still did not understand every Latin word. But he understood enough to be able to make the recitation an authentic prayer.

He had just returned to *Second Vespers* when another penitent entered the confessional. The penitent settled in on the kneeler. Another traditional confession. That was perfectly all right with Koesler. Before turning off his light, he glanced at his watch. A quarter to 9:00. This would be the final penitent of the evening—unless somebody decided to throw Louie in.

Koesler leaned toward the screen, quite unconsciously assuming the classic position of the confessor, head slightly bowed, elbow on the arm of the chair, palm cupping chin.

Nothing happened. Not that the silence was unusual. Many times the priest had to speak first to let the penitent know it was all right to begin. But there was something out of the ordinary about this particular situation, although Koesler could not identify exactly what was wrong. Perhaps it was the total lack of sound. The penitent, once he or she had entered the confessional, had made no sound at all. No shifting about to try to discover something comfortable about this position of kneeling upright. Not even the sound of breathing.

Whatever, it was making Koesler a bit nervous. More than once he had thought about how vulnerable a priest was in a confessional, especially in an otherwise empty church. Anyone could enter for any reason. As long as a screen or curtain separated them, the priest could not tell who was there.

"Yes," Koesler said at length, "you may begin now."

Silence.

"It's all right to begin now," he said, a little more loudly. It was possible the penitent might be hard of hearing. And Koesler supposed there was no reason to worry about volume. He was quite certain there was no one else in the church.

Still, silence.

"How long has it been since your last confession?" This might be one of those instances wherein information had to be extracted like teeth.

"Oh . . . a long . . . long time."

The voice sent a shudder through Koesler. It was like nothing he'd ever heard. Whoever was on the other side of the screen was not whispering, but speaking in a very soft tone. He couldn't tell if it was a man or a woman.

"About how long?" Koesler pressed.

"Oh, so long, so long . . . ago. I just can't . . . remember . . . oh . . ."

He tried to place the voice. Tried to compare it to anyone he'd heard. It sounded just a bit like Truman Capote's voice. The pitch was high enough that it could be a woman, yet low enough that it could be a man. There was a sing-song quality to it as if it might have been a child, yet it certainly wasn't a child. And there was an odd pausing between words, as if the speaker were slightly unfamiliar with the language and was searching for what in reality were quite common words.

"All right," Koesler said very softly. At least there was no hearing problem evident. "Let's forget about how long it's been. Do you have any sins to confess?"

"Sins? Oh, my, yes!" There was a soft little chuckle, an odd chuckle, as odd as the voice. "I think you are . . . describing my . . . life."

"Your life?"

"Oh, yes." A pause. "Do you . . . think . . . Father . . . that the devil can take . . .over a person's . . . life?"

Koesler suspected a verbal trap, but quickly decided to answer as if the question had been seriously put.

"Diabolic possession or obsession? It's happened and is pretty well documented. Yes, I believe it can happen."

"I believe it . . . happened to me . . . Father." The person said it as matter-of-factly as if announcing that he or she had contracted a cold.

"Happened to you?" Though the church was chilly, Koesler felt very warm.

"If . . . I'm right, you are talking . . . to Satan." A fiendish little chuckle. "You didn't ever . . . think that you . . . would talk . . . with the devil?"

Whoever it was, Koesler decided it was a very disturbed person who needed a level of professional help that was far beyond his capabilities. Although he had never dealt with anyone as obviously divorced from sanity as this person evidently was, Koesler had referred disturbed parishioners to a few trusted professionals in the past. The special problem in a situation like this was the situation itself. How to get this out of the internal forum into the external? How to get it out of the confessional and into an office?

"Would you make an appointment to see a very good therapist if I told you how to get in touch with him?"

A soft, odd laugh.

"Would you come and see me outside of confession sometime?"

"Oh, I . . . will see you outside . . . the confessional." Another soft laugh. "I . . . have some . . . mischief planned. I will see . . . you at the scene of . . . the mischief."

Koesler tried to stall for a bit more time. The person seemed to be making a move to leave. "But you see, if you don't confess any sin and express your sorrow for it, I can't absolve you."

The laugh was loud and utterly mirthless. "The fool," the person shouted, "thinks he can . . . absolve the devil!"

With that, the person was gone.

Koesler heard the church door close. He did not frighten easily. . . but he was genuinely frightened.

16.

FATHER KOESLER THOUGHT HE MIGHT BE ONE OF
the last guests to arrive for Frank Martin's combination
birthday and bon voyage party. Judging by the number of
cars in the Collegiate Club's parking lot, it indeed did not
seem possible for many more guests to squeeze in.

Koesler ordinarily was not late for functions. If anything, he had an unhappy habit of being early. He was
tardy this evening because he had scheduled more appointments than he should have. He had done this because he had been distracted and disturbed over the past
two days by that very odd confession from the person
who claimed to be the devil.

All day Sunday and today he had tried to figure out
who it might be. Was it possible Koesler knew the person? If whoever it was had tried to conceal his or her
identity by creating a strange sounding voice, the effort
had been a smashing success.

The Collegiate was one of a surprisingly large number
of private clubs Koesler had never visited. On the one
hand, he did not particularly care for private clubs, and
on the other, to be frank, he was rarely invited to any.

He found the unattended cloakroom to the left of the
entry. Next to that was the men's room. Next to that—

since no one was impeding him he decided to investigate a bit—was the locker room. He could hear in the distance the thud of rubber balls. Must be handball or racquetball courts, he decided.

Retracing his steps, he found himself in a long hallway. If there was any doubt the Frank Martin party was going on in the large, well-lit, noisy room at the end of the hall, the question was settled by a sign midway down the hall announcing that very fact.

Because he fully expected to find some, Koesler was amazed at the seeming absence of security measures. No one had checked his identity or questioned his presence. True, he was wearing his clericals. But anyone could dress as a priest.

From the door, he had an excellent view of the room, several steps below the hall level.

Several yards into the room, against one wall, a table had been set up for guest registration. On the other side of the doorway, against the same wall, was the bar, busily manned by three bartenders. From the number of filled glasses lined up at the bar's edge, Koesler guessed they were pre-filling orders. There were so many waiters—no waitresses—moving about that Koesler gave up trying to count them. In the center of the room was a huge table heavy with hot and cold hors d'oeuvres.

The guests, as was usual at such affairs, were clustered in tight groups, large and small.

At the extreme opposite end of the room from where Koesler still stood at the doorway were Mr. and Mrs. Frank Martin. He couldn't decide whether they were both using makeup or standing under a special spotlight, but they somehow appeared set apart from everyone else. Perhaps, he thought, it might be the nimbus resulting from being chairman and first lady of The Company.

As he watched, the dinner-jacketed figure of Frank Hoffman approached the Martins. They greeted him warmly, and the three entered into animated conversation. Martin appeared first surprised, then pleasantly overwhelmed by whatever Hoffman had told him. Koesler could not know that Hoffman had just delivered the news that he had arranged, through Bishop Ratigan, a private audience with the Pope.

After noticing Hoffman, Koesler began looking around for Charlie Chase. The Company had sprung a leak; news of at least part of what Hoffman had done to Chase had appeared on the business pages of both Detroit's daily newspapers. With little knowledge of the business world and only the sketchy account in the papers, Koesler was unsure how he should react. He was vaguely unhappy it had happened, particularly since it involved two of his parishioners.

Koesler located Chase off to one side. With him were his wife, as well as Emma Hoffman and Cindy Mercury. In light of what had happened between Chase and Hoffman, Koesler thought it peculiar that Louise and Emma should be together now. He could not know that when Hoffman had told his wife of his machinations leading to his tale of victory, she had been furious and a bitter verbal battle had ensued.

As he watched, the three women went off down the hall and disappeared into the ladies' room. Koesler tried to recall the name of the comedian, one of whose routines was to point out the custom, particularly in restaurants, of women regularly visiting the ladies' room together, and asking his audience if anyone ever saw a woman going to the ladies' room alone. Then he suggested that he knew what happens in homes all over the country. In the morning, he declared, the men go off to work and the women phone each other and announce it is time for all of them to go to the bathroom. A chauvinistic cliché at best, Koesler decided.

He thought of going over to visit with Charlie Chase,

but Chase looked relieved to be alone and quite content to be by himself for the time being. In any case, Koesler decided it was time to come down from his aerie and mingle. He moved to the table, registered, and got his "Hello, I'm Father Robert Koesler" badge.

He looked around, this time not seeking anyone in particular, just sizing up the crowd. He was not surprised at the number of Detroit notables present. The mayor, Maynard Cobb, now talking and laughing with Frank Martin as photographers' strobe lights flashed. Tom and Diane Schoenith, whose presence made it an official Detroit Party. Bill Bonds, George Sells, and Mort Crim, Detroit's local network affiliated TV anchormen. Other TV personalities included Jac LeGoff and, among the most beautiful women anywhere, Doris Biscoe, Jennifer Moore, Carmen Harlan, and Diana Lewis.

From the local legitimate theater, Phil Marcus Esser, Hal Youngblood, and, of course, Angie Mercury.

With the exception of Mercury, Koesler had never met any of these celebrities. But he recognized them and others present from having seen them on TV or their photos in the papers.

Since he knew almost no one and since he was very poor at gladhanding strangers, Koesler decided to mingle with the few people he knew.

So it was that he made his way through the crowd to a group of three men, Bishop Ratigan, Frank Hoffman, and Angie Mercury. All three presently were quite buoyant.

Hoffman had just delivered a most welcome present to his boss. After all, what sort of bon voyage present can one give one of Detroit's richest men—a $50 gift certificate? But a private audience with the Pope for a nice Catholic tycoon—now that was something! A gift that Frank Martin would not soon forget. Nor would he forget the giver.

Ratigan was happy because he felt he'd just won a game for fairly high stakes and had come in just under the wire to boot. This had been his first attempt in procuring a papal audience. Although, at first blush, he had anticipated difficulties, he had no way of knowing how many strings needed pulling, how many markers would have to be called in.

In the end, had it not been for the enormous influence of Detroit's archbishop, Cardinal Mark Boyle, Ratigan might well have failed. As it was, confirmation of the audience had come through only earlier today. Ratigan, of course, had gained nothing directly for himself from all his time and effort spent on obtaining this audience. But Ratigan, as was the case with most priests, enjoyed making people happy whenever possible. And, in this instance, he had succeeded in making at least two people very happy. Ratigan would continue to be favored by Hoffman . . . that went without saying. But it did give the bishop a satisfied feeling to pay his dues, as it were, every now and again.

As for Mercury, he was happy in just being here. This, tonight, was where the action was. There were uncounted people here who could do marvelous things for his career. For instance, his agent had been negotiating recently for an interview show for Mercury on ABC-TV's Channel 7. And who should be here, not more than a few feet from him, but Jeanne Findlater, Channel 7's vice-president and general manager. For several minutes now, Mercury had been trying unsuccessfully to catch Jeanne's eye. He would continue to try. He just knew something big was going to happen tonight.

As Koesler neared them, the three men greeted him jovially and expanded their circle to include him.

They had been discussing the papal audience. Hoffman explained to Koesler the history of the uncommon gift. The priest whistled softly as Hoffman laid the credit for the coup at the doorstep of Bishop Ratigan.

"Congratulations, Mike," said Koesler, "that's really something. I wouldn't even know where to start on a deal like that. I have trouble remembering what guy to write to for a papal blessing. I thought you had to be somebody like President of the United States for a private audience!"

"That would help, as I discovered." Ratigan's eyes were wreathed in smile wrinkles. "But exceptions can be made—depending on who knows whom. Let's just say I have had the pleasure recently of making the acquaintance of a whole host of the Roman hierarchy, some in charge of congregations."

"Don't forget any of them, Mike," said Koesler. "They'll be handy when you come into your own kingdom."

At that, Mercury, who had not been paying much attention, looked at Koesler inquiringly.

"When Bishop Ratigan becomes an ordinary." Koesler clarified. "When he gets his own diocese to run."

"Serve," Ratigan corrected good-naturedly. "When I get my own diocese to *serve*."

At this point, Emma and Cindy joined the group. Evidently, Louise had rejoined her husband. Koesler decided to excuse himself at his first opportunity and join the Chases on the mourners' bench.

"I was just telling Father Koesler," said Hoffman, "how Mike got that private audience with the Pope for Mr. Martin. I still find it incredible that you carried it off, Mike."

"But it was your idea, Frank," said Cindy. It was obvious, simply by the way she looked at him, how proud she was of her handsome, successful brother.

"Oh, no, Cindy," Hoffman remonstrated. "I did ask Mike if he could do something about getting Mr. Martin some type of special audience with the Holy Father. But a private audience? It never entered my head. No, that was Mike's idea. And to him goes all the credit." Hoffman glanced down at his glass. "Damn!" he said softly, "what the hell's wrong with these waiters? You'd think they could see my glass is empty!"

"Don't you think you've had enough?" said Emma. She had just finished her second martini and was holding the empty glass. She had, however, had several hors d'oeuvres. Emma had learned her lesson about the dangers of drinking too much on an empty stomach.

"Stay there, Frank; I'll get a waiter." Cindy, ever attentive to her brother's desires, left the group in search of a waiter.

"Thanks for being so solicitous for my good health, Em, dear," Hoffman said with barely disguised sarcasm, "but I'm no longer on medication. So I'll be able to hold my own. How about yourself?" He looked pointedly at her empty cocktail glass. "Have you had something to eat? You know how you tend to run off at the mouth when you don't balance your booze with a little food."

She just looked at him. But, if looks could kill . . .

"Yes, indeed," Ratigan tried to field the conversational ball from its awkward bounce, "*ne potus noceat*—lest the drink harm. Maxim's been attributed to the Jesuits, though I don't know that they invented that, too."

Cindy returned, followed almost immediately by a waiter who silently removed Hoffman's empty cocktail glass from his hand and replaced it with a fresh drink.

Koesler wondered at this maneuver until he recalled that Hoffman was a member of this club and a frequent visitor. The bartenders would well know his drink was a perfect Rob Roy.

"Could build quite a meal around it," Ratigan was saying. "Worked out best on fast days. You remember fast days!'' he quipped, and was surprised to find that no one was paying very much attention to him.

Frank and Emma Hoffman were silently seething at each other. Cindy, concerned, gazed at her brother with a troubled expression. Angie was making surreptitious gestures at Jeanne Findlater, but had not succeeded in attracting her attention. And Koesler was trying to decide if this was the time to break away and join the Chases.

Yet Ratigan, for whatever reason, plowed on. ''We weren't supposed to eat between meals. But nobody said anything about drinking. And that's where the Jesuits come in. Oh, I don't suppose collectively—but some unknown Jebbie is supposed to have figured out that if you can drink, then you can, of course, make that drink alcohol.''

Still furious, but having been stared down, Emma's gaze fell from her husband's eyes. Her attention wandered about the periphery of their circle.

Suddenly, she did a second take at someone who was standing just outside their group but who was looking very intently at Frank Hoffman. Hoffman had not yet noticed the newcomer. Emma thought she had seen this individual before. But where and when?

A passing waiter relieved Emma of her empty glass and asked if she would care for a refill. She simply shook her head no.

''However,'' Ratigan concluded, ''taking alcohol on an empty stomach can be dangerous . . .'' He stopped, suddenly realizing that in the light of Emma's embarrassment at their recent party, he was on tender ground here. But immediatley he also realized he had nothing to be concerned about: Neither Emma nor Frank was paying any attention to him. ''So,'' he went on regardless, ''that was the start of the famous maxim, *'Ne potus noceat,'* literally, 'Lest the drink harm.' So that the alcoholic beverage, which was permitted, didn't cause any problems, one was allowed to eat something, which, without the drink, was not permitted. Could build quite a meal around a drink or two in those days.''

Ratigan's protracted and undesired explanation died of its own dead weight.

In the awkward silence that followed, Ratigan managed to save considerable face when his glance lit upon J.P. McCarthy, Detroit's foremost radio personality and TV talk show host. Ratigan and McCarthy were occasional golfing buddies and, at this moment, McCarthy became Ratigan's emotional life preserver. Ratigan waved; McCarthy returned the wave. Ratigan excused himself and left the awkward silence behind him.

In an unguarded moment, Jeanne Findlater's eyes met those of Angie Mercury. He smiled brightly. She smiled wanly. She knew why he wanted to talk to her. The same reason she did not want to talk to him. There had been some discussion with his agent about Mercury's hosting a daytime interview show on WXYZ-TV. Mrs. Findlater thought the idea had merit. But she did not want to muck it up by, at this stage, discussing it with Mercury. Not while she was negotiating with his agent. Talking about it with Mercury now simply was premature. But, he had caught her eye . . . .

"I noticed your glass is empty, Jeannie." Mercury stepped from his circle to hers. "Can I get you a drink?"

"Oh, no. There's no need to do that. A waiter . . ." She wished he wouldn't be so familiar.

"No trouble. What are you drinking?" He noticed an olive along with ice in the otherwise empty glass. "A martini?"

"Well, no. Gin, actually. Just ask the bartender for Mrs. Findlater's drink."

"Be right back." Mercury took her empty glass and departed, leaving Jeanne Findlater wondering how to end the coming conversation before it began.

"Don't I know you? Have we ever met?" Emma Hoffman addressed the person who had continued to stand alone at the fringe of their group.

"No, not really. We've never been introduced."

For the first time, Frank Hoffman noticed the newcomer, who had been standing to one side, out of his direct line of vision. His face seemed to drain. He grew so pale that his sister moved toward him, fearful he was about to be stricken as he had been at the party.

"Well, someplace," persisted Emma, "I know I've seen you someplace." Emma leaned toward the attractive blonde to read her identification tag. "Jackie Le-Blanc . . . no; I don't recall that name. But someplace . . ." Emma was about to add that she couldn't forget that face, when it occurred to her: It wasn't the woman's face she couldn't forget; it was the body that went with it that had proven memorable.

At this moment, Ratigan returned. Taking appreciative notice of the newcomer, he smiled at Jackie. He, like Koesler and so many others of their calling, considered that a celibate life could include room for at least studying and savoring the view of women, God's greatest work of art. And he thought Jackie stunning in her off-the-shoulder gown and lacy shoulder covering that set off her blonde hair. She looked as pretty as a Christmas tree and was shaped much, much better.

"It was the spa!" Emma pointed at her. "Madame Tirana's spa!" She had the look of triumph that springs from a tortuous ratiocination leading to recognition. Then, puzzlement replaced the triumph. "But, who, why—?"

Jackie looked significantly at Hoffman, who was licking his suddenly dry lips. "I thought it was time we met."

Emma looked from this stranger to Frank. Gradually

but heavily the truth came. "You," she pointed at Jackie, "you . . . you're his mistress!"

Ratigan instantly regretted having returned to this group. But there was no getting away from it now.

For a few moments there was dead silence. Emma had made her charge so forcefully that people in nearby groups had stopped talking and started listening. Carol T, *Free Press* gossip writer, sensing an entire column from this apparent confrontation, stepped closer to Emma.

Cindy was horror-stricken for her brother's sake. Koesler tried to recall when he had been more embarrassed. Several occasions came to mind, but this, he decided, ranked. God, why hadn't he broken away earlier! There was no civilized way he could make his excuses now. Nor did he feel he could just walk away from what promised to develop into a formidable scene. Bishop Ratigan unsuccessfully searched his memory for some anecdote that might relieve this confrontation.

"God damn you, Jackie!" Hoffman's words came through clenched teeth. "What the hell are you doing here?"

He spoke just loudly enough for the immediate circle to hear. But the immediate circle had grown. Carol T was in the van of several other representatives of the various news media.

It was obvious from his speech that his fury had served to sober Hoffman completely. If ever he needed a drink, it was now.

Cindy noticed her brother's nearly empty glass. She caught the arm of a nearby waiter. "Would you get Mr. Hoffman another drink, please?"

The waiter nodded and headed off toward the bar.

"I thought," Jackie replied calmly, "this might be a good time for us," she nodded at Emma, "to meet."

If she had not been absorbed by her husband's embarrassment and fury, Emma would have been enraged.

"A good time to meet! What the hell is that supposed to mean?" Hoffman demanded.

"It means, Frank," Jackie was getting up a head of steam, "that it's time for me to come out of the closet. It's time for us to appear publicly together!"

"You're out of your mind! You're out of your goddamn mind! How did you get in here?"

Jackie gestured to what she may have intended as a comment on the lack of security. "There seems to be an open-door policy."

"Do you realize what you've done? You bitch! This was a night of triumph for me! I was sitting on top of the world. Things couldn't have been better for me at The Company. The only bad thing that could have happened was your showing up!"

"Isn't that the way with Murphy's Law, Frank?" Jackie was again calm, deliberately contrasting her manner with his.

"Well, I'm glad she came, and I'm glad she's here." Emma glared defiantly at her husband. "Because, as I told you before, Frank, all bets are off! I told you if I ever met your girlfriend, it was back to square one."

If any of the uninvited bystanders felt any shame about being present at this intimate marital explosion, it didn't show. The only exceptions appeared to be Father Koesler, who looked as if he wished he could slip through a crack in the floor, and Cindy Mercury, who seemed intensely embarrassed. And of course Bishop Ratigan, who wondered where J.P. McCarthy was now that he was needed.

"What do you mean by that?" Hoffman had abandoned any effort at keeping this an affair between the ménage à trois. He was almost shouting.

"I mean it's time little Em lived it up. Without an encumbrance called Frank Hoffman!" Her eyes were blazing.

A waiter was standing at Hoffman's side holding a cocktail. He seemed undecided about what to do with it in the face of the furor.

"Here's your drink, Frank," Cindy said rather meekly.

The waiter removed Hoffman's nearly empty glass and replaced it with the fresh drink.

"From now on," Emma stormed, "what's good for the gander is good for the goose! And that goes for your precious perfect Rob Roy!" She snatched the glass from Hoffman's hand and, as he looked on, too startled to react in any way, she downed the contents of the glass in a single swig.

"Em! What the hell—!"

But Em did not reply. Her eyes clouded as the massive impact of several ounces of alcohol hit her at once. Then, her eyes rolled back as something more powerful than even the liquor seemed to shake her to her core. The glass fell from her hand and bounded harmlessly on the thick Persian carpet. She crumpled to the floor, then stiffened. A series of convulsions threw her body about as if she were a rag doll. It was a terrifying sight. Some felt compelled to watch; others turned away. A few women screamed. Some men shouted. But there were so many shouts that none could be clearly comprehended.

Ultimately, Emma's body appeared to be jerked by some invisible force into boardlike rigidity. Then, after a horrible gurgling sound, as if she were drowning, Emma Hoffman fell into deathly stillness.

More screams, more shouts.

Father Koesler dropped to his knees beside Emma's body and whispered the words of absolution. She was obviously unconscious at best. Bishop Ratigan was certain he would be able to recall the formula for absolution, if it just weren't for all these damned crises.

Two men joined Koesler on the floor beside the body.

One began attempts at mouth-to-mouth resuscitation, the other began rhythmically pumping Emma's chest.

A well-dressed woman also knelt. She removed one of Emma's shoes, and with long fingernails, scratched Emma's sole. There was no response. Then she lifted one of Emma's eyelids. Next, she removed a hand mirror from her purse and placed it to Emma's mouth and nostrils as the man who was attempting resuscitation raised up. She then ran her finger along Emma's eyebrow and squeezed.

"What are you doing?" Koesler asked quietly.

"I used to work in a hospital emergency room. I'm checking vital signs. I'm no doctor, but I'm pretty sure this lady is dead."

The shouts became more intelligible as they grew less diverse. Some were urging that a doctor be called; others were shouting for the police.

Koesler sat back on his heels. Could it have been a massive heart attack? Even as the thought came, he dismissed it. He could almost hear that frightening disembodied voice as it promised, "Oh, I . . . will see you outside . . . the confessional. I have some . . . mischief planned. I will see . . . you at the scene of . . . the mischief."

Had Satan been here?

17.

WHAT HAD BEEN—WITH THE EXCEPTION OF the Hoffmans' discord—until very recently a jovial party was now the very embodiment of organized chaos. The chaos was being supplied by some of the very important people now confined to the Harvard Room, the scene of Frank Martin's party. The organization came from a contingent of Detroit police who were conducting a homicide investigation, which, somehow, is never routine. Surely this investigation into the death of a member of Detroit's automotive society and involving some of the prime movers and shakers of the Motor City could hardly be termed routine.

Some of the VIPs objected to being involved in any sort of police investigation. Others additionally objected to having their pictures taken by police photographers and being subjected to questioning. TV anchor people were anxious to return to their respective stations in time for the 11:00 P.M. newscast.

None of that mattered. This was, or, from all indications, was assumed to be, a homicide. And as such, this investigation took precedence over all other considerations.

The uniformed officers who responded to the emergency call had first sealed off the area so no one could leave. Then they had called the homicide division.

When Detective Sergeants Charles Papkin and Ray Ewing arrived and saw the number of people involved, they had called in the reserves. In addition to the other homicide detectives and technicians now on the scene, there were several from the robbery division and the medical unit.

Emma Hoffman had been taken to Receiving Hospital, where a doctor pronounced her dead. Her body was then taken to the Wayne County Morgue, where an autopsy would be performed the following morning by the medical examiner.

Sergeant Ewing was standing meditatively at the spot where Emma Hoffman had fallen. A chalk outline demarcated where her body had lain. He was mentally recording every detail.

There was a small, square hole in the carpet to one side of where the body had fallen. The dregs of Emma's final drink had seeped into the carpet. Ewing had ordered that patch of the carpet removed. Along with the still-moist glass, it had been given to the police technicians for analysis. What the technicians might identify in the carpet or glass could prove the quickest route to determining what had killed the woman. The manager of the Collegiate Club had objected strenuously to the violation of his carpet, but, as with so many similar objections, to no avail.

With all the hubbub in the large room, it was a testament to Ewing's powers of concentration that he could even appear to be oblivious to all but the precise spot of the crime. Gradually, he became aware of another presence. He looked up and smiled at his partner Papkin. "How's it going?"

"Cast of thousands." Papkin gestured at the room in general.

"Yeah."

Each detective stood a fraction of an inch under six feet. Papkin, with a full head of salt-and-pepper hair, a face that had been tanned too many times so that the lines and creases were etched deeply, and hazel eyes that seemed to see through people, was fortunate enough to be doing the only thing he had ever wanted to do—be a cop. He dressed fashionably. Ewing, on the other hand, usually dressed down. His present outfit of corduroy trousers and ill-matched jacket was characteristic. Sandy-haired, he resembled singer Steve Lawrence, more so when he smiled, which was often. "Whatcha got so far?"

"Mostly bad news. We've pretty well ruled out a stroke or any kind of heart attack. The bar was wide open. If what killed her was in that drink, anybody had access to it. Even anybody wandering in from the street."

Ewing shook his head. "Isn't that the way of it? Especially when the VIPs gather, you'd think there'd be security up to their eyeballs."

"But you'd be wrong."

"How about the waiter who brought the drink?"

"We got him. He didn't make any attempt to get away. In fact, he stayed right here even after she collapsed. Henderson's with him now. Claims he didn't know there was anything wrong with the drink. He's agreed to take a polygraph."

Ewing smiled broadly. "Charlie, Charlie, Charlie! You and the polygraph. The only people who rely on lie detectors are the people who are trying to sell them."

Papkin obviously did not share the humor. "They're not infallible, but they can prove something."

"Yeah. In this case, whether a little waiter is nervous about the possibility of being a suspect in a murder case. Frankly, if I were he, I would be."

"I've got a feeling he's not a strong lead, in any case.

The bartenders were keeping one drink ahead of the orders. They'd keep a manhattan, a martini, a Tom Collins, a rum-and-Coke, and so forth on the rim of the bar so the waiters wouldn't have to delay in delivering the drinks.'' He shook his head. ''These people must be some drinkers!

''Anyway, in the case of guests who had some special kind of drink, like straight gin, or, in Hoffman's case, a perfect Rob Roy, not only did the bartenders stay one drink ahead, they'd put the special drink on top of the person's name card.''

Ewing whistled. ''So, if somebody wants to fool with Hoffman's drink, all they have to do is find the drink that's sitting on Hoffman's card. Talk about a red carpet invitation to commit murder! But what about the wife grabbing his drink and downing it? What the hell was that all about?''

''Crazy! They were having a quarrel—no mufflers on—a good part of the room was in on it. At the moment his drink is served, she is saying something about what's good enough for him is good enough for her. With that, she grabs his drink and downs it.''

''Wow! Talk about being in the wrong place at the wrong time and doing the exact wrong thing.''

''Somebody,'' Papkin referred to his notepad, ''a Mrs. Louise Chase, said that Mrs. Hoffman herself had said that she was always doing things impulsively. And the others who knew her agree. Doing things impulsively seems to have been a bad habit with her.''

''The worst. It killed her.''

''I've impounded all the booze. I don't know that we'll find anything, but it couldn't hurt.''

''Good.''

''By the way, the TV anchor people are trying to get out of here so they can do their eyewitness accounts of this on-air.''

"Tough. They're staying till we're done. That's what they've got backups for."

"That's what I told them—in a diplomatic way. Oh, and did you know that we've got a bishop in the crowd?"

"Catholic?"

"Uh-huh. And another clergyman, too." He paused for effect. "A Father Robert Koesler."

"Koesler?"

Father Koesler, having been involved in several murder investigations, was generally quite well known to Detroit's homicide detectives.

"Think we should tell the Inspector?"

"If we found Watson here, would we tell Holmes?" Both laughed.

"How about Mayor Cobb? How's he bearing up through the ordeal?" Ewing asked.

"Just fine. He's holding court. You can never tell about Maynard Cobb. He'll surprise you every time."

For the first time in many minutes, Ewing surveyed the room. It presented the sort of scene with which he was very familiar. Police personnel were scattered about, not unlike football's specialty teams, each officer doing his or her thing: guarding evidence, gathering evidence, answering questions, blocking all avenues of egress, taking photos, interrogating.

These were highly trained professionals who understood that these minutes were, by far, the most important of the entire investigation. This was The Scene of the Crime. It would never be repeated and could never be precisely duplicated. There were clues here, physical clues as well as questions to be asked and responses given that could and possibly would tell the whole story, reveal the motive and even the prepetrator. The police, then, were carefully carrying out their responsibilities.

"Where's Hoffman?"

"Over there." Papkin indicated a man slumped in a

straightback chair against the far wall. "The people around him, as far as I've been able to determine, are relatives and friends."

"We'd better get over there."

As they crossed the room toward Hoffman, Ewing made a mental note of those surrounding the widower. Many of them he recognized on sight. There was Koesler, of course, and Frank Martin. The sergeant thought he recognized Ratigan and Mercury from their newspaper photos. The others undoubtedly were auto executives and their wives.

Introductions were exchanged and condolences offered.

Ewing did a quick study of Hoffman. Hair meticulously styled, silver at the temples; tanned; handsome; tailored dinner jacket; maybe mid-fifties but holding on to the forties. Ewing could well imagine what Mr. and Mrs. Hoffman might have been arguing about.

"Mr. Hoffman," Ewing began solicitously, "I know this is awfully soon after your wife's tragic death, but I've got to ask you some questions."

"Of course." Hoffman remained seated. He was obviously shaken.

"Until we can determine the contents of that glass, we must assume it contained poison—a pretty powerful poison at that, judging by your wife's reaction."

Hoffman nodded.

"But what we seem to have here," Ewing continued, "is almost certainly a case of murder in error. The drink was intended for you, was it not?"

Again Hoffman nodded.

"Then do you have any idea why your wife would have taken it from you and drunk it?"

Hoffman shook his head, but did not look up. "Em was angry—very angry. She had a habit of doing things impulsively, as the spirit moved her. She'd already had a couple of martinis and she was raving. She was saying something about how, from now on, whatever was good enough for me would be good enough for her. And it was just at that moment the waiter handed me my drink. It was as if she were giving some sort of demonstration of what she'd just said. I have this drink that I favor, a perfect Rob Roy. It was as if she were saying that if a distinctive drink were my drink, it could as easily be hers. But that's only my conjecture. I have no way of knowing what was in her mind at the moment."

"It sounds as if that would be a pretty good guess, sir," said Ewing. "But could you also interpret what she meant by that, 'Whatever is good enough for you will be good enough for me'?"

Hoffman still had not looked at either Ewing or Papkin since the introduction. "No, I have no idea."

A lie. Good. Always nice to have a lie on record. Later one could always bring it up. As in, "You lied to me when I asked what your wife might have meant by what she said to you. Is this a lie too? When should I start believing you?"

"OK, then," Papkin said, "let's say your wife acted impulsively, grabbed the glass before you could do anything about it, drank the contents, and died from the effects of a poison that someone had placed in it. In that case, Mr. Hoffman, you were the intended victim. Whoever put the poison in that drink intended it for you. We are looking, then, for someone who wanted to kill you."

It was an obvious conclusion, but one that seemingly had not occurred to Hoffman. "Someone kill me?" He appeared stunned at the notion.

"Mr. Hoffman, just a few minutes ago, we talked with headquarters. They ran a check on you and found that just last month there was an incident at your company's glass plant in which you were nearly killed. The file is still open on that incident. It could have been an industrial accident. Or it might have been attempted murder. With what has happened here tonight, there seems little remaining doubt.

"Mr. Hoffman, it would seem that someone wants you dead. Can you think of anyone who might want to kill you?"

Hoffman did not so much seem to be considering anyone who might want him dead as he seemed to be mentally busy denying the possibility. "Why, no. No one. Perhaps there's some mistake. . . ."

"No mistake, Mr. Hoffman. Your wife is dead. Receiving Hospital has confirmed that. She died drinking something that was intended for you. There's every indication that if she had not 'impulsively' taken the glass from you, it would be your body now resting in the Wayne County Morgue." Papkin intended to shock Hoffman into facing facts and thus providing some answers that could be helpful in this investigation.

Hoffman appeared to respond to Papkin's statement; he seemed to be considering any possible assassins. But, "No, it's no use. I can't think of anyone who would want me dead, let alone try to poison me. Enemies, perhaps a few. But not mortal enemies. No!"

"Let's look at it this way then," said Ewing. "Who would profit from your death?"

Hoffman hesitated. "Well, lots of people, I suppose. Isn't that the case with almost any relatively well-off person?"

"It would help a lot if you were more specific, Mr. Hoffman," said Ewing. "As a matter of fact, rather than have you try to think of specific people off the top of your head, a look at your Last Will and Testament should help us find the answers to that question."

Both Ratigan and Mercury standing nearby, winced slightly. Each had good reason to expect to be favorably mentioned in Hoffman's will. Ratigan because Hoffman had so informed him; Mercury due to his wife's being Hoffman's beloved sister.

For the first time, Hoffman stood and faced the two detectives. Slightly taller than they, he tried to use his height to imply a position of power. "My will is a private, personal document, Sergeant. It contains privileged information between my attorney and myself. And no, you may not see it."

"I trust there's a copy of it in a safe deposit box at your bank?"

"Yes, of course."

"Yes, well, then you must forgive us, Mr. Hoffman," Ewing's tone intimated that the step he was about to take troubled him more than anyone, but that his was an unpleasant and inescapable task. "But we'll just have to get a probate court order to have a look at that document. Sorry about that, Mr. Hoffman, but it's for your own good."

"For my own good?"

"Mr. Hoffman, somebody out there is trying to kill you."

For a fifty-one-year-old woman, Emma Hoffman had preserved a good bit of her considerable beauty. Even death had not robbed her of that. But very soon her body was going to be in several pieces.

Sergeant Ray Ewing watched as Wayne County Medical Examiner Wilhelm Moellmann prepared to make the first incision. Most who dealt with Moellmann called him Willie, but not within his hearing. Despite his many eccentricities, Dr. Moellmann ranked among the best in the business.

It was neither a rule nor a law, but most good homicide detectives attended the autopsies of the cases they worked on. Ewing always did. Over the years, he had de-

veloped four rules of thumb by which he lived his professional life: Make the scene of the crime; attend the autopsy and examine the body; establish a good relationship with the deceased's family; and get familiar with the
area surrounding the scene of the crime. Presently he was
touching the second of these four bases.

"So, what have you got for me this morning, Ray-
mond? No punctures, no bullet holes, no stab wounds! A
nice clean corpse for a change?"

Moellmann did not expect a reply. He was beginning a
performance. An audience of one was all he needed.

Ewing simply smiled.

"All the organs seem rich in blood," Moellmann pronounced.

As the medical examiner continued his work and his
commentary, Ewing's mind wandered to other autopsies
he'd attended. He recalled the woman who had been
beaten to death by her husband. As the autopsy had begun, the medical examiner had been puzzled by strange
marks on the woman's face and forehead. Ewing had
been able to solve the mystery when he recalled the tile
floor in the kitchen, the scene of that particular crime.
The pattern of the tile was the same as the indentations on
the woman's face. The man had hit his wife on the back
of the head so hard that the imprint of the floor tile had
been impressed on her face.

One of Moellmann's assistants leaned through a doorway. "Call for you, Ray."

"Thanks." Ewing stepped into the nearby office, and
picked up the phone. "Ewing."

"Papkin here."

"Yeah, Charlie. How's it goin'?"

"I'm at Manufacturers Bank." It had been a simple
process both to ascertain Hoffman's bank and to get the
court order. "I'm about to make a photostat of Hoffman's will. And I just talked to our technical guys."

"They find it?"

"Yup. Nicotine."

"Nicotine! I've never had a nicotine poisoning before."

"And I'll bet you thought you'd seen everything. Well, what next?"

"Let's meet back at the office. I'll be there as soon as Moellmann finishes the autopsy."

"You got Willie? Enjoy the show."

Ewing returned to the examining room. "It was nicotine, Doc."

"Nicotine! That's different." Moellmann prepared a section of liver and kidney plus a blood sample for his toxicology department. "You just saved us all some time, Sergeant."

"Yeah." Ewing well understood the time factor. The medical examiner's technicians undoubtedly would have found the traces of nicotine poisoning. But without knowing what they were looking for, it easily could have taken them a week. Now that they knew what had caused the woman's death, it would still require two or three days before they would be able to isolate the poison from the specimens Moellmann would give them.

Funny, Ewing thought as the autopsy proceeded, how we each have our own little kingdom.

The medical examiner eventually would officially determine the cause of death. Then he would pronounce the category: murder, suicide, natural causes. Of course he would incorporate in his own analyses the information contributed by the police. But, as far as he was concerned, it wasn't murder unless and until he declared it so.

The police had their kingdom. A murder investigation had begun last night when the police had arrived at the Collegiate Club. It became somewhat more "official" when the police toxicologists established the presence of a lethal dose of nicotine in the glass and carpet sample. No way would the police delay their investigation until the medical examiner had made his pronouncement. The police knew that. The medical examiner knew that. But they all played the game.

The final point in the triangle in the crime of homicide was the prosecutor's office. The medical examiner could pronounce, the police could investigate, but until the prosecutor decided to make the charge and bring to trial, the game was not complete.

The autopsy concluded with a "negative" finding, at least until the toxicologists inevitably found what they were now looking for.

It was only a few blocks from the morgue to police headquarters at 1300 Beaubien. Ewing walked it. He arrived in his squad room to find Papkin studying the reports that had been filed after last night's investigation. He had collated the findings of the various officers who had been at the Collegiate Club.

Ewing took a seat opposite Papkin at a long wide table which, with several other similar tables in the room, also served as a desk. He commenced sifting through the reports. He had read them all earlier, before the autopsy. But that was before they'd been collated.

"I think," said Papkin, "we've just set a new record for raw material gathered in the shortest time."

Ewing chuckled and hefted the huge pile of paper—reports that had been turned in by the many officers who had participated in last night's investigation. "I suppose so. But how many times have you found that many people present at the scene of a crime?"

"And very articulate people, at that. I mean, if you had your pick, who would you rather interrogate for juicy details than some gossip columnist?"

"Right!" Ewing laughed again. "Plus all those media people. It certainly was a shortcut to a lot of information.

I hadn't known, for instance, about the feud between Hoffman and Chase.''

''It was in the business section of the paper. I keep telling you, you've got to start reading more than the sports pages.''

Ewing smiled broadly. ''OK, OK, let's get on with it. Remember when Hoffman claimed last night that he couldn't think of anyone who might want to kill him? Enemies, maybe, but no mortal enemies?''

''Maybe,'' Papkin responded, ''he just wasn't thinking of half the people in that room.''

''With the possible exception of Chairman Frank Martin and Hoffman's sister. But when you're looking for the strongest motives, it pretty well comes down to a tight little group of four, doesn't it?''

''You're thinking of Charles and Louise Chase, Angie Mercury, and Jacqueline LeBlanc. Right?'' Papkin lit a cigarette. He was trying to quit smoking and was using the slow, painful method of cutting back on his daily allotment of cigarettes.

''That's right.'' Ewing consulted his notes, partly taken from his own investigation and partly a potpourri of the findings of other officers at the scene. ''Charles' motive is revenge. Hoffman seems to have damn near deep-sixed Chase's career. Ditto to Louise Chase. Revenge for her husband's disgrace plus getting rid of somebody who was after her husband's position in The Company. Angie Mercury would have gotten rid of the embarrassment of having to accept virtual handouts from his brother-in-law. Plus, he could have been pretty sure Hoffman would have amply taken care of his sister in his will.'' He paused. ''He did, didn't he?''

Papkin, who had read and made a copy of Hoffman's will, nodded.

''So,'' Ewing continued, ''if Mercury takes out Hoffman, he gets rid of a major league nuisance while not los-

ing the cash value. Then, there's always the mistress. In
this case, she's sure he isn't going to make an honest
woman of her, plus she shows up at the scene just in time
to pull it off.''

"There's more." Papkin exhaled through his nose. He
was the more serious smoker who inhaled down to his
toenails. "She, also, is not only mentioned in the will,
but gets a healthy sum. Two hundred thou, to be exact.''

"So, she not only gets revenge for his using her, she
also profits.''

"And you may have to add one more suspect to your
list.''

"Oh? Who?''

Papkin shoved the photostat of Hoffman's will across
the table. His finger pointed to an underlined name.

Ewing whistled softly. "Bishop Ratigan!''

"Like Miss LeBlanc, the good bishop collects two
hundred grand, passes Go, and it remains to be seen
whether he gets sent to jail.

"This estate, Ray, is worth one point two million dol-
lars.''

Ewing whistled again.

"From what I've been able to learn," Papkin continued, "Frank and Cindy Hoffman come from a middle-
class home. The bond between them is remarkably tight.
Frank got a job with The Company as an engineer. For
most of his career, he climbed the corporate ladder steadily but slowly. Until he finally attracted the attention of
the right people. Then the career really zoomed." Papkin
extinguished the cigarette and resisted the urge to light
another. "Recently—well, for about three years—he was
in the hundred-thou-a-year category. But, for the past
two years, he's been in the two-hundred-grand-a-year
group.

"He's always taken care of his sister. But since he
came into the bucks, he's really been supporting her—

and by association, her husband—in a style she could never maintain without him.

"There's a minimal trust for his wife. And that wouldn't be significant because she came from money and was wealthy in her own right. Except . . ."

"Except," Ewing continued Papkin's line of thought, indicating they were in agreement, "that Hoffman and his wife were on the outs. And when Jackie LeBlanc shows up, Emma Hoffman lets the world know there's trouble in paradise.

"Say," Ewing rubbed his chin, "it comes down to Hoffman's having plenty of motive for killing his wife. Everybody thinks he is the intended victim while he turns the tables and offs her."

"That's right, except for a couple of things."

"Yeah, I know. How could he get her to grab a glass out of his hand at just the moment he was holding a poisoned drink? She had to do that spontaneously. How did Louise Chase put it—on impulse. Hoffman couldn't have controlled that. And if somebody doesn't grab it, he ends up holding onto a drink he knows is poisoned."

"Right, plus one more thing." Papkin, losing his private battle, lit another cigarette and promised himself he would make up for the indulgence later. "Hoffman may have had a motive for killing his wife, but he lacked the opportunity. And here we come to another consideration. By actual count, the poisoned drink was Hoffman's fourth perfect Rob Roy last night. So, the poison had to be put in the drink the bartender set up after Hoffman's third drink. That's the crucial time: between the third and fourth drink. That's when the killer had to act."

"So?"

"So, between the third and fourth drink, the only people who remained together and thus had no opportunity to fix the drink were Hoffman, who doesn't figure in the picture; his wife, who becomes the victim; Hoffman's sister and Father Koesler, the only two in this little group who had nothing to gain from Hoffman's death and who are not suspects.''

"Run that by me again.''

Papkin took another deep drag. God, it was good. Why was smoking so bad? "OK. Take Charles and Louise Chase.'' He was consulting the notes he had collated from the general investigation to date. "Neither of them was a part of Hoffman's group last night. Nor were they together at all times during the party. Either of them could have slipped over to the bar at any time and deposited the poison in the glass that had been placed over Hoffman's name. Then, there's Angie Mercury. Between Hoffman's third and fourth drink, he went over to talk to that TV executive—"

"Jeanne Findlater.''

"Right. That gives him the opportunity to go to the bar, and drop the poison. Jackie LeBlanc: Between drinks three and four, she makes her first appearance with the group. She could have entered the room, registered, dropped the poison, then joined the group.

"Finally, there's the good bishop. He's been standing with the group throughout. Then, between drinks three and four, he goes over to talk with J.P. McCarthy. The big thing is, he's away from the group. After he talked to McCarthy, he could easily have wandered over to the bar, deposited the poison, then rejoined the group.

"So, all our suspects had not only motive but also opportunity. The only ones who had neither motive nor opportunity were Koesler and Cindy Mercury. So, we end up with five bona fide suspects.''

Ewing shrugged. "We've started with better and we've started with worse. By the way, what about the waiter?''

Papkin frowned. "He passed the polygraph.''

Ewing smiled. "Not such a nervous little fellow after all."

"He's been at the club a few years." Papkin consulted his notes. "Before that, he worked at just about everything—a short-order cook, night watchman, manager of a hotel, a few stints as an extra in some local theater and nightclubs, and, off and on, a waiter in local restaurants and hotels. No motive for attempting to kill Hoffman. Matter of fact, Hoffman always tips him pretty good. He'll finally get his name in the papers only because he happened to deliver a poisoned drink.

"Well, what next?"

"I suggest we start visiting some of these nice people and ask some more questions. And, while we're at it, look around for a source for this nicotine poison."

"Want to stop off and get some search warrants?"

"Oh, I don't think so." Ewing smiled one of his more charming smiles. "If I can't wheedle my way into the confidence of these five people, one of whom is undoubtedly our murderer, I'll turn in my Dick Tracy two-way wrist radio."

"It has been too long!" Inspector Walter Koznicki rose to greet Father Koesler.

The gesture was typical of Koznicki, head of the Detroit Police Department's homicide division. A student of modern police work and methods, indeed, avant garde in his use of modern technology, when it came to religion, he was old world, a conservative, in the best sense of that word, to the core. It was natural for him to stand at the entrance of a priest, even though the priest happened to be an old friend. He reverenced the priesthood and he expressed this reverence through courtly manners.

Koesler smiled and grasped the outstretched hand, or rather, lost his hand in Koznicki's.

They were seated at a table in the Kingsley Inn on Woodward in Bloomfield Hills. Once they had taken their places on the upholstered banquette that ran the length of the wall, the hostess gently eased the table close to them—or rather, close to Koznicki. At which point, it was still several inches away from Koesler.

Koesler was a large man. But Koznicki was one of those rare people who are metaphorically described as bigger than life. He wasn't fat. He was big. When Koesler saw the table stop as it reached Koznicki and noted the distance still remaining between the table and himself, the priest placed both palms against the underside of the table and continued the movement of his side of the table. They would dine with their table on the bias, as they had many times before.

"How are things at St. Anselm's?" Koznicki moved the ashtray to a neighboring table. He had never smoked. Koesler had quit smoking several years before.

"In general, quite well. In particular, not so good."

Koznicki ran a large hand through his full head of dark hair. "You would be referring to the murder. Terrible thing!"

The waitress brought bread, butter, and water. They would study the menu later. Meanwhile, Koesler would have a bourbon manhattan, Koznicki sherry.

"It's hard to imagine that last night at this time there was a party going on at the Collegiate Club and Emma Hoffman was alive," said Koesler.

"I know how you must feel, Father. It must have been particularly shocking to you since you were present."

How did Koznicki know that, Koesler wondered. The Inspector caught his inquiring look. "One of the detectives investigating the case knew of our friendship and informed me of your presence. Normally, at this stage of the investigation, the detectives would not make any report. But when you asked that we meet, I asked Sergeants

Ewing and Papkin to brief me. It is only the first day, but they have made considerable progress. Of course, this is to be desired. As we have discussed before, the more time elapses the less chance there is that the case will be solved.''

The waitress brought their drinks. The small glass of sherry looked as if it were a miniature in Koznicki's meaty fingers.

"Will the funeral be held at St. Anselm's?"

Koesler nodded. "Thursday morning. Bishop Ratigan will be the main concelebrant of the . . . Mass.'' He smiled. "I almost said 'funeral Mass.' Sometimes it's hard to remember it's called the 'Mass of Resurrection' now.''

"Bishop Ratigan? Are you certain?''

"Why, yes. It's at the request of Frank Hoffman. They're friends, you know. I'll concelebrate and there should be other priests concelebrating. The Hoffmans are prominent Catholics so we're expecting quite a few priests. But Bishop Ratigan will be the principal concelebrant.

"You seem surprised.''

Koznicki took a sip of wine. "Bishop Ratigan was interrogated today by Detectives Ewing and Papkin.''

"Interrogated!'' Somehow the word sounded more ominous than "questioned.'' "Why in God's green world would they interrogate Bishop Ratigan?''

Koznicki explained in detail the finds and conclusions reached by Ewing and Papkin that morning.

As the explanation proceeded, Koesler recalled the events as they had transpired. He remembered standing with Hoffman, Mercury, and Ratigan as they were joined by Emma and Cindy. He recalled Hoffman's complaining that his empty glass had not been replaced with a fresh drink. He had not been aware that he had joined the group during Hoffman's second drink. Now that

Koznicki had so informed him, Koesler thought of the lucidity of Hoffman's speech and marveled at the way the man could hold liquor when not groggy from medication.

Cindy had left the group for a short while to fetch a waiter. The waiter had first removed Hoffman's empty glass—that would be drink two—and brought him a fresh drink—that would be number three.

At this point, the bartender would make up the fourth perfect Rob Roy and place it on the bar atop Frank's name card. While that fourth drink rested on the bar, someone would pour poison into it. Who?

Neither Charles nor Louise Chase had been present in the Hoffman circle. Nor, according to Koznicki, had the couple been together at all times last night. Either of them could have had the opportunity. But Koesler could not imagine either of them, especially the gentle Louise, doing it.

As Koznicki continued his explanation, Koesler continued to display his self-made motion picture against the screen of his memory.

This was the crucial time. The Chases were off somewhere in the room. Was one of them poisoning a drink? He could see Angie Mercury depart from the group. He could see Mike Ratigan leave. A bishop poison a drink? Impossible. It was medieval! He could see Jackie LeBlanc join the group. Where had she been?

Koesler could agree that each of these people might have a motive for murder. But, with the exception of Miss LeBlanc, whom he didn't really know, he could not imagine anyone actually doing the deed. It was one thing for a civilized person to consider murder—anyone could think of anything. But it was quite another thing to actually take someone's life.

As he mentally rewound this imaginary film, Koesler recalled that the only ones not to leave the scene during this crucial span were Frank, the intended victim; Emma, the actual victim; himself—and God knows he had nothing to do with it; and Cindy, who would be the last to try to harm her brother, and who certainly had no reason to.

For a moment, Koesler pitied the police. Everyone who would not have committed the crime also could not. While everyone who might have committed the murder also could have.

"Our technologists," Koznicki continued, "using a technique involving washing with distilled water, early this morning discovered the toxic substance used in the drink. It was nicotine."

"Nicotine! As in cigarettes? I agree with the surgeon general that smoking can be dangerous to one's health, but that takes a while. Emma just collapsed and died."

"I must confess, Father, that as a result of this case, tonight I and some of my officers know a great deal more about nicotine than we did last night.

"As it happens, nicotine is one of the most toxic of all drugs. It can be as potent and fast-acting as cyanide."

Koesler's mind immediately focused on a number of the war movies he'd seen. When the spy was about to be interrogated, more often than not under torture, if the spy were lucky—lucky for the purposes of the film's plot, that is—he or she would slip a pill into his or her mouth and promptly drop dead. Koesler, as the police had been, was impressed.

"The reason," Koznicki continued, "that the nicotine in cigarettes, cigars, and pipe tobacco does not have this effect is that the toxic elements are burned up before they are ingested. In a manner of speaking, the deadly poison goes up in smoke.

"But when we come to pure nicotine, a single drop is sufficient to cause death."

Koesler, still deeply impressed, considered this. "But where does one get pure nicotine? If I tried to find some, I wouldn't know where to look."

"But Father, it is so powerful one does not need to find it in some pristine condition."

"Still . . . where?"

"That is where our technicians were particularly helpful. You see, when we are looking for something toxic, we do not first search for some exotic substance. Usually, there will be general household products that will serve very well as a poison of one sort or another. With nicotine, we were told to look for some sort of insecticide. And that is precisely what Detectives Ewing and Papkin did today as they visited with our five suspects." Koznicki took another small sip of sherry.

"And—?"

"It turns out that nicotine in one form or another was available to all of them."

"All? Isn't that rather odd?"

"Oh, yes, indeed, Father. But in this case somewhat explainable, through the good offices of your friend and house guest, Bishop Ratigan."

"Mike? What's he got to do with this?"

"You will know that, in his youth, Bishop Ratigan worked for a number of years for a plant nursery."

"He never lets me forget it."

"Insecticides are very important to those who work with flora. Some would say they are, not to speak in contradictions, vital. There is a product called Black Leaf 40 that is very powerful as well as very popular, although its sale is now restricted. It seems that the Chases and the Hoffmans, as well as the Mercurys, all have greenhouses. And each greenhouse held a supply of Black Leaf 40.

"To give you some idea of how potent this chemical is, users are directed to dilute the substance by one teaspoonful to one gallon of water, or one pint to 100 gallons of water. Our technicians tell us that only a few drops of Black Leaf 40 can be fatal to a human.

"They also tell us it has a very bitter taste. Mrs. Hoffman very probably would have caught that taste in the drink if she had not downed it so quickly. One gulp, wasn't it?"

"Yes." Koesler would never forget the incident, nor the look on Emma's face after she downed her husband's drink. "It seemed as if she was hit by two very powerful blows, first the drink, then, as it turns out, the poison."

"But what has Mike Ratigan got to do with all those people having—what was it?—Black Leaf 40 around?"

"He supplied it."

"He supplied it!" It sounded to Koesler's ears as if Ratigan had been involved in some sort of conspiracy.

"You see, Father, in 1976, Black Leaf 40 became a restricted substance and, by law, only certified pesticide applicators could buy the drug and only from specific wholesalers."

"What if someone were to break that law?" Koesler had a vision of his friend the bishop behind bars.

"A high misdemeanor."

Still the same vision.

"But you see, Father, Bishop Ratigan had purchased a large supply of Black Leaf 40 prior to 1976 and had given some to the Hoffmans for use in their greenhouse. Mrs. Hoffman, in turn, gave some of her supply to Mrs. Mercury and Mrs. Chase. None of them, apparently, was aware that they were in possession of a restricted substance.

"Not that many urban people are acquainted with Black Leaf 40 nowadays. And, of those who are, few know it is a restricted substance. Unless they try to purchase it now.

"The thing we must keep in mind, Father, is the significant toxic effect of nicotine. Black Leaf 40 is called '40' because the substance contains 40 percent nicotine and that, as I have noted, is, even in a very small quan-

tity, extremely poisonous to humans. Whoever chose a
nicotine product to place in Mr. Hoffman's drink could
depend on its being fatal."

"So, Mike gave the Hoffmans a supply of this insecticide while it was still legal to do so. And Emma Hoffman
gave it to her friends probably not realizing that it had become restricted. So far, there seems to be a good bit of
invincible ignorance going on. But what about Mike?
You haven't mentioned anything about his having been
found with any of this Black Leaf 40."

"That is correct. But the bishop was found in the possession of something even more potentially powerful—
nicotine bombs."

Koesler recalled the sign Ratigan had placed at the
door of the greenhouse in the rectory. And of Ratigan's
warning of how dangerous was the insecticide he was
using.

"Now that you mention it," said Koesler, "I recall
seeing the things around Mike's greenhouse. But they're
canisters, not in liquid form."

"That is true, Father. But now we are dealing with the
principle that anything that has been put into a compound
can be removed again. Along with other substances, nicotine, of course, is prominently present in a nicotine
bomb. And a press applied to the canister can extract a
liquid nicotine more potent even than Black Leaf 40.
And, since Bishop Ratigan remains on good terms with
his one-time employer, he has access to as much of this
as he wants."

Their waitress returned. They quickly consulted the
menu. Koesler, as he almost always did, orderd chopped
sirloin; Koznicki ordered scrod.

As the waitress took their order, Koesler studied her as
if seeing her for the first time. As she left the table, Koesler said, "My God! The waiter! I forgot the waiter—the

one who brought the drink to Frank Hoffman. How could I have overlooked him? He's so obvious!''

"A little too obvious." Koznicki smiled. "For one thing, Father, the waiter passed a polygraph test. Which does not prove very much, but it is an indication in his favor. The investigating officers do not consider him a suspect. He appears to be one of those jacks-of-all-trades. A waiter at the Collegiate Club and many other local restaurants, some local stage and nightclub work, managed a hotel, night watchman, that sort of thing. It is, of course, possible, but very unlikely. We are keeping an eye on him, Father, but not an extremely sharp eye.''

"That leaves Miss LeBlanc, I guess. Don't tell me she had some of that Black Leaf 40? If so, how did she get it?'' Koesler nibbled on a breadstick.

Koznicki finished the sherry and with his index finger pushed the empty glass across the table. "No, no Black Leaf 40. No greenhouse. No garden. She lives at 1300 Lafayette.''

Koesler of course recognized the address.

"Here again, Father, we are faced with the process of extracting something from a substance of which it is a component part. In this case, cigarettes.''

"I thought you said that the nicotine is burned up when cigarettes are smoked.''

"That is correct, Father. But the nicotine is part of a cigarette. Most cigarette advertising notes the nicotine content. Since the nicotine is a part of the tobacco, it is possible to extract this extremely potent poison. Although it is not a simple process, it is entirely feasible.'' Koznicki took a notepad from the inside pocket of his jacket and consulted several pages. "One needs an aqueous alkali such as sodium carbonate, sodium bicarbonate, or lime. Then some benzene ether, or some other suitable water-immiscible solvent.'' He returned the notes to his pocket. "It is by no means impossible to acquire these elements. After that, a scientific treatise available in any public library and some considerable chemical expertise, and,'' he spread his hands, palms upward, ''voila! One has an extremely toxic nicotine with which one might kill someone.''

The waitress brought their tossed salad. Each had selected the creamy garlic dressing.

Koesler speared a morsel of lettuce and dabbed it in the dressing. ''And in Miss LeBlanc's case?''

''The detectives found half a carton of cigarettes in her apartment.''

''That's unusual?''

''Miss LeBlanc does not smoke. A number of her friends can testify that to the best of their knowledge, she has never smoked. She herself admitted as much.''

''Then—?''

''She claims that she has been so nervous of late that she has taken up the practice for the first time. That, or,'' Koznicki paused with a forkful of lettuce in mid-air, ''she got them in order to extract a lethal substance.''

''And she has the skill to do that?''

''A brilliant student all the way through school. And an accomplished chemist throughout college.''

Koesler absently let his fork rest in the salad dish as he pondered all he had just heard.

''Then each of your suspects had motive, means, and opportunity to kill Frank Hoffman.''

''That would appear to be correct.''

''What happens next?''

''Detectives Ewing and Papkin have made a rather comprehensive list of the suspects under the factor of probability. They will continue their investigation, heavily concentrating on those they feel are the more likely suspects.''

As Koesler finished the salad as well as his drink, it occurred to him that his friend had been giving him more of the details of this investigation than Koesler had any right to expect. They had discussed homicide investigations in the past, but never in this great detail.

"Inspector, is there a reason you've gone into such great detail in telling me about this investigation?"

Koznicki allowed himself a brief smile. "It is admittedly rare that we have a homicide investigation that interests or involves you. But when we have, you have a history of being very helpful, to understate your past contributions. This is another of those times when you have some involvement, since, with the exception of Miss LeBlanc, you know everyone connected with this investigation. Indeed—again with the exception of Miss LeBlanc and, of course, Bishop Ratigan, who is in residence with you—all are your parishioners.

"With that in mind, I would like you to be informed of everything involved in this investigation. Frankly, in hopes that you may shed a little light on it.

"In any case, as you are wont to remind me from time to time, more things are wrought by prayer than this world knows of."

"What does that have to do with this?"

"Pray for us."

Cindy Mercury offered the two detectives coffee. Ewing declined, Papkin accepted.

The Mercurys were ill at ease. They were not used to having police officers in their home. And they knew that these detectives were investigating Emma Hoffman's murder. These same two detectives had been here just yesterday when, under the soft allaying spell spun by Ray Ewing, Angie had let the officers "just browse around." It was while browsing that they had found the Black Leaf 40. The fact that they had returned today seemed not to bode well.

Cindy placed the cup of coffee—black—on the occasional table near Papkin. Her hand was trembling sufficiently to rattle even the full cup in its saucer.

Papkin took a cautious sip of the steaming coffee. "Could I trouble you for an ashtray, ma'am?"

For a moment, Cindy could not remember where she kept the ashtrays. She hesitated, then went to the kitchen to get one.

Ewing shook his head. He didn't care whether his partner smoked. But he knew Papkin was trying to quit. Ewing wished he would do it cold turkey.

"So," said Angie, "what brings you back so soon?"

Ewing flipped open his notepad and smiled one of his winning smiles. "We just need a little more information. Just a few more questions we need cleared up. Nothing for you to be concerned about."

"But we answered all your questions yesterday," Cindy protested. She was twisting the small dish towel as if to wring it out. "We let you go all through our house. We didn't demand that you have a search warrant or anything. We've been very cooperative. What more do you want?"

Ewing turned his smile to her. "You have been very cooperative, ma'am. And don't think it isn't appreciated. But you've got to remember that less than two days ago, someone made an attempt on your brother's life. That attempt failed. But whoever was responsible is still out there somewhere. You want to do everything you can to help us apprehend the guilty party, don't you?"

Cindy nodded. She appeared to be emotionally drained.

"OK," Angie said, "what do you need to know?"

Ewing turned a few pages of his notepad. "Let's just go over the events of Monday evening again. Just the part when Frank Hoffman's third drink was delivered. Now, you got that drink for him, didn't you, Mrs. Mercury?"

"No. Yes. Well, sort of. Frank was standing there with an empty glass. He wanted another drink. Usually, the club waiters are more attentive: If a regular member has an empty glass they usually automatically replace it with a fresh drink. If the member doesn't want the new drink, the waiter simply returns it to the bar.

"But Monday, there were so many guests, it was almost impossible for the waiters to attend to everyone. And Frank was getting peeved. So I went to get a waiter. The waiter followed me back to our group. He took Frank's empty glass—I guess that had been his second drink—and then the waiter placed the fresh drink in Frank's hand—I guess that would have been his third drink."

"And then you stayed at your brother's side for the rest of the evening?" Ewing added a couple of words to his notes as Cindy recounted her actions.

"Well, until Em collapsed. Then things got pretty chaotic."

"Of course."

Papkin finished both coffee and cigarette. "Now then, Mr. Mercury, for your actions during the same period?"

Angie smiled—a bit nervously, Papkin thought.

"Well," he began, "I've told this all before . . . Monday night to one of the officers."

"Again, please, if you don't mind."

"Well, I was standing there with—let's see, Frank, Cindy, Em, Father Koesler, and Bishop Ratigan. Cindy got the waiter, just as she said. Bishop Ratigan was explaining some kind of church doctrine or practice. To be perfectly honest, I wasn't paying much attention."

"And why was that, Mr. Mercury?" Papkin was successfully fighting the urge to light another cigarette.

"Well, in the next group over was Jeanne Findlater, of Channel 7. I have a chance of getting a show on her channel and I wanted to talk to her about it."

"Then what happened?"

"You know," Mercury said apologetically, "Monday evening is kind of a long time ago. I know this is only Wednesday, but it's hard to remember every little detail clearly."

"Do your best."

"OK. Well, Frank and Em were kind of bristling at each other. Then, I think Bishop Ratigan left the group. I think he went to talk to Joe McCarthy. I suppose he really wanted to get away from the group until Frank and Em cooled off. Then, I got a chance to talk to Mrs. Findlater, and I left the group."

"And then what happened?" Papkin leaned forward.

A thin line of perspiration was forming on Angie's upper lip. "Well, I talked to Jeanne about the show—you know, the program I may get on Channel 7."

"Didn't you leave Mrs. Findlater to get her a drink?"

Mercury seemed to searching his memory. "Yeah . . . yeah, I guess I did."

"So, you went to the bar." Papkin made it sound as if going to the bar were a crime.

"I . . . I don't think I went to the bar."

"Suppose I tell you I know that you brought a drink to Mrs. Findlater?"

"I . . . I must have . . . gotten it from a waiter . . ."

"Suppose I tell you I have a waiter who saw you at the bar."

"Well . . . I must have forgotten. It's been a couple of days."

Papkin looked at his notepad. "You have a convenient memory, Mr. Mercury. Monday night you also forgot you were at the bar. According to the statement you made to Officer Henderson, you weren't anywhere near the bar all evening."

"I think it's time we called our lawyer!" Cindy was angry as well as agitated.

"There's no need for that, Mrs. Mercury." Ewing's voice had a calming tone. "Nobody's being charged with anything. We're just trying to get some things straight." He turned to Angie. "Do you want to clear up this little inconsistency, Mr. Mercury?"

Angie was rubbing his hands together forcefully. "Look, I went to the bar to get Jeanne a drink. When I got back with it, Frank and Em were really going at it. It wasn't that I was all by myself in eavesdropping on them. Everybody in the vicinity was watching and listening to the battle. I saw the waiter replace the glass in Frank's hand and then Em grabbed it, drank it, and collapsed. In a little while, it was obvious she was dead and pretty evident that she'd drunk poison that had been meant for Frank.

"I panicked. I knew that the way Frank and I feel about each other isn't exactly a secret. I didn't want to be placed anywhere near that bar. But I swear, I didn't put anything in Frank's drink! I couldn't do anything like that! Think it, maybe. Do it, no.

"Besides," he looked at the two officers beseechingly, "how could I possibly bring myself to kill somebody Cindy loves so much?"

The phone rang. Cindy went, somewhat unsteadily, to answer it.

Both the detectives knew that at least part of what Mercury was telling them now was the truth.

The media and show business people at Monday's party had been quite unanimous about the fact that Angie was not working all that much, while, at the same time, he was living well above his means. Strong opinions had been given the investigating officers that Angie was getting a healthy percentage of his income from Frank Hoffman and that neither Frank nor Angie was very happy about the arrangement. But both kept at least a superficial lid on their feelings for Cindy's sake.

The other verity, which no one questioned, was that Angie and Cindy were about as dedicatedly in love with each other as any two people could be.

Still, Angie had the motive, the means, and the best opportunity of attempting to kill Frank Hoffman of any of the suspects thus far discovered.

"It's for you, Sergeant Ewing." Cindy offered the cordless phone to the officer.

"What?" Ewing listened intently. "When? Where is he now? We'll be right there." He handed the phone to Angie.

"We've got to get right over to the Fisher Building," Ewing said.

"What's up?"

"Hoffman just got a note threatening his life."

"What?" Cindy lost what little color had remained in her cheeks. "Frank?" Her knees seemed about to buckle. Angie helped her to a chair. "Now, look what you've done!" Angie, on one knee beside his wife, turned angrily on the officers.

"One way or another she would have heard about it," said Papkin. "Sorry she had to hear it this way. But we'll want to talk to you again, Mercury, and soon. Don't go anywhere."

When last they had seen Frank Hoffman, he had been stunned at his wife's sudden death and angered that they wished to pry into his Last Will and Testament. But the Frank Hoffman Sergeants Ewing and Papkin now encountered was shaken and visibly frightened. He was seated—slumped might be a more accurate description—behind his desk in his office. A few of his associates were with him. The atmosphere was almost funereal.

The document in question was lying open atop a brown envelope, the only papers on the executive-sized desk.

Wordlessly, Ewing moved next to Hoffman in order to read the message. It was composed of words cut out of some publication and pasted onto a plain sheet of paper.

Ewing read aloud: "I missed the first time. I will not miss again. You are a dead man."

Ewing looked around. Besides the officers and Hoffman, there were three men and one woman in the room. "How many of you handled this?"

"As far as I know, just Mr. Hoffman and me." The man looked inquiringly at the others. All agreed: None of them had handled the paper.

"And you are—?"

"Kirkus. Al Kirkus. I'm Mr. Hoffman's assistant."

"I see. And how did the note arrive?"

"In the interoffice mail. In a company envelope."

Papkin carefully transferred the note and the envelope beneath it into a plastic evidence bag. He motioned Ewing to join him in a far corner of the room. "What do you think—Chase?"

"If it is," Ewing replied in a low tone, "he's being pretty obvious . . . and pretty stupid. He's the only suspect who actually works here. That is, unless we've got to add to the list of suspects."

"Don't even think that!"

They turned back to the silent group.

"Tell us about the interoffice mail," Papkin invited.

After a brief pause, during which there was some nonverbal jockeying to determine who would respond, Kirkus finally spoke. "The interoffice mail doesn't come or go through the post office. It originates in and passes through The Company."

"I assume," said Papkin, "that everyone who works here has access to the interoffice mail."

"Yes, that's correct."

"How about outsiders?"

"Why would anyone outside The Company want to use the interoffice mail?"

"Say someone did."

"If an outsider, for some reason, wanted to use our mail, and if he knew how to get into the system, I suppose it wouldn't be difficult."

"How does one plug into the system?"

"Just drop the envelope in the mailbag in the mailroom."

"Is the mailroom guarded?"

"Usually there's an attendant. But he takes the mail around to the various offices four times a day."

"At the same times each day?"

Kirkus nodded.

Papkin looked at Ewing. "I don't think we have to add to the list."

"The rest of you can leave now." said Ewing. "We'd like to talk to Mr. Hoffman."

The two detectives sat at the opposite side of the desk from Hoffman.

Hoffman quite obviously had been paying little attention to what had been said. He seemed in a daze.

"Mr. Hoffman," Ewing said. "Mr. Hoffman . . ." He had to repeat before Hoffman looked at him attentively. "Any ideas? About who sent this threat?"

"No. No, none."

"Mr. Hoffman, an attempt was made on your life Monday night. This is Wednesday afternoon. Haven't you been giving this any thought at all?"

"I've tried not to think of it. Or if I do, I try to think there was some mistake."

Ewing looked concerned and sympathetic. "I can understand how difficult this is for you. But we've trying to help you. And you've got to help us. You can best help us by trying to think of whoever it is who wants you dead."

"There's no stopping him, is there?"

"Who?"

Hoffman appeared to be self-absorbed. "If someone wants to kill me, really wants to kill me, there's no stopping him, is there?"

"We like to think we can do something about that."

"It could be in a drink. It could be in food. It could be when I'm driving the car. It could be while I'm asleep. There's just no stopping him. No stopping him if he's really determined."

There didn't seem much point in continuing what had become a soliloquy. The two officers once again urged Hoffman's cooperation; then they excused themselves.

Hoffman continued to sit at his desk looking absently at the opposite wall. "There's no stopping him. If he's really determined."

18.

MAYBE THE TRAPPISTS HAD THE RIGHT IDEA.

Father Koesler, as was his habit when driving, had his mind in neutral.

Of course one could never tell, what with post-conciliar change affecting just about everything in the Catholic Church, even the eremitical orders. But in the old days, when Trappists were into neither conversation nor Zen meditation, they used to bury their dead the next day. A monk might die today and tomorrow morning there'd be a funeral Mass. The body would be placed in the simplest of pine coffins. After the Mass, a procession of all the surviving monks would form and the coffin would be carried to the open grave. There the body was removed from the coffin and placed directly in the earth. Ashes to ashes, dust to dust, earth to earth. Maybe so. Koesler decided he would not mind if his remains were thus disposed of. As long as he was embalmed. His final desire, if he were to be buried, was that he be dead.

And that was all the time he had for daydreaming. It was a very brief distance from St. Anselm's rectory to Morand's Funeral Home on Ford Road. It was Wednesday, the evening before the obsequies of Emma Hoffman. Time, as far as traditional Catholics were concerned, for the traditional recitation of the rosary. For more updated Catholics, there were alternatives to the rosary for the vigil of burial services such as an appropriate scripture service.

Koesler smiled as he parked his car in the nearly filled lot. He recalled his own father's vigil service. All during the day of the vigil, his mother kept asking him when the rosary would be said. And all day, he kept explaining to her that some of his priest friends were going to gather that evening and have a scripture service. He kept assuring his mother that she would like the scripture service. That evening, about an hour before the scripture service was scheduled, his mother urged him to go out and get a quick dinner. While he was out, his mother secured another priest who led the rosary.

The following year, when his mother died, Koesler did not schedule a scripture service for her. He scheduled a rosary. And he led it.

But tonight he would be dealing with mostly traditional Catholics. He would lead the rosary as he had done hundreds of times before. While Bishop Ratigan would be the main concelebrant at tomorrow morning's funeral, the bishop would not attend the rosary service. Koesler sometimes wondered if, along with a general inability to remember the formula for absolution, bishops had forgotten how to say the rosary.

As he entered the majestic foyer of the Morand Funeral Home, Koesler was impressed at the bumper crowd. Mourners filled the room where Mrs. Hoffman's remains were displayed and the crowed spilled well into the foyer.

A small group surrounded Frank Hoffman, who did not seem to be paying much attention to them. He seemed to be searching for someone. As it happened, he was looking for Father Koesler. As soon as he caught sight of the priest, Hoffman excused himself and made his way past those offering condolences and over to Koesler.

"Father," Hoffman placed his hand on the priest's arm, "it isn't all that long since I've been to confession, but I want to go again—now. I really want to go to confession."

Koesler was surprised at the change that had come over Hoffman. His face was ashen, his pupils seemed a bit dilated, his lips appeared parched, and every hair was by no means in place. Koesler had seen similar changes in people who were deeply bereaved. But particularly over the recent past, he had not gotten the impression that Frank and Emma's mutual affection was such that either would have been terribly affected by the death of the other.

"Frank, don't you suppose you might be able to wait a little while? Maybe tomorrow morning we could get together before the funeral Mass." He looked at his watch. "It's a quarter to eight—fifteen minutes before the rosary is supposed to start. And if you go to confession, others may get the idea of going too."

"Father, please: Now!" Uncharacteristically, Hoffman was not angry at Koesler's reluctance to acquiesce to his wishes and hear a confession. He was simply pleading, an attitude Koesler could not refuse.

"All right, Frank. Just a minute while I get set up."

Hearing confessions at a funeral vigil, in Koesler's long experience, was neither common nor unheard-of. It was at best helpful and at worst awkward. Sometimes, at a solemn occasion such as this, people were inspired to make rather profound, soul-searching confessions. At the same time, the numbers who might avail themselves of this convenient opportunity to confess could delay the scheduled time for the recitation of the rosary; no cataclysmic occurrence on the face of it, except that Koesler's life was run by the sweep-second hand of his watch.

If he had a compulsion, it was punctuality. About the only time he was without his watch was when he showered. And, if asked, he would readily admit he missed it then.

In any case, he could not refuse Hoffman's plea.

Koesler left Hoffman and approached the funeral home's owner. They knew each other well. Koesler knew many mortuary proprietors. Death brought morticians and priests together regularly.

"Lou, the deceased's husband wants to go to confession. You know what that can start—a whole line of people who will follow suit. Can you set something up?"

"Certainly, Father."

The solicitous smile never left the mortician's face. Koesler was sure that turning his mortuary into a confessional didn't appeal to Morand any more than it did to him. Undoubtedly, the Hoffman vigil service would be delayed, thus upsetting the timing of services scheduled for the home's other two current corpses. But Morand would smile through it all. In his many dealings with morticians, Koesler had never experienced any who seemed upset by anything. If the image was the reality, then surely morticians were born, not made.

Morand set up a modest divider just inside the door of an empty "slumber room." A curtained screen was inserted in it. Long ago, Morand had converted the room-divider into a portable confessional for just such occasions.

Before taking his seat on the other side of the screen, Koesler motioned to Hoffman that his confessional was ready.

It was a peculiar arrangement. The room was large, well-lit, and empty but for this pseudo-confessional, a chair for the priest, and a kneeler for the penitent. Morand had set it up far enough within the room so that its existence would not be evident to the casual passerby.

One would need to be very observant to realize there was a confessional here. Morand did not want a long line of penitents any more than Koesler did.

The priest took from his coat pocket the narrow, short silk band, violet on one side, white on the other, that constituted a stole in emergencies. He kissed the cross on the violet side and draped the abbreviated vestment over his shoulders, violet side out. He waited. In a few moments, he heard movement on the prie-dieu on the other side of the screen.

"Bless me, Father, for I have sinned. It's been just a couple of weeks since my previous confession." Pause. "Father, I'm doomed. I'm a dead man."

"What do you mean?"

"I'm as good as dead. It could happen any minute. You know who I am. You were standing right beside me when my wife took the poison intended for me. Whoever did that hasn't given given up. I got a note today from the killer. He promised he'd get me."

Koesler hadn't known about the note, although mention of it had been made on the evening's local radio and TV newscasts.

Another leak at The Company.

"All of a sudden, it came to me . . . it dawned on me, Father: This is it. This is where life ends for me. I'm a healthy, relatively young man. I never think about death, about dying. Not until now. Now I've got to face death. I'm convinced that whoever it is that's trying to kill me is going to succeed. Maybe God's giving me a warning. I've got very little time left and I've got a lot of things to sort out, to make good before I face God in judgment. Help me, Father."

"OK, Frank, let's say you're right. Maybe God has given you an opportunity to straighten out your affairs. But we're all going to die. And none of us knows exactly when. You could be wrong—I hope you are—but it never hurts to come to a moment of self-reformation. Whatever gives you this grace, greet it sincerely. Now, why don't you tell God through me what troubles you—what you intend to reform.

Hoffman licked his lips. They were so dry they cracked.

"I hardly know where to start. Em and I practiced birth control for years. It wasn't her fault. It was my idea. I never confessed it. I suppose there were bad confessions when I didn't confess it—and bad communions.

"For years now, I've had a mistress—well, actually, a series of them. I have one now. We have sex regularly, several times a week on the average. She's a nice kid. Could have made something of her life if I hadn't dead-ended her. Maybe she still could do something with her life," he added thoughtfully.

Koesler well recalled the strikingly attractive blonde who had appeared unannounced at the Monday night party.

"I'm afraid I've plotted and schemed to undermine one of the executives at The Company. It was wrong. I took unfair advantage of him. It's possible—probable—I ruined his career. Hell!—excuse me, Father—but that's what I intended to do: ruin his career so I could climb into his place in The Company and then keep right on climbing."

So, thought Koesler, finally come the corporate sins. He didn't think Catholics could lead blameless lives from nine to five; he just couldn't recall many who ever confessed any such sins. Strange that it required the specter of death to bring business sins out of the closet.

"And I've treated my brother-in-law like dirt. I suppose I've always resented his marrying my sister. She could have done so much better. I've never given a damn about him—sorry, Father, but it's the truth. Without my sister, I wouldn't have given Angie a quarter if I met him on the street.

"But there was no way I was going to let Cindy suffer just because she happened to be married to a stage bum. So, I've subsidized them over the years. Only I've made Angie crawl. I've made him feel like what I considered him to be—dirt. It wasn't a good way to treat him. He never hurt me. I'm sorry for that now.

"Finally, I guess you know that Mike Ratigan and I are friends. But I've used and manipulated him too."

That did it, Koesler mused. He didn't know whether Hoffman was doing this consciously, but he had gone right down the list of suspects in this case. Somewhere in this confusion, Hoffman was confessing the sins he had committed against the very person who was trying to kill him. Sins that undoubtedly had motivated the would-be murderer.

"I don't think Mike knew it was happening. But the favors, the vacations, even a general bequest in my will—all of it was just a way of keeping him indebted to me so that when I needed anything from the Church I could get it from Mike. If the truth be known—and that's the whole idea of this confession—I've never respected Mike. There were any number of times when, if he had put his faith where his actions were, he would have stood up to me. But he never did. Or so rarely it didn't make any difference. Anyway, I'm sorry I manipulated him.

"That's about it, Father. If I did anything else wrong, I'm sorry for it. I don't want to die, but I'm convinced there's no way out of it. But I don't want to go to hell. I'm afraid. I'm afraid to die. And I'm afraid to go to hell." It was only with the greatest effort that Hoffman managed to keep from breaking down in tears.

Koesler could almost feel the nearly tangible relief Hoffman experienced with his confession. It happened every so often: a confession so torturous to make that the recounting of the sins became a catharsis.

"Frank," Koesler said gently, "there is a person in the Gospels you may remember. His name was Zacchaeus. He was described as a wealthy man but also as a very sinful man. One day Jesus singled Zacchaeus out from among all the other people in his town as the one with whom Jesus would stay. Zacchaeus felt very honored, and justly so. He also felt very humbled by the honor Jesus paid him. In this spirit, Zacchaeus made a little speech. He said, 'I give half my belongings to the poor, Lord. And if I have defrauded anyone in the least, I will pay him back fourfold.' And then Jesus replied, 'Today salvation has come to this house. The Son of Man has come to search out and save what is lost.'

"You see, Frank, that's what's happened for you tonight: Jesus has come to save what is lost. He's given you time and the impetus to repent and now He will forgive you your sins. That ought to make you feel as honored and grateful as Zacchaeus was. And, like Zacchaeus, you ought to want to make things right. It is one thing to ask God's forgiveness—and receive that forgiveness—and another thing to ask the forgiveness of those we have offended. But remember, Frank: Zacchaeus wanted to make everything right. Anyone he had defrauded, he intended to pay back fourfold. I think you ought to feel that way, too, Frank. And would you agree, if I made your penance to do your best to set things straight with all these people you've mentioned tonight?"

"Yes. I'll do it, Father! I'll do it!"

"Good."

As he went on to pronounce absolution, Koesler could not help but wonder whether, as a decided fringe benefit of his penance, Hoffman might not even yet thereby dissuade his would-be killer from his murderous course. If so, this could turn out to be one of the most effective confessions and penances in the history of the sacrament.

After Hoffman departed, Koesler decided to wait a moment to see if he might escape a contagion of confessions. But no sooner had Hoffman left the room than Koesler heard shuffling feet and two knees hitting the kneeler.

"Bless me, Father, for I have sinned. It's been a few months since my last confession. Say, can't I go to confession face to face?"

"We're not set up for it tonight."

"Oh. OK. Well, last time I confessed impatience with my husband and I was going to work on that. Specifically, I was going to stop complaining about how he always throws his soiled clothes in the laundry inside out. Well, I did OK with that resolution. In fact, it was perfect. But I still feel and express impatience with him. So this time, I think I'll resolve to be more patient with him when he loses patience with me."

Koesler told the woman he considered that to be both a good resolution and a good penance. And he absolved her.

She was followed by still another penitent. Koesler looked at his ever-present watch. Five after eight. He was late for the rosary. As was the case with the previous penitent, he had to fight back the urge to be impatient.

"Bless me, Father, for I have sinned. It's been two months since my last confession. And I didn't do anything."

"You didn't do anything? You didn't miss Mass or anything?"

"No. I didn't do anything. I was in the hospital."

This was by no means the first time Koesler had heard such a confession. He had no idea why patients in a hospital never did anything, much less committed a sin. But a great number of them seemed to share this experience.

"You're sorry for the sins of your past life, aren't you? Maybe especially for impatience?" He had to find something to forgive. One could not absolve from nothing. And impatience seemed to be popular tonight.

"Oh, yes, Father."

"Then for your penance say five Hail Marys."

Koesler absolved.

"One more thing, Father."

"Yes?"

"This is really neat."

"What?"

"Having confessions in a funeral home."

He might have argued the "neatness" of the custom. But there wasn't time.

As the latest penitent departed, Koesler decided to wait just a few seconds in case there was another. He did not wish to inflict embarrassment by bumping into someone entering the quasi-confessional—someone who might desire anonymity.

Sure enough, he heard slow, hesitant footsteps approaching. The penitent knelt. There was something different, something strange. He couldn't identify what it was. Perhaps the breathing. It was irregular. Was the person ill? He felt a presentiment. "Is something wrong?"

"Wrong?" An indifferent chuckle. "Yes, I'd . . . say so."

That voice again! The one he'd heard in the confessional just before Emma Hoffman had been killed.

"It's you again!"

"My, aren't . . . we perceptive."

Either a high-pitched male or a low-pitched female voice. But so blasé about such a serious matter that Koesler found it frightening. "Why are you here!" Koesler reflexively made it a challenge rather than a mere question.

"Why am . . . I here? Why . . . to confess. Why else

would anyone . . . come to confession?'' Another hu-
morless chuckle. ''This time I . . . have it for you . . .
priest.''

''Have what?''

''A sin. Just what you . . . were looking for. And not
just a slight sin. That would be . . . dull. I have a . . .
capital crime for you. I committed murder, once.'' It was
an effort to mimic an adolescent sing-song manner of
confessing. ''What is lost in . . . quantity is compen-
sated for in quality.''

''You killed Emma Hoffman!''

''As it turns out . . . yes.''

For one of the rare moments in his life, Koesler forgot
about time. There were serious things to be settled here.
There was the matter of surrender to the civil authorities,
particularly should an innocent person be harmed by an
investigation, a trial, a false conviction. More than anything was the fact that the penitent had killed the wrong
person and would very probably try again to kill Frank
Hoffman. But above all, there was the matter of sorrow,
contrition, amendment, atonement. The essentials to the
granting of absolution. He decided, before possibly wasting much time on the consequences of this sin, that he'd
better get down to the essence and see if there were any
reason to talk about undoing, to the extent possible, the
evil that had been done.

''From your tone and the manner of your presentation,
I find it difficult to believe you are sorry for what you
did.''

''Sorry? Sorry . . .'' The person seemed to be pondering the word. ''As it . . . turns out, I am not . . .
sorry for just about anything. I asked you to consider
. . . the devil living again on this earth. Do you . . .
suppose the devil can be sorry for what he does? Then do
not . . . expect me to be sorry!''

This was, by no means, a unique occurrence. In Koesler's experience, quite a few unrepentant sinners presented themselves in the confessional. Usually their presence was pro forma. They had sinned, thus it was only natural to visit the confessional. Perhaps they hoped that the priest might overlook their lack of true contrition. Perhaps they simply wanted to confide in someone even though absolution would be denied. However, Koesler had to admit that this was the first time contrition had been withheld by someone claiming to be the devil.

"Then I cannot absolve you. I cannot begin this act of reconciliation until and unless you have sorrow. Can we talk about that?"

"No! There is . . . no point. Let's just consider this . . . our little secret."

With that, the person rose and left the room, leaving Koesler badly shaken. For a fleeting moment, he had experienced the natural urge to discover the identity of this strange penitent. There was no Church rule or law against it; it simply was not in his character to dash around the screen and peek. As he respected the penitent's right to secrecy, he respected his or her right to anonymity. He considered it unseemly to violate either trust.

Fortunately, there were no more penitents. He would have had a decidedly difficult time concentrating on any more confessions. As it was, he was concerned about getting through the rosary.

The knock at the door startled her. She expected no one.

"Who is it?"

"It's me . . . Frank . . . Frank Hoffman."

She hesitated. "Just a minute." She opened the door. "You had the lock changed! Why did you do that?" A look of anger passed over his face and then it was gone. "Never mind," he added.

"Really, Frank—after all that's happened, I didn't really think we'd be getting together again. Or, if you did want to see me, I wasn't at all sure I wanted to see you. So, I had the lock changed."

"I don't blame you." Ordinarily he would have been livid at such a unilateral action. But this was the "new" Frank Hoffman. "You had every right to feel that way. But things have changed."

"That may be the understatement of the century." She was still wearing the simple yet attractive black dress she had worn at tonight's rosary service at the funeral home. "I have gone from being your closet mistress to being the occasion, if not the cause, of your wife's death. I'd say that marks a certain degree of change in our relationship!"

"No, Jackie; you don't understand. The change is in me. I saw you in the back of the crowd at the rosary this evening. I tried to talk to you afterward, but by the time I got back there, you'd gone."

In point of fact, on his way from the Dearborn funeral home to 1300 Lafayette, Hoffman had been forced once again to consider the possibility that Jackie had been responsible for the poisoned drink. However, that possibility made no difference in what he was determined to accomplish—nothing less than the radical reformation of his life.

He was thoroughly convinced that his death was imminent. There was nothing the police or anyone else could do to prevent it. Nowadays particularly, it was so simple for a determined killer to have his or her way. If it had not been for that bizarre accident of Em's grabbing the drink from his hand, he would be dead now. And they would be burying him tomorrow instead of Em.

In any case, it no longer mattered which of the suspects was the real perpetrator. What mattered was his certainty that in the relatively near future, he knew not when, he would be meeting his God in judgment. To a certain extent, he felt fortunate. God was giving him more than fair warning and a golden opportunity to make up for the past, set all matters straight, and prepare for eternity. He was determined to make good use of this opportunity.

So determined was he to make amends that it did not occur to him that in changing his life, he just might be persuading whoever was determined to kill him to change his or her mind. That Hoffman might be removing the grounds for which someone wanted to commit murder. Buying his eternal welfare by self-reformation might not have been a completely selfless consideration. But it was as close to altruism as Frank Hoffman had ever come.

"What did you want to talk to me about, Frank?" Jackie could not help but notice that some change, seemingly profound, had come over him.

Hoffman led her to the sofa near the window. Together, for a few moments, they watched absently as the Canadian Club sign continued to blink.

"After Em died," Hoffman said finally, "well, after I got over the shock of Em's death, I started thinking that perhaps it would be better for me if I never married again. Or, at least, not for a great number of years—"

"Frank, if you came all the way over here just to dump me, you needn't have bothered. I figured that's the way we were headed—Split City—without your having to tell me."

"No, no! On the contrary, I didn't come here to announce that we were finished. I came here to ask you to marry me."

"Frank!"

"As soon as possible. Before it's too late."

"Too late!"

"Never mind that. Just tell me: Will you marry me?"

"Frank! Of course! It's all I've ever wanted since we first got together. I mean, I'm sorry it had to happen this way—with your wife dying. But—oh, yes, Frank; I'd be proud to be your wife!"

"Good!" It was said with little romantic emotion. But then, he felt little romantic emotion. It was simply a base that needed touching on his circuit of reformation. And now it had been touched.

"But, Frank, how—?"

"Don't worry about it. I know this is sudden . . ." He stopped, smiled briefly, and shook his head. "Strange to say a proposal can be sudden after we've been practically living together for years. But it is sudden—at least unexpected—for both of us. But, it's the right thing to do. Yes," he nodded, "the right thing to do."

The right thing to do. When, she wondered, had she known him to be concerned about "the right thing to do"?

She was both surprised and a little frightened. Surprised, naturally, by his proposal when she had been convinced their relationship had been terminated. Frightened by the obvious change in him.

The thought crossed her mind that maybe it would be a good idea for them to date for a while before marriage. Could she be sure about entering wedlock with a man who suddenly appeared to be, in some respects, a stranger?

She quickly dismissed this thought as nonsense. If she knew any man, she knew Frank Hoffman, even if he did appear to be, in some respects, a stranger.

Perhaps he just needed a little something. He did look a bit ashen.

"Can I get you a drink?"

He considered. "I guess I could use a little something. I'll get it."

The surprises kept coming. She could not recall his ever volunteering to wait on himself. He went to the kitchen; she to the bedroom.

He dropped a large ice cube into a cocktail glass and added Dewar's. He glanced momentarily at the sweet and dry vermouth, closed the liquor cabinet and added water to the Scotch. It was a spontaneous decision. Along with all the other things in his life he was changing, he would alter his drinking habits. No more perfect Rob Roys. It was symbolic, but symbols were important indicators of change.

He stood before the window, letting the melting ice further dilute his drink and gazing at the lights of Windsor reflected in the now placid waters of the Detroit River. Gradually, he became aware of her presence.

He looked over his shoulder. She stood at the corner of the window, illuminated only by the reflected lights of the city. She wore a black lace negligee. Something from Frederick's of Hollywood that Hoffman had picked up on one of his New York trips. She had never worn it. The clinging, revealing garment accentuated her subtle youthful curves.

"Something for our celebration," she said.

The ice began to rattle against the side of Hoffman's glass. "Oh, my God!" he exclaimed with utmost sincerity. "Oh, my God, but you're beautiful!" It was evident that he was restraining himself only with great difficulty. "But we can't! We mustn't! Jackie, the flannel nightgown: Go put it on!"

"But . . ." She felt confused and not a little scorned.

"Please! The flannel nightgown!"

She disappeared into the bedroom. She felt oddly embarrassed, and tried with great difficulty to sort out her feelings. None but her parents, when they had had to diaper her, had seen her naked more often than Frank Hoffman. Why should he suddenly give the impression not only of being unfamiliar with her body but of being shocked at the sight of her in a seductive negligee. Heretofore, they had had no legal relationship. Now, they were virtually engaged.

She returned to the living room, in shapeless flannel from neck to toe, and hopeful for some sort of explanation.

"Jackie, I know this is going to sound incomprehensible to you, but I won't be able to sleep with you again until we're married."

"What!"

"I am in the state of . . . uh . . . grace for the first time in a long time, and I've got to maintain it. I can't chance going to hell."

"Well, I'll be damned! No; as a matter of fact, as long as I hang around with you, I won't be."

It all fell into place. It had finally dawned on Frank Hoffman that he was mortal: He had been scared into virtue. Enough of her Catholic training remained to enable her to recognize the signs. His was a deathbed conversion without the bed. Definitely without the bed.

She could scarcely argue with it since his change of heart had prompted him to want to make an honest woman of her.

"So," she said, open to suggestion, "what's next?"

"I think we ought to say our night prayers and then go to sleep. I've got a big day tomorrow." He breathed a quick prayer that he would have a full day. "I'll sleep on the couch."

Night prayers. All she could recall was, "Now I lay me down to sleep." Inappropriate. "You lead."

"All right."

He stumbled through some half-forgotten formal

prayer, bade her a chaste goodnight, turned out the light, and easily found the couch.

The extinguishing of the lights was noted by the occupants of a car parked on East Larned.

"Looks like they've gone to bed," noted Sergeant Ewing.

"But not necessarily to sleep," added Sergeant Papkin.

They continued their protective surveillance of Frank Hoffman. They would be relieved at midnight. Till then, they would sip coffee from a thermos and imagine how nice it would be to be home with their wives.

19.

IT WASN'T WHAT IT USED TO BE. OH, NOT THAT there hadn't been division among the clergy even in the good old days. But the major split of yore had been between the older and younger priests. Or, more specifically, between pastors and assistants.

These thoughts occurred to Father Koesler as he welcomed the visiting priests to St. Anselm's rectory. They were gathering for Emma Hoffman's funeral.

Koesler recalled an incident that had taught him his place as a very young priest in the sacerdotal pecking order. He had been ordained only a couple of years when he attended a priests' retreat given by the noted Redemptorist theologian, Father Francis J. Connell. During one of Connell's conferences, Koesler found himself seated in the rear of the chapel directly behind an enormous, bald pastor.

Connell was referring to the relationship between pastors and curates, when he stopped and corrected himself. "I'm sorry," he said, "out here you call curates 'assistants,' don't you?" At which the fat pastor had stagewhispered to his companion, "Out here we call them assholes." The two had laughed heartily. Only respect

249

for the elderly had kept Koesler from knocking their heads together.

It had been as if a tight-knit group of pastors had to circle their wagons to protect the territorial imperatives of their parishes from the covetous hands of their eager assistants.

But even then, with vast differences in age and position, there had existed a strong fraternity of like-minded clerics. Virtually no one had argued about theology. Everyone had believed in one doctrine and one morality.

Now, the divisions among priests frequently were sharp and profound. And one, particularly one who was familiar with the old camaraderie, could see evidences of this in just such a gathering as this in St. Anselm's rectory. Whereas a few years before there would have been one or two groups and much intermingling, now there were quite a few very small groups and almost no intermingling. Greetings at the door were hearty enough, but then the newly arrived priest would find the appropriate companions in one of the rooms of the rectory and in compatible company don his Mass vestments.

Popularly, the blame for the recent sharp divisions in the Church was laid at the door of the Second Vatican Council. The Council was indeed responsible for drastic liturgical change. But the substantial change in hierarchical structure, the free-wheeling questioning of the Council's utterances, its brave entry into the modern world, all had been pretty well stifled by Roman curial authorities. With the exception of some very bad new hymns and pedestrian vernacular texts, Vatican II was now, by and large, an ineffectual memory.

Koesler had long thought the far more likely, if subtle, cause of divisions among the clergy as well as laity must be ascribed to the decision made by Pope Paul VI to override the majority opinion of his own birth control commission. On July 29, 1968, the Pope had released his encyclical, *Humanae Vitae*—Of Human Life—and Koesler now dated everything from that.

He could well recall when, shortly after that encyclical was published, Archbishop Boyle and his auxiliary bishops, Bishop Ratigan among them, were going about the archdiocese, meeting with territorial groups of priests, trying to explain the meaning and implications of the encyclical.

As far as many of the older priests were concerned, the Pope had made his decision; there was no need of further explanation. Nothing had changed; all methods of artificial contraception were condemned. Again. *Roma locuta est, causa finita.*

As far as many of the younger clergy and the majority of younger Catholic laity were concerned, the Pope clearly had been wrong. His citing of the natural law as the basis for his reasoning was misplaced at best and quite incorrect at worst.

And if the Pope could be mistaken, or dead wrong, on what or whom could one—at least a loyal Catholic—depend?

As far as Koesler was concerned, it was not the closing of the Vatican Council in 1965, but the promulgation of *Humanae Vitae* in 1968 that had split the Church asunder.

For the most part, the laity and some of the clergy had resolved the question of family planning quite apart from the Church's magisterium. The remainder of the clergy and the hierarchy were holding fast to a moral teaching that was backed only by longevity. Koesler wondered whether the Church would ever again be able to teach with its former authority. He doubted it.

He kept these thoughts in mind as he wandered from room to room, identifying each group by the century they seemed to inhabit. He attempted to get the various groups to intermingle but was largely unsuccessful.

There was only one clear-cut conclusion to be drawn from a rectory full of priests in various stages of vesting: A funeral involving wealthy, influential Catholics draws a bumper crop of clergy.

The usual funeral home procedure was being turned topsy-turvy.

Ordinarily, the bereaved family remains in one place near the coffin while visitors approach to offer condolences and, perhaps, pause at the bier to offer a prayer.

In the case of the Hoffman wake, Frank Hoffman's two sons and his daughter and their families occupied the traditional position by the bier. But Frank seemed to flit from one spot to another in the large room, with little rhyme or reason.

He had been standing with his daughter when his sister and brother-in-law entered. Immediately, he crossed to them, greeted his sister perfunctorily and took Angie Mercury aside.

"I've got to talk to you."

"Sure, Frank." Mercury couldn't put his finger on it, but there was something different about Hoffman.

"Listen, Angie; we both know I've been giving you a monthly allotment and we both know it's only because you're married to my sister."

Mercury nodded with ill-disguised bitterness.

"I haven't asked that you repay any of it; we both know you couldn't have—let alone considered any interest.

"But I have exacted payment from you, and I want to acknowledge that right now. I've forced you to eat humble pie not only when I gave money but at every moment of our relationship. I've insisted that you admit your dependence on my money. I've insulted your profession. And there was no good reason for that. However you happen to be doing in it, the theater is a very viable way of life and I shouldn't have belittled it—or you."

Mercury's jaw was beginning to hang loose.

"And I know that when we competed at anything, you had to lose and I had to win no matter whether you could have beaten me in a fair match. And that's not all: I cheated on a pretty regular basis."

Mercury's mouth was just plain open.

"I just wanted to tell you, Angie, that all that shit . . . uh . . . nonsense is going to stop, as of now. I'm going to use every contact I have, in whatever time is left me, to help you get the good, fat parts. And if you continue to need any help, it'll be there. Only in a quiet unobtrusive way."

"Frank, you don't have to—"

Hoffman held up a hand. "Along with the promises I've just made goes my apology for the way I've treated you."

"Frank, I . . . I just don't know what to say."

"No need to say anything, Angie. That's the way it's going to be. Now, why don't you rejoin Cindy. And be sure to see me after the funeral."

Hoffman returned to his place near the bier. Mourners and those offering condolences continued to stream by. After greeting the bereaved family, visitors would try to find a place to sit or stand in the fast-becoming-congested room.

Hoffman's height allowed him to see over the heads of most of the visitors. He spotted Charles and Louise Chase entering at the rear of the room. They did not appear to be making any effort to enter the line of those proceeding to the bier. Hoffman approached the Chases and maneuvered them into an alcove where he could speak to them in relative privacy.

"We're sorry about Em's death." Louise Chase intended to make it clear from the outset that Emma's demise was the one and only reason they had come.

"Thank you, Louise. It was good of you both to come. But I have something to say to you and I've got to say it while I have time.

"Charles, what I did to you through the assistants I sent you was unforgivable. So I am not asking your forgiveness. But I do want to apologize."

Charles Chase's face remained immobile, his expression severe.

"I know an apology is small coin for the damage I did to your career as well as to you personally. So I have gone a step further than an apology. This morning, I sent a hand-delivered letter to Frank Martin, with copies to the other members of the board, detailing my responsibility for what happened at the meeting. I also tendered my resignation.

"I understand that even this cannot erase the harm I've caused you. But it should go a long way toward correcting the damage. It is both the least and the most I can do."

There was an embarrassed silence that was almost broken by Louise. But, sensing that Hoffman had addressed his apology to her husband, she decided that if either of them were to respond, it would be her husband's place to do so.

But he did not.

"Well," Hoffman shrugged, "that's about it. Sorry I entered your life. I will now leave it."

Hoffman returned to his place in front of the room.

"Don't you think you should have made some sort of response, dear?" asked Louise. "After all, it was a most generous move on Frank's part. He's sacrificed his career for yours. Granted he's the one who ruined yours; still, it is a rather remarkable act of reparation."

The stern expression had not left Chase's face. "I'll

believe that son of a bitch when I see the letter with my own eyes and not one second before.''

Along with relatives, friends, and neighbors, quite a few representatives from The Company were gathering. The time was nearing to close the proceedings at the Morand Funeral Home and move on to St. Anselm's Church. The large room was now almost completely filled. It was Standing Room Only.

At long last, Hoffman spotted the last two people he had intended to speak to before the funeral. Fortunately, both Al Kirkus and Clem Keely, along with their wives, were together in the line of those offering condolences. And again fortunately, they were near the end of the line. It was relatively simple for Hoffman to steer the two men off to one side.

"I did something this morning that you two should know about." He looked from one to the other. Both met his gaze. He had their attention.

"I sent a letter to Frank Martin and the other board members explaining what we did to Charles Chase."

"You did wha—?"

Hoffman's upraised hand stopped Kirkus. It was indicative of his shocked reaction to Hoffman's statement that Kirkus would dare question his superior.

"In explaining what caused Chase to miss the mark so badly in his report, I naturally had to include the role you two played." He sensed their agitation and anxiety, so he quickly added, "Of course, I took complete responsibility for the entire affair. I don't think The Company will come down on you too hard. After all, you were only following my orders."

Keely appeared ready to offer a rebuttal, but Hoffman's raised hand put an end to that before it had a chance to begin. "That's the way it is, gentlemen, and the way it's got to be. Thanks for coming. I'll see you after the funeral."

They passed Hoffman's grieving family and the bier. Keely was numb with fear for his future with The Company. Kirkus was lost in thought: Now this is a strange turn of events. Who would think that Hoffman would do anything so completely stupid? All I hoped to accomplish was to scare him into getting out of there—taking an early retirement and opening up a position for me. I wonder how serious I would have been about actually killing the bastard if I had known he was going to blow the whistle on us. No, I don't think I could actually have killed him. Not even Hoffman. Threatening is one thing; actually killing is something else.

Louis Morand ushered the visitors out of the room and into their cars, almost all of which were products of The Company. Small flags with a cross insignia were attached to fenders. It would be one of the largest funeral processions in Morand's memory. Inside, a curtain was drawn to spare the bereaved family the sight of the closing of Emma Hoffman's coffin for the final time.

Kirkus, sitting silently in his car, continued to ponder the threatening note he had sent to Hoffman. He was beginning to second-guess himself. Would that note become a problem sometime in the future?

Kirkus could not know that it had been his threatening note that had brought about Hoffman's change of heart and compulsive need to confess and repair. Kirkus, all unknowing, had scared Hoffman into a wave of virtue that might very well imperil himself.

Mike Ratigan looked like a bishop should, thought Koesler.

The vested clergy stood in the rear of St. Anselm's as the cortege approached. Koesler looked about. No one could claim that they turned priests out on an assembly line. They came in every variety. But Mike Ratigan, tall, slender, athletic, looked every inch the bishop with the miter on his head and crosier in hand.

Finally, everyone was parked and assembled. The pallbearers, all Company men, bore the coffin into the vestibule, where they placed it atop the wheeled cart.

Bishop Ratigan sprinkled the coffin with holy water and prepared to drape it with a ceremonial white cloth. Frank Hoffman, first in line behind the coffin, circled it and rather urgently whispered something to Ratigan. The two conversed, in whispers, but intently, for several moments.

The others wondered what they could be saying. Koesler, if he had had to guess, would have supposed that Hoffman was carrying out the penance that had been imposed last night. Scarcely ever had Koesler encountered a penitent more genuinely frightened and—at least seemingly—repentant than Hoffman.

But one confession reminded Koesler of another.

Actually, the bizarre penitent who had now confessed twice to Koesler was never far from the priest's thoughts and concern. Whoever it was had managed to maintain anonymity not only by confessing on the other side of a protective screen, but also by creating—that was the only word to describe it—a strange, if not unique, vocal sound, secure in the knowledge that the rules of the confessional oblige the priest to do nothing that might enable others to connect the penitent to the sin.

The classic case held up to the newly ordained was the possibly apocryphal story of the new priest hearing confessions for the first time. Afterward, he emerges from the box to join the party his relatives are throwing for him. "You wouldn't believe it," he says to an assembled group of kin and confreres, "but the first penitent I heard confessed adultery!" Not a minute later, an attractive woman in a nearby convivial cluster was heard to say, ". . . I was the first one to go to confession to Father."

Of course the thought had crossed Koesler's mind that it was always possible that the strange person who had confessed the killing had been lying. But it was not very likely. Koesler was well aware that police throughout the world had their "professional confessors"—people who had a pathological need to confess to crimes they had not committed. But these were public penitents of a sort, who needed the attention and notoriety. It would be unlikely to find such a person getting his or her gratification in the internal forum and secrecy of the confessional. Besides, the cardinal rule of thumb for confessors was that they were to believe the penitent no matter whether he was accusing or excusing himself.

The procession reformed and began making its way up to the front of the church. There were too many priests to all fit into the sanctuary. So the two front pews on the left side had been reserved for the visiting clergy.

Koesler watched the long line weave its way up the middle aisle. Pity they never taught marching in the seminary. Priests' processions were notorious for their serpentine conformation.

As he pondered the goodly number of priests present, Koesler was reminded of a similar occasion at another parish years before. Instead of a funeral, it was the silver wedding anniversary of a couple who happened to have many priest friends. As was the case now, the sanctuary had been overflowing with priests. The altar boys, whom Koesler had trained but not prepared for such a priestly onslaught, were mightily impressed by the sight of more clergymen than they knew existed. So, for their own unfathomable reasons, they placed at the communion rail the six large black candleholders with their unbleached candles. Candles that were used exclusively for funerals. The couple was henceforth forced to endure predictable jokes about this ecclesial commentary on their twenty-five years of marital bliss. Father Koesler's clerical friends had never let him forget it either.

The Mass of Resurrection for Emma Hoffman proceeded without incident.

A few years before, Koesler would have had to train altar boys in the then complex ceremonies of the solemn pontifical Mass. But now, bishops put on their own miters, had no gremiels placed on their laps when seated, and no one any longer followed them about with a lit candle.

All of the priests present pronounced aloud the words of consecration. Words which, according to Catholic dogma, transformed the bread and wine into the real presence of Jesus Christ, while the appearance of bread and wine remained. Koesler was once again impressed that this, the Mass, was the thread that held together the fabric of the Catholic priesthood. Each priest present— slender, fat, old, young, traditional, liberal, conservative—found his common denominator in these common words of consecration.

At communion, Koesler watched as many came forward to received the consecrated wafers. Among them were those suspected of Emma's murder: Angie Mercury, Charles Chase, Louise Chase—even Bishop Ratigan himself, though he seemed to be taking his official interrogation rather lightly. And, although she did not present herself for communion, Jacqueline LeBlanc was present. Koesler could see her near the rear of the church.

Amazing to think that in all probability one of them had killed Emma Hoffman in an attempt on the life of Frank. Here they all were in the same church at the same time, attending the funeral of the woman one of them had killed.

It was like a mystery story.

And whoever had done it had been to confession to Koesler—twice. And he had no idea which one it might be.

And even if he were able to cut through the disguise and anonymity and identify the culprit through his or her confession, what could he do with the knowledge? There was the storied—by now clichéd—seal of confession to deal with.

Koesler looked about and marveled at all the secrets that were being kept by all the priests here today. One more thing that united them in a unique fraternity.

Although he could never envision himself violating the seal of confession, Koesler had a long-standing, at least theoretical, problem with the secrecy of the confessional. Was there, he wondered, no possible exception to this rule?

Jesus may indeed have commissioned His Apostles and their successors to forgive sin when He said, "Receive the Holy Spirit. Whose sins you shall forgive, they are forgiven. Whose sins you shall retain, they are retained." But there was no record of His having said anything about keeping sins a secret. That was what was termed a theological conclusion.

Koesler noticed Father Leo Clark in the front pew. The avant garde theologian from the major seminary was seated next to Father John Schwartz, who customarily identified himself as a retired veteran of World War I. The twenty-first century sitting next to the thirteenth. They wore identical vestments and, given an after-dinner drink, could find any number of Catholic traditions they could share and agree upon.

Koesler had recently spoken to Father Clark about a more contemporary view of the seal. It was Clark's opinion that the very nature of confession bound the confessor to do nothing the penitent would find odious. Obviously, this would include not revealing what any specific penitent had said in the confessional and certainly not connecting any particular penitent with any particular sin. But the notion that there could be absolutely no exception to this rule was no longer alluded to. While, in theory, this made the fabled seal slightly more open-ended, Koesler still could not envision any circumstance that could justify the violation of such a sacred trust.

In any case, there was no purpose in even contemplating using in any way what he'd learned from the person who had confessed murder. All Koesler knew from two encounters was that someone—male or female, he didn't know which—had confessed to murder. Whoever it was was able to project a strange ambiguous speaking voice. And finally, the person seemed to be under the delusion that he or she was either possessed or obsessed by the devil. Of course, the possibility of a genuine diabolical influence could not be completely dismissed. But it surely was not very plausible.

The Mass of Resurrection was concluded, as were the prayers for the deceased as well as the bereaved. The procession reformed, the clergy again preceding the coffin, which was followed by the laity. At the door of the church, the procession halted as Bishop Ratigan once more sprinkled the casket with holy water, a gesture that would be repeated by each priest in attendance.

As Koesler concluded his rite of sprinkling the casket and handed the aspergillum to the next priest in line, Frank Hoffman approached him.

"You're going to the cemetery, aren't you, Father?"

"Certainly, Frank."

"And you'll be coming to the hall for a bite to eat?"

"I'd like to Frank, but I'm pressed for time. I've got an important appointment early this afternoon. I am sorry."

"That's OK, Father. But I wanted to thank you for hearing my confession last night. I feel like a new man, literally. Whatever happens now, I'm ready."

"Good, Frank. God bless you."

Koesler stepped back against the wall and thought,

whoever might doubt the axiom that confession is good
for the soul ought to consult with Frank Hoffman.

It was not the sort of appointment that Koesler favored.
But he had agreed to meet with the lad. So he would.

The priest sat at the desk in his office. He was studying
several brochures and newspaper clippings. He had decided it would be a good idea to make some preparation
for the upcoming appointment.

The prospect of this meeting was beginning to depress
him. In no little manner he had been buoyed by the apparent spiritual rebirth of Frank Hoffman. It was good to see
a penitent put his spiritual house in order. Unfortunate
that it had to be caused by the threat of imminent death.
But, Koesler reminded himself, the beginning of wisdom
was the fear of the Lord.

What most distressed Koesler about the coming meeting was that the person with whom he had the appointment didn't really want to meet with him. The young
man's parents had arranged for the meeting. Koesler was
not the type to impose himself on an unwilling listener.
He would have made one of the world's worst salesmen.
Every once in a while, he thanked God for the law
obliging Catholics to attend Mass. Although he was
rather good at preaching, he was pleased that he did not
have to "sell" his services. He pitied his Protestant confreres who had no such law to enforce attendance at Sunday services.

The doorbell rang.

Koesler checked his watch. Precisely 1:00 P.M. Good;
he appreciated promptness. He had informed Mary
O'Connor, the secretary, that he was expecting an appointment at one, so he would answer the door himself.

"Good afternoon, Father." Tom Costello, an
eighteen-year-old college freshman, stood at the door.

He wore a black topcoat over a dark blue suit, white shirt, and dark blue tie. His hair was cut in an Ivy League style. Koesler knew that one could scarcely find that cut anymore.

"Come in, Tommy." Koesler led his visitor down the short hallway into the small office. They sat at opposite sides of the desk.

Koesler moved the clipping he'd been reading to the center of the desk.

"Your parents tell me you're transferring to the Maharishi International University."

"That's right."

"That's quite a transfer—from Henry Ford Community College to MIU. And all the way from Dearborn to Fairfield, Iowa."

"Sometimes a person's life has to change drastically, Father."

"I know." Koesler had just finished encouraging one man, Frank Hoffman, to do just that—make a drastic change in his life. Now, he would try to convince a younger man that his proposed radical change in life would prove unwise. "But are you sure you're doing the right thing?"

"Who can be sure, Father? It seems right. It sure got me to clean up my act."

"That it did," Koesler was forced to agree. Until recently, Tom Costello had been a dropout from polite society. Over his parents' constant objections, he had stopped going to Mass during his high school years and began associating with a tough, boisterous crowd. Now, in a 180-degree turnabout, he was headed for a pseudo-religious institution and, as his meticulous grooming attested, he had indeed cleaned up his act.

"Speaking of cleaning up your act, Tom, when did all this happen? Last time I saw you, you were in Levis and your hair was down to here. And look at you now."

Tom smiled self-consciously. "A couple of months ago—just after we began classes in September. A representative of MIU came on campus. There was a notice on the bulletin board."

"But why would that attract you, Tom?"

"I'm not sure, Father. Someplace down deep inside, I had this uncomfortable feeling. Like my life was going in sixteen directions at one time. This representative of MIU maintained that transcendental meditation could put my life together again. So, I went to see. Well, I saw. And I bought."

Koesler leaned forward, resting his elbows on his desk. "You know, Tom, this business of Eastern gurus on our campuses is a comparatively recent phenomenon. Think back as early as the sixteenth century, when Francis Xavier, on the orders of Ignatius Loyola, went to India, China, and Japan, evangelizing in the East. From that time on, a constant stream of Christian missionaries, Protestant as well as Catholic, has been carrying the message of Christianity to the East. But, in just the last quarter century, approximately, there has been this growing trickle of Eastern gurus becoming evangelists, as it were, for everything from Confucianism to Zen to TM, and some really bizarre offshoots, to boot."

"Well, fair is fair. We did it to them. Now it's their turn to do it to us." Tom's jaw was becoming fixed. Since making his decision he had had to face one challenge after another.

"But doesn't it make you wonder, Tom? Transcendental meditation, under one form or another, has been around as long as Christianity, some two thousand years. Yet it was only in 1957 that the Maharishi Mahesh Yogi brought TM to this country."

"I guess it was just time."

"Time, Tom, and, I would suggest, money."

A smile crossed Tom's face. He had fielded this question many times. "Everybody needs some operating capital. What was it somebody once said about the marks of the true Church—One, holy, Catholic, apostolic, and bingo?"

"OK, score one for your side. Everybody needs some capital. But I don't think you could say that Francis Xavier went to India and the East to get rich. Nor do most Christian missionaries go from the richest countries in the world to the poorest in order to get rich and build up operating capital. On the other hand, most of the gurus of the East come from very poor countries to the richest countries of the world. I would only submit for your consideration, Tom, that there may be a less than purely altruistic intent in this latter-day missionary activity."

"Well, for God's sake, Father, I don't know what everybody's getting so excited about. After all, I'm hardly going off the deep end. I mean, I'm not joining the Moonies or Hare Krishna!"

"I know you're not, Tom. And thank God you're not. But, have you given any thought to the fact that you're about to enter a foreign culture?"

"Foreign culture!"

"Tom, the Maharishi's transcendental meditation comes from India's Vedic Science of Enlightenment. It was born, grew up, and developed as a part of Eastern civilization. It is part of Eastern culture. But you are a product of Western civilization. No matter what happens, you're never going to be comfortable immersed in a culture that is foreign to you."

"For God's sake; I'm going to learn to meditate. You don't have anything against meditation, do you?"

Koesler couldn't help smiling. He was reminded of the old Bing Crosby film, *Going My Way*—specifically, the scene where Father Fitzgibbon, played by Barry Fitzgerald, shows Father Chuck O'Malley, played by Crosby, around the cloistered parish gardens. Fitzgibbon observes that the garden is a good place in which to meditate, and quickly adds, "You do meditate, don't you?"

"Yes," Koesler replied, "I believe in meditation. But even there we are going to find differences. When you reach the ultimate in meditation—contemplation—you also encounter the phenomenon of an altered state of mind . . . almost a programmed unconsciousness."

Tom nodded. He was familiar with the terms.

"OK," Koesler continued, "now, in the East, this altered state of consciousness is the whole goal of the contemplative exercise . . . a kind of nothingness, nirvana. Whereas, in our culture, the altered state of mind sometimes achieved in contemplation is not the end in itself, but a means to another end. In the altered state of consciousness, one is better able to unite oneself with God. For us, the altered state of consciousness is a vehicle for prayer. For perhaps the most sublime prayer man can achieve."

Tom hesitated. "I . . . I didn't know there was any mysticism but Eastern mysticism."

"Oh, but yes, Tom. Western civilization would not have developed as it has—perhaps would not have developed at all—without its heritage of a distinctly Western mysticism.

"There is nothing 'wrong' about Eastern mysticism and such great religious movements as Confucianism, Buddhism, and Zen. Nor is there anything 'wrong' with those of us who are products of Western civilization using some of the Eastern methods—as long as we know what makes us what we are. Many Trappists use the methods of Zen to achieve an altered state of consciousness. But they never forget that what they've achieved is not an end in itself, but an effective and beautiful means toward prayer."

"I . . . I never quite thought of it that way, Father.

I've got to admit, you've given me something to think about,''

"Why don't you let me help you rethink the whole thing? What you are interested in, transcendental meditation, is an altered state of consciousness. It can be an end in itself, or it can be a means to an end. It is not altogether different from self-hypnosis—''

There was an awkward silence wherein the priest appeared to become lost in his own thoughts.

To fill the vacuum, Tom Costello began to talk, though he didn't really have anything to say. "I think that's really interesting, Father, about how the purpose of contemplation is so different in the West from the East.''

Tom continued to talk. Koesler was aware the young man was saying something, but the priest was off in another world.

It resembled the conclusion of a famous musical: In New York, Tommy Alcott's fiancée is talking to him. But, though her lips continue to move, Tommy doesn't hear a word she's saying. He hears the singing of his friends and his true love, Fiona, back in Brigadoon.

". . . self-hypnosis . . .''

". . . self-hypnosis . . .''

". . . hypnosis . . .''

". . . hypnosis . . .''

Something someone had told him recently. But, what? It was as if Koesler had stumbled upon the final missing piece of a jigsaw puzzle, but paradoxically he didn't know where it fit.

". . . hypnosis . . .''

". . . hypnosis . . .''

Yes, that's where he'd heard it. But why was it important? He'd have to think it through. Now, while the thought was fresh.

"Tommy," Koesler interrupted the young man in mid-meaningless sentence, "excuse me, but I just re-

membered something and I've got to follow it through
right now.'' He turned in his swivel chair and took a
small paperback from the shelf behind the desk and
handed it to Tommy. "I'd like you to read this. It's *The
Cloud of Unknowing*. It's by an anonymous fourteenth
century mystic and it's a classic. It will help show you the
contemplative treasures of Western civilization. After
you've read it, let's talk again. It may work out that you
will go to MIU. But I'd like you to agree with me that
you will get a lot more out of an authentic Eastern mysticism if you know who you are and a lot more about the
culture that produced you. OK?''

They stood, shook hands, and, armed with the small
paperback, Tom Costello went out to rethink things.

Koesler stood in the rectory corridor smiling. What
would Father Dowling do in a spot like this? Probably
light his pipe and ponder the thing in a cloud of smoke.

But Koesler had quit smoking. And, while Dowling
was on the wagon, Koesler definitely was not. However,
it was much too early for a drink. He decided to go over
to the quiet church and think things through. Yes, he decided, Dowling would approve.

Koesler sat in the rear pew. Somehow, he always
found that an empty church was more quiet and condu-
cive to thought than any other place he'd ever experienced.

Perhaps he ought to try to put himself in an altered
state of consciousness. Short of that, he would try to recall everything he had witnessed the night Emma Hoffman died and see if he could fit this piece of the puzzle in
place.

He had arrived a little late and parked in a crowded lot.
He'd given himself a private tour of the ground floor of
the Collegiate Club and had been surprised at the lack of
security in such an exclusive private club.

He'd entered the room where the party was being held.

No, he hadn't. Not quite. He'd stood in the doorway for a while, getting the lay of the land, as it were.

He'd noticed the registration desk and the bar. Both busy places.

He'd seen Frank Hoffman approach the Martins and give them the good news, as Koesler later learned, of their scheduled private audience with the Pope.

Then he'd seen Charles Chase with his wife and Emma Hoffman as well as Cindy Mercury. The three women had gone off to the ladies' room together. Koesler remembered wondering about that custom that seemed to preclude any woman's going to the ladies' room alone.

Funny, but he couldn't recall seeing them come back.

Looking for familiar faces, he'd spied Hoffman, Mike Ratigan, and Angie Mercury together. He'd joined them. They were later joined by Emma and Cindy.

Frank had started a quarrel with his wife. No . . . no, that's not the way it happened. Frank had been rather happy over the papal audience. Emma had started the quarrel. Then Cindy had left the group to get a waiter to serve Frank another drink. Then the quarrel had heated up considerably.

Angie Mercury had seemed distracted. There was someone nearby he wanted to talk to. Koesler couldn't remember her name . . . some woman executive of a local TV station, as he recalled.

Then Ratigan had left the circle, presumably to talk to someone. He had been followed by Mercury, who finally got to speak with the lady in question.

Next, a new person had intruded on their small circle. It had turned out to be Hoffman's very attractive mistress, Jacqueline LeBlanc. At that point, as the expression goes, everything hit the fan.

While the argument between Hoffman, his wife, and his mistress intensified, first Ratigan, then Mercury had returned to the group. Now Koesler tried to remember what had happened next in as great detail as possible, since it was the instant Emma had surprisingly grabbed the poisoned drink from her husband and downed it.

There had been a waiter standing on the fringe of the circle. It was he who had held the poisoned drink. Koesler could see him in his mind's eye. The waiter, as was nearly everyone else, had been embarrassed by the vicious argument. Cindy had called her brother's attention to his drink. Frank had taken the drink from the waiter. With a defiant cry, Emma had grabbed the glass from her husband, downed it quickly, and had seemed to be hit by two successive blows. First by the highly alcoholic beverage, then by the poison. She had collapsed, gone into convulsions, and died. Rather quickly—all things considered. Koesler later thought, mercifully quickly.

Now, Koesler asked himself, where, in that scenario did his tentatively identified piece of the puzzle fit?

If it fit at all, it would be applicable to only two people. Koesler considered each separately.

If he applied the hypothesis to the one—no; that didn't make any sense at all. But if he applied the hypothesis to the other—? Yes . . . everything seemed to fall into place.

He tried to keep his exuberance in check. It was, after all, no more than a hypothesis. But, if he were correct, he had solved the murder.

He needed only to make a few phone calls. If they checked out, his next call would be to the police.

Father Koesler hurried from the church back to the rectory.

20.

"WANT SOME MORE COFFEE?" Sergeant Ewing was pouring himself another cup.

Sergeant Papkin shook his head. "I'll float."

Ewing returned to the large table that served as a desk in their squad room, and sat opposite Papkin. He stirred the steaming brew before him. "Well, the Hoffman woman was buried this morning, and this is the third day of our investigation. I think we ought to branch out a bit. What do you think?"

"Where?"

"I'd say Ms. LeBlanc. I know that all our suspects have motive, means, and opportunity. But I just like her motive best. The mistress who's been on the back burner too long. Well set up, but no public life at all. Can't be seen with her john. Maybe begins to believe she's about to be dumped. She figures to see enough dough from his will to set herself up pretty good. Move away from here. Start over somewhere else. You know, hell hath no fury and all that.

"I like her opportunity too. The others' whereabouts are pretty well on record. But she comes in out of nowhere. No one knew she was there till she came and stood on the fringe of the group. Finally recognized by Emma, then sighted by Frank Hoffman.

"She could have just walked into the room. Walked over to the bar. Who would notice? The room was crowded. She finds Hoffman's standing drink. No problem; his name identifies it as his. She drops the nicotine in the drink. Goes over to the reception table. Gets her sticker. Walks over to the group. She knows her presence will cause a scene. More than likely, Hoffman will want another Rob Roy. You know, 'This calls for a drink' kind of situation.

"So Jackie just stands there, waiting for her Frankie to take the poison. But, unexpectedly, his wife grabs the drink from his hand and swallows it before anyone can stop her. Jackie couldn't stop her in any case since that would be an admission that she knew something was in the drink."

Ewing sipped his coffee and smiled at his partner. "Well, what do you think?"

Papkin had listened to the scenario behind unrevealing eyes. "I don't swallow it. For one thing, if Ms. LeBlanc could enter unnoticed, and put the poison in the drink unnoticed, why bother joining Hoffman's group and making herself noticed? Why not just drop in, drop the poison in, and then leave, with nobody the wiser?"

"No," he shook his head, "your problem is you're always looking for the subtle suspect."

"What do you mean?"

"We've got somebody else at the bar."

"Who?"

"Mercury. Angie Mercury. You're assuming LeBlanc might have gone to the bar and dropped the poison. You don't have to assume anything when it comes to Mercury. He went to get a drink for someone. He was at the bar. All he'd have to do is move over, by actual count, two feet from the spot where he picked up the lady's drink to stand right in front of Hoffman's. At that point, he takes a small vial—he only needs a few drops—from his pocket. It's hidden in his palm; he holds his hand over Hoffman's drink, pours in the poison, turns, brings the lady her drink. Then all he has to do is wait for Hoffman to have one more perfect Rob Roy.

"But, the same thing then happens as in your scenario: He watches in satisfaction as Hoffman takes his drink. Then he can't believe it when Emma grabs the drink and downs it. He can't stop her for the same reason you proposed. If he did, he'd be admitting he knew something was wrong with the drink. Besides, she drank it so quickly no one could have prevented it."

"Except someone standing right next to her."

"But none of the subjects was."

Ewing drained his cup. "So you say it was Mercury."

"Right."

"Charlie, we questioned him just yesterday."

"Yes, and we were reaching him. If we hadn't gotten that call about the threatening note that Hoffman received; if I had had just a little while longer with him, he would have cracked."

"He's also got a nervous wife, who was on the verge of calling their attorney."

"Let her, I say."

"Charlie, we're three days into this thing. A few more days and you know as well as I that the Inspector is going to want us to move on. We can't take a chance of concentrating on just one suspect. We've got to play the field as long as we can before we decide to come down on one of them.

"So what about the LeBlanc woman? And don't forget, we haven't scratched the surface with either Charles or Louise Chase. Then, there's the bishop—the one who could immediately put his hand on a ton of nicotine."

"I've got it in my guts, Ray. An hour, maybe two, I

could crack Mercury. Don't forget: He lied to us about not being at the bar. And if he lied to us once . . . I know if I can get those lies he's telling us lined up, we'd have him cold.''

Without knocking, Inspector Koznicki opened the door to the squad room. He was wearing blue, pin-striped trousers, a matching unbuttoned vest, and a white shirt open at the neck. "Good," he said, "you're still here. Father Koesler just phoned."

Father Koesler? Papkin had been concentrating so hard on the suspects in the Hoffman killing that the priest's name did not ring an immediate bell. Then he remembered that the priest was the Inspector's personal friend.

Koznicki was, for him, somewhat excited. "In his characteristic humble manner, Father told me he thinks he may have stumbled across the solution to the Hoffman case.''

Oh, he has, has he? thought Papkin.

"He would like for us to meet him," said Koznicki.

Big deal, thought Papkin.

"Where?" asked Ewing.

"At the Mercury home," Koznicki responded.

Smart man, thought Papkin.

As the car bearing the three police officers turned onto the street where the Mercurys lived, they saw Father Koesler in his yellow Cheetah parked several houses the other side of the Mercury home.

The unmarked police vehicle, Papkin driving, pulled up directly in front of the house. As soon as it came to a stop, the occupants of both cars emerged. There was a man whom none of the officers recognized with Koesler. They all met on the walk leading to the Mercury house, where Koesler introduced the officers to Rudy Scholl, whom Koesler identified as a friend and a doctor of psychology.

"As I explained to the Inspector," Koesler addressed Papkin and Ewing, "this is no more than a hypothesis on my part. However, I checked out its plausibility with Dr. Scholl here, and he told me I was operating at least in the realm of possibility. I've thought this out quite carefully, and I think at worst, my hypothesis will not cause any harm and at best, it might just provide the answer to this case.

"And, I hasten to add," Koesler was painfully aware that he, an amateur in the field of crime investigation, was speaking to professionals, "I have arrived at this hypothesis mostly from information I don't think you had access to directly.

"With that, gentlemen, shall we try it out?"

All five men approached the door. Koesler pressed the bell. After a few moments, Cindy Mercury opened the door. Quickly, she scanned the serious faces of the men. She appeared apprehensive. None of her visitors could blame her.

After a slight hesitation, she stammered, "M-my husband isn't home."

"We didn't come to see your husband," Koesler replied. "We came to see you, Cindy."

Her countenance clearly expressed fear and confusion. Nevertheless, she invited them in. They found seats in various locations in the living room, leaving Cindy only a straightback chair for herself. Her eyes darted from one to the other of the men.

"Cindy," Koesler broke the silence, "we've come to talk to you about Emma's death."

"To me?"

"Since Monday night when this terrible tragedy occurred, everyone has assumed," he paused, realizing that he was including professional crime investigators, "everyone, with very good reason, has assumed that the intended victim of the killer was your brother Frank. And that Emma became the unintended victim when she impulsively took the poisoned Rob Roy from him and drank it."

"Of course everyone assumed that." Cindy's voice was strained. "Everyone saw what happened. The drink was Frank's, a perfect Rob Roy. He would have drunk it if Em hadn't taken it from him. What else could it be?"

"What if, Cindy . . . what if Frank were not the intended victim? What if the person responsible for poisoning the drink actually intended to kill Emma?"

"But . . . but that's ridiculous! If anyone wanted to poison Em, they would have put the poison in Em's drink. She drank martinis. Everyone knows that. In fact, she'd had a couple of martinis earlier in the evening."

"That's right, Cindy. Emma drank martinis. But she was not one of those celebrities who had their specialized drinks prepared. With Emma, there was little opportunity to poison a drink that never left her hand after the waiter had given it to her. Besides, if someone were to poison Emma's drink, then everyone would know that Emma was the intended victim. Just as all 'knew' Frank was the intended victim because it was his drink that had been poisoned."

"And what difference would that make?"

"Quite a bit of difference, I think. For about three days now, the police have been operating under the assumption that Frank was the intended victim. They have been looking for someone who had the motive," Koesler tried to recall Inspector Koznicki's words, "the motive, the means, and the opportunity. There has been the added pressure of the fact that, under this assumption, whoever tried to kill Frank failed, and so that someone is still out there someplace. And Frank's life is still in danger.

"Now, if Frank was really not the intended victim, the

police are looking for the wrong person and for the wrong reason."

There followed a significant pause during which it became evident that the only person who was ill at ease was Cindy. And she was very ill at ease. "I . . . I think I'd better call my attorney."

"You may do that, of course, Mrs. Mercury," said Koznicki. "But, at most, he can advise you on which questions to answer and which he finds it advisable for you not to respond to. And I believe that, up to this point, Father Koesler has not asked you any questions. He has been explaining a theory he has. You are the one who has been asking the questions. Now, Father can continue the explanation of his theory whether or not your attorney is present. That is what you intend to do, is it not, Father—to continue the explication of your thoughts on this matter?"

Koesler nodded.

After a moment, Cindy shrugged.

"So," Koesler continued, "let's suppose that Emma was the real intended victim—"

"It's an impossible assumption, Father," Cindy interrupted. "It's so obvious that whoever put that poison in Frank's drink meant it for him! Em's grabbing his glass could be nothing but an impulsive gesture.

"Even granting, just for the moment, that someone would poison Frank's drink to throw the police off the track—how could that 'someone' possibly get Em, if she were the real intended victim, to take it from Frank and drink it herself?"

The identical question was in the mind of the three officers. They, naturally, had not expressed it. But now that Cindy had, they turned to Koesler for his response.

"How about the power of suggestion?"

The blood seemed to drain from Cindy's face. She appeared about to faint. Dr. Scholl moved toward her, but she waved him away. She sat very still and very upright, the fingers of her right hand pinching her forehead, eyes closed as if she were enduring a very painful headache.

"I am so sorry, Cindy," said Koesler. "But I think we're getting at the truth now. You see, I learned a lot of things at the party you had here a week ago. They weren't things I was trying to learn about you in some gossipy context. It was information that in some cases was almost forced on me.

"All of us who were at that party will remember what a central role Emma Hoffman played and how she sort of orchestrated the events of that evening to their unhappy conclusion."

Koesler was aware that, of the six people presently seated in the Mercury living room, only he and Cindy had been present at the party in question. Thus, he would have to recap briefly the sequence of events leading to Emma's revelation of some dark family secrets.

It was also important for Koesler to make clear that his knowledge derived from what had transpired at that party and not from any privileged communication. Cindy certainly had made apparent in the confessional their living far beyond their means as well as their dependence on her brother's dole. But Koesler, in the explanation of this part of his theory, was basing it on what he had learned at the party, not on what Cindy had told him in the confessional.

"Undoubtedly, it was because Emma was . . . uh . . . in her cups and at least slightly intoxicated that she began to reveal some of the family secrets. Among them was the obvious statement that Angie was not working in the theater that much or that well. She then made the equally obvious implication that you were living far beyond the rather meager income that Angie was able to eke out of show business. Emma also made plain that your income was being substantially augmented by her husband, referring to him as your rich relative. She also made evident her disapproval of the entire affair. From all she said, I think it safe to assume that should she have had her way, Frank's contribution to your income would cease.

"That put you under enormous pressure, Cindy. So much pressure, indeed, that you ran to your room weeping uncontrollably.

"The pressure you felt was completely understandable. You love your husband. You realize that in his profession, the appearance is quite as important as the substance. You understand this because at one time you shared that profession with him. Angie told me about that earlier in the evening.

"You knew that Angie was determined to stay in show business whether or not, at the moment, he was achieving success. You were determined to support him in what had become a facade.

"The only thing that permitted you to keep up appearances was the subsidy from your brother. His contribution might have been somewhat demeaning, but it was dependable. You are justly confident of your brother's love and care for you. All others might desert you, but not your brother. You could be sure that in life or in death, he would provide for you.

"If your brother were to die, naturally, accidentally, or by homicide, you could trust his will to provide for you amply. But you had no reason to want him dead. You loved him and he would continue caring for you while he lived.

"The only possible fly in this ointment was Emma. As Frank's wife, she was arguably at least as close to him as anyone else, perhaps closer than anyone else. She was being openly sarcastic about Angie's inability to maintain your lifestyle without Frank's continued assistance. What if she tried to cut off these funds? She was the only one who might try. And who was to know what sort of pressure she might bring to bear on Frank? Who could be sure she might not find enough of a threat to Frank to finally discourage even him from continuing to help you?

"Your only ultimate security was in the elimination somehow of Emma. But how to do it? If even you want to be objective about it, Frank has a lot of potential enemies. But Emma apparently had few. Her greatest enemy, judging by the violent argument they had the night of your party as well as at the party at the club, was her husband.

"Now, if an attempt were made directly on the life of Emma Hoffman, successfully or not, the prime suspects very likely would have been Frank and you. Frank because they obviously were not getting along. And you because it could easily be demonstrated that she was a threat to the lifestyle you are, in effect, being forced to live by the vagaries of Angie's career.

"So you devised the ingenious plan of going after Emma through Frank. Then the authorities would logically be searching for someone who might want to kill Frank. Which certainly would not be you. They would have no reason to try to find someone who might want Emma out of the way.

"Frank would not be a suspect because he obviously had no control of his wife's seemingly impulsive action in taking his glass and drinking its contents. You would not be a suspect because the attempt at murder was made against Frank, and you would be among the last persons who would want him dead for any reason whatsoever."

Koesler paused to allow his explication, still incomplete, to sink in. Cindy had not moved. She still sat upright, eyes closed, fingers pressing into her forehead.

"Father," said Inspector Koznicki, "if you do not mind my intruding, your explanation of motive was very strong. No stronger, however, than the police might have made had Mrs. Mercury been a viable suspect. But your hypothesis that Emma Hoffman was the real intended victim remains as unlikely as ever. The charge you are making is most serious. And you have said nothing that would alter the extremely logical assumption that Frank Hoffman was the intended victim. It was his drink that was poisoned. Emma Hoffman has been described by many who knew her well as an impetuous, impulsive woman. It would seem that her action in taking a drink meant for her husband would have been right in character.''

"I agree, Inspector. I must admit I was astounded by her behavior the moment I saw her grab that glass. But when so many of her friends as well as her husband described her as a most impulsive person, I could understand what she did in that context.

"Now that I look back at it, I think I tended to believe her action to be spontaneous partly because she had the reputation of being such an impulsive person and partly because because there simply was no other credible explanation for what she did.

"But I remember thinking all the while, as I'm sure all of us did, what a fantastic coincidence! Think of the odds against her picking the precise moment that her husband is holding a poisoned drink to snatch it from him and drink it! Undoubtedly, he had never before held a lethal drink or, in all probability, he would not be with us today. So, the one time in his life he is about to drink something someone has poisoned and intended for him, he doesn't drink it because of his wife's impetuosity. What a coincidence.

"But," Koesler made a gesture of helplessness, "what else was there to believe? There was no other explanation. I do not believe that God needlessly multiplies miracles. And, ordinarily, I do not credit miraculous sorts of coincidences such as this one. But, as I've said, and as we would agree, there was no other explanation.

"Until . . . until earlier this afternoon. I was talking with a young man about transcendental meditation and contemplation. And I mentioned to him a theory that the altered state of consciousness sometimes achieved as an element of contemplation is a form of self-hypnosis.

"Then, suddenly, I recalled that at that party, in this very same room, Angie Mercury was telling me about their early life together. How Cindy had dived right in to join him in his theatrical career. How, together, they had done musicals and almost every imaginable form of show business entertainment, including nightclub acts.

"And part of their act was the ever-popular hypnosis shtick. Where volunteers from the audience come up on stage. They are hypnotized and given sometimes silly, sometimes awe-inspiring, post-hypnotic suggestions. I think we've all seen such acts. As a result of a post-hypnotic suggestion, a perfectly normal person will cluck like a chicken. Or another will find it impossible to lift his right arm.

"Recall, gentlemen, because it is important in what we will consider now, if a subject is going to slip into a hypnotic state, it takes a qualified hypnotist only a few moments to induce the trance."

The three officers and the doctor nodded in agreement. Each was familiar with such demonstrations. Cindy remained immobile.

"Well, according to Angie, this was one of the acts he and Cindy had performed. And he had added that, possibly to relieve boredom, or for whatever reason, they had switched roles from time to time, one of them working the audience, the other playing the part of the hypnotist.

"So, Cindy is not only capable of hypnotizing people; from all indications, she is proficient in it.

"At this point in my reasoning, I began to put together

another concept. An alternative, if you will, to the plot that had Emma acting spontaneously and impulsively.

"We already know that the Chase, Hoffman, and Mercury households had on hand a supply of Black Leaf 40, which comprises a powerful nicotine poison. Jacqueline LeBlanc had the potential of extracting nicotine from cigarettes. And poor Bishop Ratigan, God save him, not only had a nicotine bomb, he was all unwittingly responsible for the others having a supply of a controlled substance. So, everyone, including Cindy, had access to the type of poison that was actually used.

"And, as a result of what I have just postulated, we know that Cindy had a motive for wanting Emma silenced.

"Now, let me combine what I witnessed at the scene of the murder with what I think went on behind the scene.

"When I entered the Harvard Room, where the Martin party was being held, I naturally looked around for people I knew. The first ones I saw were Emma, Cindy, and Louise Chase, who were standing together talking with Mr. Chase. Then I watched the three women—as it turns out, they were the only women in the whole room I actually knew—anyway, I saw the three of them cross the room, go down the hall, and enter the ladies' room. I remember reflecting on the phenomenon of women never visiting the rest room alone, but always in couples or groups.

"That was when Cindy had the opportunity of quickly inducing in Emma a hypnotic state and offering the post-hypnotic suggestion that, at a given signal, she would take her husband's Rob Roy and drink it herself.

"There is nothing in that suggestion that would conflict with either Emma's morals or standards. It would be in keeping with her usual custom of doing things impulsively—and show up her husband at the same time. And Dr. Scholl here has assured me that the usually strong-willed Emma would be even more apt to submit to the hypnotic state and suggestion since she had been drinking."

"Just a moment, Father," Inspector Koznicki felt that he must play the devil's advocate since someone eventually would, "do you not think you are assuming too much at this point? All you saw was the three women going into the ladies' room together. You have no way of knowing what went on while they were in there."

"That's true, Inspector. But remember, I'm trying to build a hypothesis that will stand or fall only when it has been completely explicated and examined.

"However, at this point, I should tell you that before coming here this afternoon, I called Louise Chase and asked her if she could remember anything unusual or out of the ordinary happening when she and Emma and Cindy visited the ladies' room at the club. After some thought, she told me that one thing had surprised her. Cindy had asked if she would mind leaving her alone with Emma for a while, saying she had something personal to discuss with her sister-in-law. So, Louise had left the other two in the powder room adjacent to the toilet section. The two of them were alone, then, for several minutes."

The other men in the room seemed to gaze at Cindy more intently.

Father Koesler shifted in his chair. Though eager that the others understand his hypothesis, he was in no great hurry to rush through its explanation lest he omit a vital consideration.

"After I saw the women enter the ladies' room, I looked about for other people I might know. I spotted Frank Hoffman, whom I had seen earlier talking to the Martins. Frank was with Angie and Bishop Ratigan, so I joined them. We talked a bit about the private papal audience that the bishop had secured as a gift Frank could present to the Martins. Then, Cindy and Emma joined us.

"Frank got angry because he was standing there with an empty glass in his hand and no waiter had come to serve him another drink. A nasty argument began between Frank and Emma. At this point, Cindy left the group to find a waiter. It was the only time Cindy was away from the group. She was with the group, as was I, during the crucial time when the drink was poisoned. So, how could she have poisoned the drink? How, unless she had arranged for someone else to poison it for her?"

"The waiter," suggested Koznicki, softly.

Koesler pointed at the Inspector as if he had won a game of charades. "The waiter," Koesler affirmed. "I believe the newspapers mentioned that the waiter in question had a work history of a lot of odd jobs, among them some in show business."

The others nodded.

"If you check into it, and I'm sure you will," Koesler nodded at Koznicki, "I think you will find that this particular waiter may have worked with the Mercurys or at least in a hypnotic act. Which doesn't really matter.

"In any event, I believe what happened at this point was that Cindy quickly beckoned the waiter into a quiet corner, and just as quickly led him into a shallow hypnotic state and suggested that besides bringing him the presently called-for drink, that at a future signal from her, he would fetch Frank another drink. Only this time, he would pour the contents of a vial—she may even have told him the vial contained something like cold medicine—into Frank's drink before presenting it. None of which would have offended the waiter's hypnotized sensibilities. And which would not have interfered with his passing a polygraph test, as she would have programmed him to forget the posthypnotic suggestion had been made.

"So, Cindy returns to the group and the waiter re-places Frank's glass with another—harmless—Rob Roy, the one already mixed.

"The argument between Frank and Emma intensifies; and, when Jacqueline LeBlanc arrives on the scene, the volcano erupts. I remember that while the furor was going on, Cindy summoned the waiter and asked him to get Frank another drink. I thought it a bit odd since Frank had not completely drained his previous drink. But I believe *that*—asking the waiter to get Frank a fresh drink—was the prearranged signal of the posthypnotic suggestion. The waiter picked up Frank's perfect Rob Roy, and poured into it the contents of the vial—possibly the so-called 'cold medicine'—Cindy had given him.

"Next, I remember that when the waiter returned with the drink—which we would later learn was poisoned—he simply stood on the fringe of the circle. Then Cindy said something again—something like, 'Your drink is here, Frank.' That, I believe, was the verbal cue that triggered the posthypnotic suggestion for Emma, who took the glass from her husband, downed the contents, and died, almost instantly.

"And that, gentlemen, is my theory of what happened Monday evening. The wrong person did not die. Emma was the intended victim all along. As the result of a rather complex and ingenious plot, Cindy was able to make everyone think her brother was the intended victim, and everyone's attention was thus diverted from the actual victim and the actual perpetrator.

"And," Koesler emphasized, "just in case anything went wrong with her plan, as a sort of fail-safe measure, Cindy was able to be right on the scene. If, for example, Emma did not reach for Frank's glass, or if she had hesitated—if for any reason the posthypnotic suggestion did not work, Cindy was right there to, say, take Frank's glass from him or even 'accidentally' knock it out of his hand.

"And Cindy," Koesler addressed the still immobile woman, "Dr. Scholl assures me that we will more than likely be able to induce another hypnotic state in the waiter. And, in such a state, he should be able to recall the events of Monday evening and tell us about your leading him to an altered state of consciousness, and also about the posthypnotic suggestion you gave him. I came here first, rather than to the waiter, out of deference to you. So that you could tell us why you did it.

"Even though we know that you were trying to protect your husband—his career as well as his lifestyle, which was just about as important to him as life itself—I still don't understand how a good woman, good mother, and good wife could actually plan and carry out a murder. It just doesn't make sense to me."

At this point, Koznicki raised a cautionary hand to Koesler. "Mrs. Mercury, it is my duty to inform you that you have the right to remain silent . . ." As the Inspector continued with the Miranda warning, a strange thing happened. Slowly, Cindy removed her hand from in front of her face. She looked up at Koesler with a most peculiar smile. Suddenly, she no longer resembled Cindy Mercury. Something had transformed her. Or at least there was enough changed about her eyes and mouth that she looked like a completely different woman. Koesler had seen such a transformation before only in movies with the aid of cinematical special effects.

"That's right, priest . . . Cindy could . . . not have . . . done it."

It was Cindy speaking, but not with her voice. Not even close. It was the same peculiar, androgynous voice that Koesler had heard twice before in a confessional setting.

"Cindy *what*—?" Koesler half rose from his chair.

"No . . . let her talk, Father." Dr. Scholl, from behind Koesler, put a restraining hand on the priest's shoulder. "If Cindy didn't do it, who did?"

"You're smart men—or, at . . . least you're supposed
to be . . . smart men. You figured out . . . everything
else. Why . . . couldn't you figure out . . . it was me?"

"I guess we weren't so smart after all," Scholl replied. "Tell me, who are you?"

There was a long pause while Cindy's lips worked
wordlessly. Then, "Why, I'm . . . Audrey, of course."

"Of course you are," said Scholl. "How stupid of us
not to recognize you. Have you been with us before?"

"With the . . . priest, twice." She sneered. "But, he
didn't . . . recognize me. Even when I . . . promised
him I . . . would see him again." She laughed; it was a
diabolical sound.

Koznicki looked inquiringly at Koesler, who shook his
head and soundlessly mouthed, "Confession: the seal."
Koznicki nodded and returned his gaze to Cindy—or
Audrey.

Sergeants Ewing and Papkins's attention was riveted
on her.

"So," said Scholl, "you were with us more than just
the two times you visited with Father. When else were
you here, Audrey?"

"At the party at the . . . Collegiate Club, fool! How
else could I . . . have killed Em."

"So, it was you who killed Emma Hoffman! Did you
do it the way Father described?"

She looked at Koesler with loathing. It almost seemed
as if she were going to spit on him. "Yes! Lucky . . .
guess, priest."

"Tell us about it, Audrey."

She smiled crookedly, as if envisaging something both
satisfying and evil. "I made sure Emma had . . . enough
to drink so she wouldn't be too . . . . alert. I waited until

there were no others in the . . . powder room. Then I asked . . . Louise to leave us alone. I . . . massaged Em's neck while she . . . sat in front of the mirror. It took only a few . . . moments and she was under, at least enough to accept the suggestion.''

"Didn't your voice frighten Emma?"

"I used . . . Cindy's voice. I also borrowed her skills as . . . as hypnotist.'' She giggled, a little girl who had done something naughty.

"What was the signal that would trigger the post-hypnotic suggestion?"

"When I . . . said, 'Here's your drink, Frank,' she would show him who's boss, take the glass from him and drink it down.''

"How about the waiter?"

"Him . . . too. I . . . never worked . . . with him before. But I'd seen him in . . . a hypnosis skit once. He was a . . . good subject. I recognized him once . . . before when I was at . . . the club. In fact, when I saw him there . . . before, that's when I began to build my . . . plot. I . . . knew I could hypnotize him. When I was confident I could . . . hypnotize Em, the plan was complete.''

"It was a clever plan, Audrey.''

"Satanic. . . . Would you go so far . . . as to say it was . . . Satanic?'' she cackled.

"Maybe, maybe not,'' ventured Dr. Scholl. "That will take a little study and involve our working together. You know you will have to be arrested, don't you, Audrey?"

"It . . . doesn't matter. You can't hurt me!'' she shrieked. "You can only hurt Cindy!''

Everyone was chilled by the weird, eerie cacophony.

Suddenly, the woman's expression changed radically. Her eyes softened and her mouth smoothed. "I . . . I . . .'' It was unmistakably Cindy's voice.

She collapsed. But before she slumped to the floor, Dr. Scholl, who had been inching forward during his conversation with "Audrey," caught her.

The three officers exchanged glances. Without a word, each asked the other if he had ever had a case like this. Each silently communicated: "Never."

21.

"THE PHONE IS FOR YOU, MR. HOFFMAN."

Hoffman was surprised. He had not told anyone he had planned to stop off at the Collegiate Club after the funeral. His loose schedule called for a brief stop at the club. He wanted to pick up his athletic gear and make sure all his bills were paid. That would pretty well tie up all loose ends.

He never would have thought the preparation for his own death could be such a satisfying experience. By now, he'd become quite at ease with the idea of his impending death. He was convinced that whoever was intent on killing him would succeed. Who could stop it? But with a good confession behind him and all the amends he was making for past sins, he was in pretty good condition to meet his Maker. Most of all, he hated the thought of having to part from the body he had taken such pains to keep youthful, trim, and healthy. What a waste!

After the club, he planned on seeing Jackie and making plans for their wedding. He was quite sure he would not live long enough to see that wedding, but it would be a kind touch to at least give her the pleasure of planning it. He considered the way he was feeling might be akin to what Ebenezer Scrooge felt after his encounter with the Ghosts of Christmas.

"Hoffman here."

"This is Father Koesler, Frank. I've been trying all over to reach you."

"What can I do for you, Father? I'm in a bit of a rush."

'I've got some important news for you, Frank. Something you should know as soon as possible. That's why I've been calling everywhere for you. The police think the case is closed."

"The case? You mean they know who tried to kill me?"

"It's a bit involved. There are parts of it you'll find hard to believe. It's important that we meet so I can explain this in detail."

"Wait, Father. This is terribly important: Tell me all you can about it now."

"OK, Frank. I'll sketch it out now and later we can go over it more specifically.

"First of all, Frank, you were not the intended victim."

"Not the—! Then, who—?"

"Your wife."

"Em? That's crazy. She took the poison from me."

"That's one of the reasons I want to go over this with you later."

"But who do the police think did it?"

"Your sister."

"Cindy? That's ridiculous! My sister wouldn't harm anyone. Why, she ushers spiders out of the house rather than kill them."

"I told you this was complex, Frank.

"Listen to me: Your sister appears to have a serious pathological disorder. The psychologist seems to think she can be cured. But I want to assure you: If I were you,

I wouldn't worry about Cindy's being convicted or sent to jail."

"Do I have this correct, Father: There was no attempt made on my life? My wife was deliberately murdered by my sister, who may have been, say, temporarily insane?"

"That's about it, Frank. At least in outline."

"I . . . I don't know quite what to say. Let me think about this. I'll be in touch."

Hoffman hung up the receiver and stood beside the phone in a numb state. He finally walked away without purpose or direction. He found himself seated at the bar. He knew not how he had gotten there.

"Yes, sir, Mr. Hoffman."

The bartender approached, polishing the ever-spotted glass. "Sorry to hear of your loss, sir."

"Uh-huh."

"Your regular, sir?"

"What? Oh, no; just give me some Perrier."

The bartender raised his eyebrows but quickly lowered them. He dropped ice in a glass, filled it with effervescence, and added a twist of lime.

Hoffman tried to assimilate what he'd just heard. He felt as if he had been flipflopped twice by the spatula of life.

Somehow, when Em grabbed that glass from him, she had neither intentionally saved his life nor committed suicide. Someone had murdered her. But . . . Cindy? His own sister?

The priest wouldn't lie to him. Somehow it was all true. Father Koesler would explain. Pictures at eleven.

But wait: If Em had been the intended victim, then *he* had *not* been.

He tried to absorb that single, simple fact. No one had tried to kill him. He was as alive and as likely to stay alive as he had been before the party Monday evening.

And before the party Monday evening, he had not given death a serious thought.

Reprieved! What do you know about that? Just as alive as he had been before the party Monday evening.

It was beginning to take. He was getting used to the idea of being alive. Being alive means there is no one out there lying in wait for you, plotting your death.

Being alive means having a healthy, strong body that no one is going to puncture with bullets or knives or invade with poison. Being alive means having a life expectancy of maybe twenty or thirty more years. Being alive put the roses back in his cheeks.

"Andy . . ." He beckoned to the bartender. ". . . get rid of this water and bring me a perfect Rob Roy."

"Yes, sir!" The bartender's spirits often reflected those of his customers. Down when they were down. Up when they were up. At the moment, he mirrored Frank Hoffman's ebullience.

Hoffman sipped his drink. It was the elixir of life and he'd been away from it too long.

"Call for you, sir." The bartender held the phone aloft. "Take it here?"

Hoffman nodded, took the phone, and put the receiver to his ear. "Hoffman."

"Yes, sir. This is Kirkus . . . Al Kirkus."

"Yeah, Al. What's up?"

"Your letter, sir. I think it set a world's record in getting here."

"That's what happens when you hand-deliver, Al."

The letter! The goddamn letter! He'd forgotten about the letter! He hadn't had any reason to think of it until this minute. When he'd had the letter and its copies delivered to the secretaries of the members of the board, he had figured he'd be dead by the time they read it.

But he wasn't going to be dead.

This was very definitely a problem. But, he was certain, not an insurmountable one. "Wait a minute, Al . . . how do you know it's been delivered?"

"Because, sir, Clem Keely and I have been dismissed. When we got in this afternoon, we were given our notice. And just this morning, you said—"

"This morning, I was guessing at the reaction of the board."

"Yes, sir. I know that, sir. But we were thinking, Clem and I, that with your record and experience—not to mention your contacts—you probably won't have much of a problem finding another position. Probably right in town, too. So, Clem and I were thinking that . . . well, sir, to be perfectly frank, whether you can do anything for poor Clem or not, I was hoping, as your trusted aide, you would be able to take me with you."

"Take you with me, is it? You know better than that, Al. Fortunes of war and all. You take gambles in the game we're in. We lost. Now, we recoup as best we can. I'm going to have enough trouble getting relocated myself, pal, without having you as an albatross around my neck.

"Good luck, Al. Oh, and Al: Don't call me again." He disconnected.

Kirkus sat dejected and deflated in an office that was no longer his. He wondered whether he should reconsider following through with the threat he'd sent Hoffman. If winning all the marbles became impossible, there was something to be said for revenge.

Back at the club, Hoffman continued to sit at the bar, reflecting on his new, if not uncluttered, lease on life.

That damned letter! If only he had held off long enough to be certain he was about to die. No, that wasn't correct: When he'd sent the letter confessing to sabotaging Charlie Chase, he had thought he was a dead man. But now, he was very much alive. And, due to an excess of premature virtue, out of a damn good job.

Well, hell, there was still GM and Ford and Chrysler and AMC . . . and the foreigns. Somebody out there had to be interested in a top exec who knew and was willing to share the secrets and the plans of The Company in exchange for a good position wherein he could write his own ticket.

The future didn't look so bleak after all.

"Andy," he slammed his glass on the bar, "another!"

"Yes, sir, Mr. Hoffman."

Hoffman sipped his second perfect Rob Roy.

The future. Goddamn, that's right. The future.

"Andy, hand me that phone."

Hoffman dialed.

"Yes?"

"Jackie?"

"Frank! Frank, how are you? *Where* are you?"

"Jackie, about that . . . uh . . . wedding . . ."

22.

IF THERE WERE ANY PRECIPITATION, IT WOULD BE snow. It was cold enough. But even in the depths of a Michigan winter, longtime residents of the state knew that from November through April they could expect anything from a blizzard to a heat wave.

The present cold snap had occasioned a rare log-burning in the fireplace of St. Anselm's rectory, where Father Koesler was hosting his friends Inspector Walter Koznicki and Dr. Rudy Scholl.

Koesler had made dinner. His was not the skill to attempt anything as complicated as a roast. When one was invited to a Koesler dinner, one could be quite sure of a steak or chops, a tossed salad, and cooked frozen vegetables. As Koesler did not believe in dessert, so neither did his guests.

They were batching it this Tuesday evening. Koznicki's wife, Wanda, was attending a confirmation ceremony being conducted by none other than Bishop Michael Ratigan. Scholl's wife, Sonya, a psychologist like her husband, had appointments scheduled. She would join them later only if she got a cancellation. Koesler was batching it by order of Holy Mother Church.

Dinner completed, the three men had repaired to the

comfortable living room and were sitting around the fire-place. Koznicki, aware of Koesler's strange inability to brew a decent cup, had volunteered to make the coffee.

Most of their dinner conversation had revolved around the murder of Emma Hoffman. Which conversation was continuing.

"Dr. Frank Putnam, of the National Institute of Mental Health, is responsible for a significant break-through in this field," said Scholl. He had been com-menting on the condition of Cindy Mercury, who had been diagnosed as a multiple personality.

"Dr. Putnam," Scholl continued, "had sort of inher-ited a forty-five-year-old woman who had been diag-nosed as everything from an epileptic to a schizophrenic to manic-depressive, and even as having a brain tumor.

"She had been given dozens of standard medications, as well as some experimental drugs. When you find a medical history like that, you know the men of science are just plain baffled. No one could understand her rapid changes of behavior. She was lethargic and listless one moment and vibrant and charming the next.

"But it was that very swing in emotions which sug-gested to Dr. Putnam that she very well might be a multi-ple. And he was right. What had been thought to be a variety of mental diseases was really an internal struggle between personalities battling for control of the woman's body."

"Not to digress," said Koesler, who was forever di-gressing, "but it reminds me of something I once heard Sammy Davis, Jr., say in his nightclub act. Davis said that since he is both black and Jewish, when he wakes up in the morning he doesn't know whether to be shiftless and lazy or stingy and mean."

"And only somebody like Sammy Davis could get away with such a racist comment," said Scholl. "But, it does help to illustrate the point. You see, in very stressful situations, frequently the subject's only perceived alternatives are to stay and fight or to run. But what if you can do neither?

"Say you're a child, perhaps, or someone like Cindy. Cindy feels the embarrassment of her husband in having to accept a dole given in ill grace. She cannot fault the brother she loves. At the same time, she empathizes with the husband she loves. She cannot insist that her husband live within their means, even with Frank Hoffman augmenting those means. She knows Angie's show business career demands a certain degree of ostentation. Yet, she is left to balance books that will not balance.

"People have worked her into a tight little corner. She cannot fight them, nor can she run. On top of it all, there is the threat that her sister-in-law will pull down the whole house of cards by putting a stop to Frank's contributions.

"Finally, it becomes too much. She certainly can't fight it. She'd like to run away, but she can't do that either. She can only run away symbolically. Dissociation is symbolic flight.

"It's such a simple and successful way to handle unbearable stress that it becomes pathologically compelling. A different personality develops to handle each problem. One multiple named Pauline, for instance, has an alternate named Annie, who appears once each week to do the laundry. I've got a patient now, in fact, who, so far, has revealed eighty-one alternate personalities."

His listeners looked properly impressed.

"When we were gathered at the Mercury home, as soon as Audrey began to speak, I was sure she was a multiple. Either that, or Cindy was giving an Academy Award performance. By the way, it is not unusual for multiples to sound and even look different from the host.

"Under all the stress and pressure that Cindy felt, she probably subconsciously tried any number of psychological defenses. None of them solved the problem, until, again subconsciously, she chose dissociation. Her personality fragmented, creating Audrey, a very hard dame, who borrowed Cindy's voice when it was appropriate, and even Cindy's skill as a hypnotist, and created a damned clever solution to the problem of killing Emma Hoffman.''

"Yes," agreed Koznicki, "it is noteworthy that all the forensic psychiatrists called in by both defense and prosecution agreed that Cindy suffered a multiple personality. In all my experience, I have never seen such unanimity among psychiatrists called in to testify.''

"Well," Scholl commented, "Fritz Heinsohn did waffle a bit.''

"What's new?" remarked Koesler.

"I think," said Koznicki, "everyone agreed with the verdict of not guilty by reason of insanity.''

"Audrey's assertion that she could not be punished, that all we could do was hurt Cindy, was certainly on the mark," said Scholl.

"The court was forced to send her to the forensic center in Ann Arbor before they determined to give her a civil commitment," Koznicki observed.

"Yes," added Scholl, "and with Frank Hoffman's money helping, she should get excellent treatment at the Brockport Home in Massachusetts. It's one of the best facilities in the country. I visited her there the other day, at her brother's request, and she's doing remarkably well. Of course, with these fusion attempts, it has to be anybody's guess. But I really believe her prognosis is excellent.''

"Well, for one thing, the pressure that caused the initial split disappeared with Emma's death," said Koesler.

"And she certainly ought to find reassurance in her husband's new job," said Koznicki.

"Have you seen his new show on Channel 7?" Koesler asked.

"I believe," Koznicki answered, "even those of us who do not watch daytime television have tuned in that program at least once just to see how Mr. Mercury is coming along."

"I think he was made for that kind of show," Koesler enthused. "He's got a steady supply of local and visiting show business personalities. He knows most of them and their chatter is always interesting. At least Angie keeps it interesting.

"But most of all, now he's got a steady—and, from all I've heard—a very respectable salary. He doesn't have to go on the road anymore. And, with his exposure on that show, he's getting all the better parts in local theater and commercials. I'm really pleased for them both. Cindy should recover, please God, completely. And she'll have a much more normal home life waiting for her."

"Speaking of a normal life," said Scholl, "weren't you pleased to see Jacqueline LeBlanc return to her native Fall River? She's still young enough to pick up the pieces and start over."

"Yes," added Koesler, "she'll probably marry some nice Irish Catholic lad and become another example, in Fall River's peculiar view, of a mixed marriage between Irish and French Catholics."

"And what of Charles Chase?" Koznicki asked. "From what I read in the papers, he seems to be doing well."

"From what I've heard, that's true," Koesler responded. "I guess Frank Martin was eager to find out what was the cause of that disastrous presentation Mr. Chase made. On face value, his career seemed virtually over. But once it got out that he had been sabotaged by Frank Hoffman, Mr. Chase's star took off again. According to most of our people in the parish who work for

The Company, Mr. Chase may yet indeed, one day become chairman of the board.''

"He will have to do it without the help of that Al Kirkus." Koznicki smiled. Not only was he dismissed from The Company, but it was not difficult to establish that he was the one responsible for the threatening note sent to Frank Hoffman. One of the cleaning people noticed an interesting looking magazine in Kirkus' wastebasket. But when she retrieved it to look at it, she was disgusted to find that it had been all cut up and clipped out.

"If he can't cover his tracks any more thoroughly than that, for his own welfare, I trust Mr. Kirkus will not turn to a life of crime."

"I was wondering about him," said Scholl. "Wasn't he charged with anything?"

"It is a very gray area," Koznicki answered. "In the final analysis, we decided to scare him within an inch of his life. We gave him an official talking to and told him what would happen if he ever crossed the line again . . . especially if he ever were to bother Mr. Hoffman or interfere with his life.

"And speaking of Hoffman, with the solution to this investigation, we were able to close the books on two files. The earlier incident, when he came close to being killed at the glass plant? The Prosecuting Attorney's office has ruled that an industrial accident. It seems, after all, that no one wants—at least actively wants—Mr. Hoffman dead."

"Ah, yes, Mr. Hoffman," Scholl mused. "Is it true that he is now postmaster for an affluent Detroit suburb?"

"Yes, it is," said Koesler. "I'm afraid none of the other automotive companies would have him."

"Sort of restores your faith in the automotive community, doesn't it?" Scholl laughed.

"Yes, but what does it do to one's faith in the U.S. Postal Service?" Koesler replied with a grimace. "I hear that they welcomed him as just the kind of man they needed. Of course, he had to take a whopping cut in income. But mere money is not what Frank Hoffman needs just now, what with his own savings and investments, and the inheritance from his late wife.

"No, the position of postmaster is a political appointment. And that's where Frank is headed—into politics. And I wouldn't be surprised to see him climb steadily up the political ranks. Wouldn't that be something—Frank Hoffman, president of the United States . . ." Koesler thought for a moment, then added, "God preserve us."

"Amen," echoed Koznicki and Scholl.

The coffee cups were empty. Koznicki offered refills. All declined. Koesler offered after-dinner liqueur. All declined. The evening was winding down.

Suddenly, a bell jangled, startling everyone. It was the only discordant sound they had heard this evening. Scholl, for one, had forgotten he was in a rectory where anyone could call at any hour.

"For the love of Pete!" Koesler exclaimed, rising. "It's the phone. You might get the impression people normally call at this time of night. I assure you, they don't." He left the living room to answer the phone in his office.

Scholl thought the statement a refreshing bit of candor. Most people complained about being too busy whether they were or not. Enjoyment of a leisurely work place seemed to be a cardinal sin to most Americans. And here was this suburban priest assuring them that the phone did not normally ring itself off the wall.

Koesler reentered the room.

"It's Wanda," he said to the Inspector. "You can take it in my office."

As Koznicki left the room, Scholl returned to a subject

he had been pursuing earlier. "You'd be surprised, Father, how much company a dog can provide. And I'm sure you'd feel more secure. You must be alone in the rectory frequently. Few things scare off unwelcome visitors more than a barking dog."

Koesler, who had no intention of living with animals of any description, tried to humor his friend. "Well . . . I suppose St. Anselm's could afford a small dog."

Scholl shook his head. "Father, if you're going to get a dog, get a big dog. If you're going to get a little dog, get a cat."

With that, Koznicki reentered the room, smiling broadly.

"Something funny?" asked Koesler.

"Does Bishop Ratigan normally enter into a dialogue with the children he confirms?"

"Why, no . . . no. As far as I know, Mike has never even liked kids very much."

"Then he is even less likely to do so after tonight." The Inspector shook his head. "For some reason, instead of preaching at the confirmation, the bishop began to ask questions, pretty much letting the children's streams of consciousness take over."

"That's certainly not like Mike," Koesler commented.

"I did not think so. Well, at one point, they had gotten into Bible history and one young lad mentioned Abraham. The bishop asked if any of the others knew who Abraham was. And one youngster volunteered, and I quote, 'Abraham Lincoln was our first president.' "

They chuckled.

"Later—Wanda believes it was because the pastor of that parish is a monsignor—the bishop asked the children if any of them knew what a monsignor is. And one answered that a monsignor is a cross that hangs around a bishop's neck."

They laughed.

"The old pectoral cross confusion, eh?" Koesler commented. Then, to Dr. Scholl: "You've never met Bishop Ratigan, have you? He should be home soon. Would you like to stay and meet him?"

"I think that may not happen this evening, Father," said Koznicki.

"There's more?"

"Wanda did not see the bishop's Oldsmobile anywhere outside the rectory, so after confirmation she offered to drive him here. He thanked her, but said that he was being picked up by the Chases for a late dinner."

"The Chases!" Scholl was impressed.

"God never closes a door without opening a window," Koesler murmured.

"What was that?" asked Scholl.

"Oh, nothing. It just occurs to me that as Hoffman is waved out of the game, Chase is sent in. And Mike Ratigan lands on his feet again."

"What do you think the future holds for him, Father?" Koznicki asked.

"Mike? Well, I don't think he'll be Pope. But I'm sure he'll get his own diocese. And soon."

Koznicki smiled. "And you, Father?"

"Me? I'll be right here at the old stand," Koesler replied, forgetting, for the moment, that police headquarters was becoming a home-away-from-home. "Just leading the quiet, unassuming life of a simple parish priest."

About the Author

William X. Kienzle, author of five best-selling mysteries, was ordained into the priesthood in 1954 and spent twenty years as a parish priest. For twelve years he was editor-in-chief of the *Michigan Catholic*. After leaving the priesthood, he became editor of *MPLS* magazine in Minneapolis and later moved to Texas, where he was director of the Center for Contemplative Studies at the University of Dallas. Kienzle and his wife, Javan, presently live in Detroit, where he enjoys playing the piano as a diversion from his writing. His previous novels include *The Rosary Murders, Death Wears a Red Hat, Mind Over Murder, Assault With Intent,* and *Shadow of Death.*